Death at the Drive-In

ANGIE FOX

Also by Angie Fox

THE ACCIDENTAL DEMON SLAYER SERIES

The Accidental Demon Slayer

The Dangerous Book for Demon Slayers

A Tale of Two Demon Slayers

The Last of the Demon Slayers

My Big Fat Demon Slayer Wedding

Beverly Hills Demon Slayer

Night of the Living Demon Slayer

What To Expect When Your Demon Slayer is Expecting

SHORT STORY COLLECTIONS:

Haunted for Christmas: A collection of Southern Ghost Hunter short stories

A Little Night Magic: A collection of Southern Ghost Hunter and Accidental Demon Slayer short stories

Death at the Drive-In

The Southern
Ghost Hunter
Mysteries
Book 13

NEW YORK TIMES BESTSELLING AUTHOR
ANGIE FOX

DEATH AT THE DRIVE-IN

ISBN: 978-1-957685-27-4

Moose Island Books

Chapter One

The sun dipped low in the sky, its golden light filtering through the stately old apple tree shading the pond out behind my house.

"C'mon, Lucy! You can do this!" She was the smartest skunk in six counties. I knew because she was mine.

My furry companion hesitated in front of the Hula-Hoop I'd propped up between two metal stakes. Her shiny black eyes peered up at me, and her nose twitched as if considering the absurdity of the contraption in front of her.

She might have been too smart for her own good.

Luckily for me, she also liked homemade Banana-Walnut Skunk Tasties. And luckily for her, I'd baked up a fresh tray this morning. "I have a scrumptious treat with your name on it."

I really did. I'd cut it into a heart shape and written *Lucy* on it in pet-safe, pink frosting.

With renewed energy and a lick of the lips, Lucy burst into an animated waddle and cleared the hoop as if she'd been born to it. I cheered the same as if she'd just won the Purina Classic and presented her with her grand prize. She gulped it down in three bites and spun in a happy circle.

"You're a natural," I said as I scratched the white stripe down her back. We were in training for the annual Sugarland Pet Parade and Festival to be held next spring. Every year, I'd watched the dog agility course and thought—why not skunks? This year, I checked the rules, and there was nothing about contestants being dogs. "Just a few more obstacles and we'll call it a day."

I wanted to get her back inside before dark. I also wanted to call my boyfriend, Ellis, before he went to work. His parents were going through a complicated divorce, and he'd been acting as peacekeeper after his dad made it back to town the night before. I hoped he was doing all right. And that an invite to a cozy dinner at my place tomorrow might cheer him up.

Lucy eyed the treat bag. "Ramp," I instructed, thrilled when she dashed for the incline I'd made from an old washboard.

She barreled up the metal rungs, not even hesitating at the top this time. What did I say? A natural. Then she zipped straight through the canvas tent that served as our tunnel and came trotting out the other end, her little legs moving double time.

I couldn't take it. She was too darling. Not to mention talented. I scooped her up and nuzzled my cheek into her fur. "I'm so proud of you," I declared. "But how am I going to let you finish a race when I can't keep my hands off you?"

She buried her face under my arm, which meant she was either snuggling or about to go after my bag of banana-walnut treats. Probably both.

Then she suddenly stiffened.

"What's up, girl?" I asked at the exact time I saw the reason for her fear.

The ghost of a 1920s gangster shimmered into existence between Lucy's tunnel and the small pond in my backyard. He appeared in black and white, but I could see through him. Almost. He wore a 1920s-style pin-striped suit coat with matching cuffed trousers and a fat tie. His chest was level with my line of sight, which made him appear unnaturally tall.

Until you realized he liked to hover about a foot off the ground.

The gangster's mouth settled into a frown as he glided through the tent and straight for us. "What did I ever do to that skunk?" he muttered as Lucy wriggled out of my arms and scampered away from us, straight under my white-painted porch.

Lucy and Frankie didn't tend to get along. Well, he liked her. She didn't fancy him.

He was an acquired taste.

"Give it time," I said to the gangster by way of encouragement. Technically, he had eternity.

His gaze followed her until the tuft of her tail disappeared. "Fine, but she's going to miss the unveiling of my greatest achievement." He turned to me with a twinkle in his eye. "It's new. It's one of a kind. It's, dare I say, epic."

Wow. "I hadn't even realized you were striving for epic-ness." He spent most of his time entertaining his old gangster buddies and romancing his girlfriend. That and trying to steal stuff.

Old habits die hard.

His face brightened. "It came to me in a dream last night."

Wait. "Can ghosts dream?"

He pointed a finger at me. "Don't get technical." He lifted his hands to the sky. "In a flash of brilliance, I knew I had to build it."

"Oh no." I didn't like it when Frankie built things in my backyard.

He dropped his hands. "I recognize that look. It's the same one Tommy Three Sticks had when I laid out the plan to swipe the mayor's diamond cufflinks smack in the middle of his big speech."

I raised a brow. "Did it work?"

"No, but that's beside the point. My point is you need to see this," he declared, his power washing over me.

"I'm not so sure that's a good idea," I countered. In fact, I knew it wasn't, but it was too late. The energy cascaded over me in a flurry of tiny pinpricks that made my skin dance. I stiffened as the sensation spiraled down my spine and anchored itself into my very marrow.

On my own, the only ghost I could see was Frankie. But when he tuned me in to his power, I could see the other side exactly as he did.

Sometimes, I'd rather not.

I had a feeling this was one of those times as a curious contraption began to take form directly behind the ghost.

"Ta-da!" he exclaimed, beaming at me like Lucy did the first time she'd mastered the tunnel. Only Frankie was no cute skunk training for the blue ribbon. The gangster was up to something.

As usual.

He swelled with a showman's flair. "Feast your eyes on the future."

I blinked once. Twice. "The future of what?"

My mouth dropped when it came into focus. It reminded me of a mad scientist's experiment gone very wrong. But trust me, Frankie was no academic. He was a thief and a whiskey runner at heart. And as a Southern girl, I recognized all too clearly what he'd built beside my gorgeous pond.

A dented old oil drum stood on rickety legs, connected by a twisting maze of rusty pipes to a copper coil that looked salvaged from an ancient water heater. The whole thing had been haphazardly welded together with what seemed to be paper clips and old gum wrappers. An ominous, foul-smelling vapor oozed from several leaks in the pipes, and the entire structure tilted at a precarious angle as if it might collapse into a heap of scavenged junk at any moment.

Of course, Frankie mistook my wide-eyed horror for awe. He flung his hands out like a demented *Price Is Right* model. "Meet Betsy Sue the Third," he crowed. "Isn't she a beaut?"

If beaut meant large and ugly and smelly, then yes.

"What happened to Betsy Sue one and two?" Maybe I didn't want to know. "Did they fall apart?"

This one was well on the way.

Frankie scowled. "For your information, Betsy Sue the First

was glorious. She had an actual bathtub attached, and her gin-infused hooch put more crooks and congressmen under the table than a lawyer laying down a bribe."

Charming. "She exploded, didn't she?"

He notched up his chin. "She burned bright and left her tub in a tree."

"So Betsy the Second fell apart," I concluded.

The gangster hitched up a shoulder. "After she exploded."

"Frankie!"

"I refuse to justify my stills to you or to anyone," he snapped.

"Fine, but Betsy Number Three isn't staying there. Not under my apple tree." I didn't want anything on my property—ghostly or otherwise—exploding so near the house. And I didn't know what I'd do if the undead police got wind of the thing and decided to raid my property.

I'd had enough trouble in the past when it came to Frankie bringing unwanted paranormal attention to my lovely, formerly quiet home.

"Relax," said the ghost, who'd probably been running illegal alcohol since he could say the word *still*. "It's not permanent. I built it to impress my girl," he explained as if that were the only reason men did anything. "Molly is coming over tonight, and I'm making a special recipe just for her."

I chewed my lip. I supposed it was nice when two people who cared about each other spent quality time together. Even if those moments were fueled by lighter fluid.

At the same time... "I'd recommend roses instead," I told him. Big ones. Especially when she saw this still. "I'll even let you pick some from the bushes next to the back porch." The ones my grandmother had planted.

His expression soured. "Those rosebushes are the reason I can't be with Molly anytime I want."

Not exactly true, but he did have a point.

I'd tied Frankie's spirit to my land when I'd emptied his

funeral urn onto my rosebushes. In my defense, I'd believed my ex-fiancé had gifted me a slightly ugly antique vase long overdue for a rinse with the hose. And perhaps a fresh flower. But as it turned out, there was a reason ashes were customarily scattered to the wind, or at least spread out a bit. When I poured the entirety of Frankie's remains in one spot and then hosed him into the ground, the poor gangster had become quite stuck.

As soon as he'd been tied to my land, I could see him clear as day. He could also show me the ghostly realm if and when he chose to lend me his power to see it.

Spoiler alert: I didn't always want to see.

Still, I had to give the ghost some grace. Where he'd once had the run of the world, Frankie was now confined to my property. The only way he could leave was if I brought his urn with me. It still contained a smidge of his earthly remains, which I kept secure by keeping the lid taped down tight.

In the years since the unfortunate incident, we'd tried everything to get him free. So far to no avail. We'd only seen one ghost manage the feat, and she did it by changing and growing and essentially becoming a different person than the one trapped in the dirt.

Only Frankie the gangster wasn't always so keen on change. Case in point: the moonshine still in my backyard.

"Okay," I conceded. "Maybe instead of roses, you could make your girlfriend something nice, something personal to make her feel extra special."

"I did," he concluded, standing proudly beside the still.

And we were back to square one.

I sighed. I hoped Molly would be more impressed than I was.

At least he'd made an effort.

Frankie had been dating a gentle, pretty Victorian ghost who thought the world of him despite his rough-and-tumble past. I supposed she liked the bad boys. Although, I had hoped some of her good nature would rub off on him.

I was still hoping.

"Okay, Frankie, I'm not going to ask you to get rid of that still before your date tonight," I conceded, not saying that tomorrow was another matter. "But you can't give that sweet girl moonshine." She was a true lady. "She won't be able to handle that toxic sludge."

"Sludge?" Frankie balked as if I'd called his baby ugly. "This is my famous pine needle and chili pepper 'shine, smoother than a silk stocking. I'm known countywide as the Rembrandt of moonshiners. My still is precision meets craftsmanship!"

"Meets battery acid," I added.

"It does have a kick," he said fondly. "I just wish I knew what was holding Molly up," he added, glancing at the sun lowering over the horizon. "She promised she'd be here well before dark."

I stiffened as the coils above the contraption began to shake. "Her days haven't been exactly predictable lately. I'm sure she'll be along soon."

Frankie's girlfriend lived with several Civil War-era ghosts at a former bordello that now housed the Sugarland Heritage Society, a historical preservation club. Molly had been an orphan, taken in by the working girls. She'd kept up the house while they'd entertained their guests. The house was mostly a warm, welcoming place, but every once in a while, a few of the more dangerous ghosts from the cemetery out back tried to move in. When that happened, Molly and her friends worked together to clear them out. This time, they'd been at it off and on for weeks. It seemed they had a few stubborn spirits on their hands.

I knew the feeling.

While Frankie focused on the horizon, the still began to rattle and wheeze, and a loud pop of heated air burst from where the coil met the barrel.

I took a step back. "So, when you said it wasn't permanent, you didn't plan for it to explode tonight, did you?"

Frankie's eyes bugged. "Betsy Sue the Third is my greatest creation yet. She has a double filtration system at the cost of both my socks, and she's perfect the way she is."

"Right." I nodded one too many times.

At least we weren't dealing with the bank robber he'd stashed at my place, the goats he'd tried to raise on my porch, or the illegal race track he'd tried to open in my backyard.

No, it was more straightforward than that. It was my fault Frankie couldn't build his still in the backwoods or down by the river or anywhere else. I alone had trapped Frankie "The German" on my ancestral property. And unfortunately, I'd told him to make himself at home until we could free him.

"Just as long as Betsy Sue is gone by tomorrow," I said. Maybe then we could avoid any trouble. If not the smell.

"You never support my dreams," Frankie lamented as if his goal in life were to build a still by my pond. "You shoot me down every chance you get."

More like I had a home and had standards. "Maybe Ellis will lend us his truck so she can go live in the country," I suggested. "We could pick her out a great spot down by the river."

"That I could never visit by myself," he snapped.

True. Also, I wasn't so sure Deputy Sheriff Ellis Wydell should be moving an illegal shine operation, even on the ghostly plane.

I was saved from answering when Frankie's attention whipped toward the road at the front of the house. "Make yourself scarce. I hear Molly's carriage," he said, running his fingers through his hair and straightening his jacket.

A second later, I heard it too—the pounding of horse hooves from the direction of my driveway.

"Be good," I couldn't resist adding, pleased when the hardened gangster's cheeks flushed.

I turned back toward the house, ready to fish Lucy out from under the porch for her supper, when a faint shriek echoed in the distance. I paused and heard a string of panicked shouts.

A ghostly carriage barreled into my backyard like a runaway train, kicking up dust and startling the birds from the trees. It slammed to a halt in front of the gangster, and three ghostly women in low-cut, frilly dresses plunged out in a mad rush.

The first one tripped over her skirts and nearly sent the rest tumbling after her. "Frankie!" she called.

He rushed to the trio. "Lottie! Violet! Ruth!" he demanded. "What's wrong?"

"It's awful," Lottie wailed, catching her balance.

The ringleader of the group, Violet, zipped past her, her angular features drawn tight, wisps of hair escaping from her bun. "It's Molly. Something's wrong with Molly."

Frankie steadied her. "What do you mean something's wrong with her? Where is she?"

Ruth gasped and began trembling. "We don't know."

The gangster grabbed Violet by the shoulders. "What happened?"

She gulped, unable to speak.

"We were clearing out the cellar, same as always," said Lottie, clutching her cameo necklace, "when Molly started acting peculiar. Her eyes went glassy, and she said in a strange voice, 'Well, isn't this the cat's pajamas!'"

"Cats don't wear pajamas." Ruth shook her head, fighting tears. "It made no sense."

"Then she said she was a woman named Kitty Cunningham," Violet added.

Molly had never mentioned anyone by that name. I looked at Frankie. "Kitty Cunningham? Who's that?"

"Your guess is as good as ours," Violet insisted.

Lottie shook her head, hair in loose ringlets tangling at her shoulders. "Before we could ask, Molly jumped up on the washroom folding table and started dancing like, like..."

"A wanton," Violet finished. "We should know," she added with a nod to her friends. "Then she declared there was no stopping Kitty ever again, and she ran off before we could stop her!"

"That doesn't make any sense," I said. "How can she suddenly decide she's someone else?"

"She's possessed," Frankie said with a rare tremble in his voice. His hands clenched into fists and went white.

I gasped.

Ruth let out a wail.

"How can we be sure?" Violet challenged.

"Because Molly would never run off like that," Lottie insisted.

"Wait," I said. "*Possessed?*" I hadn't known it was possible. "How can a ghost possess a ghost?"

The gangster tensed his jaw. "It's a lot like a ghost possessing a live person, only worse." He brought his hands to his head. "A ghost can take over a human body for a time. It's rare because it takes a boatload of power. Not to mention only the crazy ones do it because it hurts like a shotgun blast. Eventually, the ghost loses the power to maintain the connection and gets kicked out." He ran a hand down the side of his face. "The living person comes back, and the ghost develops an awful hangover that's been known to last for centuries." Frankie dropped his hand. "Ghost-on-ghost possession is more dangerous and deadly. Once the invading spirit attaches itself, it begins to drain the energy of the host, taking it and transforming it into itself." He looked to the girls, then to me. "A ghost that is possessed by a spirit that can't manifest will first think and act like that ghost, then slowly *become* them."

Ruth let out a small cry.

"That's awful," I said on an exhale. I couldn't imagine what Molly must be going through.

Frankie's expression went cold. "The more powerful the spirit, the faster the change, until the second spirit manifests completely and the first spirit is lost."

"Lost?" I didn't even want to think it. "Gone?" To be taken like that. To be drained of your energy, your life force, what makes you...*you*.

The gangster shot me a frigid look. "Yeah, well, it ain't gonna happen to my Molly." His mouth set in a grim line as he turned to her trembling friends. "Tell me what happened right before Molly said she was Kitty. Leave nothing out."

Violet nodded. "Molly was coaxing out a dark shadow from

the corner. I'd tried it right before her. It was sticky, but it didn't act like it was about to attack."

Frankie's lip curled in a silent snarl. "That's the best way to get the jump."

Violet brought a hand to her mouth. "I figured Molly was fine on her own. I went to help Ruth and Lottie dispel that creepy guy who likes to steal our hairpins."

"I turned to ask Molly to join us," Lottie warbled. "Then I saw her face. For a split second, Molly had a different face. The face of some girl I'd never seen before."

"You most likely saw Kitty's face." Frankie's voice thudded dully. "That's fast." He gritted his jaw. "Faster than I'd expect."

Violet blinked hard. "What does it mean?"

The gangster had gone paler than I'd ever seen him. "It means we don't have much time. We have to find her, now."

"But we don't know where she went," Lottie said helplessly. "Right after that face flashed, she said she was Kitty, and then she was gone."

Then we'd just have to think. "Who is this Kitty Cunningham, and why would she do this?" I asked, trying to recall if I'd ever met a ghost by that name. "That might lead us to where she is now."

"We've never met her," Violet insisted.

I didn't think I had, either.

"She could be a wandering spirit," Frankie said tightly. "With nowhere to manifest except in my Molly."

"She could be an outsider," I suggested. We'd never been warned of a ghost by that name. And this Kitty was definitely dangerous.

Lottie shoved a lock of hair behind her ear. "We checked the cemetery records. There's no one by that name in the ledger."

Ruth nodded and wrung her hands. "No Cunninghams alive, either. At least none who belong to the Sugarland Heritage Society."

"I don't know of any Cunninghams in Sugarland," I agreed.

And I knew pretty much everybody.

"Okay, an outsider, then," Frankie determined, his eyes as sharp as broken glass. "Or wait. It could be an alias."

Or it could be a matter of looking in the right place. "I think I know a way to find Molly," I told the group. "Follow me."

Chapter Two

I ushered Molly's friends into my vintage yellow kitchen. The late afternoon sunlight spilled across the polished countertops neatly lined with cookbooks and jars of spices. The squat refrigerator hummed quietly. I pulled up a chair at the white oak heirloom farm table and flicked on the copper pendant lamp overhead to chase away the lingering shadows.

Frankie halted right inside the door. "We're not going to find Molly in your kitchen."

"We're not going to find her at all unless we know where to look," I said, firing up my laptop.

We needed to determine who Kitty Cunningham had been to know where she might be now—and how to convince her to let Molly go.

"It's simple," Frankie said, striding straight through Lucy's favorite banana toy. "We'll take your car, drive around town until we spot her, and then shove this Kitty Cunningham into your trunk and keep her there until she agrees to leave Molly alone."

His answer to everything was shoving someone into a trunk.

Ruth gasped in shock. I went for practicality.

"You don't know where Kitty is," I reminded him, typing in my password.

"She's *in my girlfriend*!" Frankie shouted.

Technically, yes.

"If we want to solve this fast, we need a solid idea of where to start," I urged, wishing my computer would boot up quicker.

"You need to get my urn in the car and get me out of here," Frankie shouted.

"I realize you're upset—" I began.

"You think so?" he asked, spinning in a circle. "You never want to shoot anybody. You've never used arson as a motivational tool. You never even want to shake anyone down. And you still think you should be in charge?"

"Yes," I said, causing him to loom two feet taller.

It wouldn't work.

And I refused to add mob tactics and intimidation to my toolbox.

Besides, my fact-based approach had worked for us before. "Remember, I helped you discover who shot you in the forehead."

The gangster lowered his Panama hat over the ragged hole etched permanently between his eyes. "By getting me trapped inside a haunted asylum."

I never said my methods were perfect.

My home screen came up, and I turned back to my computer. "I worked it so that ghostly federal mob investigator didn't put you under house arrest for eternity."

"You made me solve a crime like some do-gooder," the gangster shot back.

"*We* solved a crime," I corrected.

His frown deepened.

Hey, it wasn't all sunshine and roses for me, either. "You brought home a pet racehorse," I reminded him.

"That's it. I'm calling in the mob," Frankie announced, disappearing through the wall that led out to the backyard.

Absolutely not. "Leave the South Town boys out of this!" I called after him. At least until we knew what we were dealing with. We needed to think about this logically, and Frankie's guys tended to shoot first and ask questions later.

Anytime a ghost got "killed" again, it knocked them out for at least an hour. And with Molly in danger with every minute that passed, we didn't have time for half the town's ghosts to be lying around ghostly dead and unable to help us if we needed it.

Ruth's frigid hand brushed near my shoulder, sending a chill straight down to my bones. "I believe in you," she said shyly.

"Thanks," I said, rubbing a hand up my arm and turning back to my computer to begin my search.

Ruth and Lottie gathered to peer over my shoulder.

Violet stood on the opposite side of the table from me, her body stiff, her mind working. "While we're at it, we could start looking in the places disembodied spirits tend to linger. With any luck, this Kitty entity is attached to one of those spots. She could have gone back to gather her strength."

Which would be terrible news for Molly.

Lottie inhaled sharply. "Well, there's usually one or two unformed spirits hiding out in the air vent in room 13 in the old Sugarland Hotel."

I forced myself to keep typing but found all the wrong keys. "That's oddly specific."

"It attracts restless spirits," Violet explained. To her friends, she added, "Last I heard, it was haunted by that silent-movie actress who likes to throw fits."

Lottie nodded. "Her old dressing room went kaput when the theater burned down. She's a mess. I doubt she'd even notice another spirit horning in on her air vent."

"But would Kitty want to be with *her*?" Ruth clicked her tongue. "More likely Kitty is hiding out inside that haunted doll in the New For You antique shop."

"Haunted?" My fingers clenched and slipped off the computer keys.

Oh my. I'd have to warn my sister's friend who owned the place.

"I hear it's fun to blink the eyes," Ruth offered.

"Like we've ever gotten a turn," Lottie countered. "It's like Grand Central Station inside that doll. Malicious spirits feed off the dark energy. The strongest ghost gets to stay."

I found the thought oddly terrifying. "She'd have to be strong to take possession of Molly."

Poor Molly.

"Don't forget that abandoned mine shaft by the river," Violet suggested with a shiver.

I realized I had one big typo, hit Delete, and prepared to start again. "Just how many creepy haunted places are there in Sugarland?" I mean, sure, I'd visited more than a handful on my various adventures, but I still considered my town to be the kind of warm, friendly place most people dreamed of calling home.

Lottie touched a finger to her chin. "I could make you a haunted guidebook. By which, I mean a guide to the most haunted places in Sugarland, not that the book itself would necessarily be haunted."

"Sometimes, there's no avoiding it," Violet pointed out.

Lottie ignored her. "I do my own watercolor illustrations," she added without a hint of guile. "I haven't had a scrapbooking project in years."

"I appreciate the thought, but no, thank you," I said, turning back to my computer. Yes, a supernatural guide to Sugarland could come in handy, but I liked to give everyone the benefit of the doubt, to judge each ghost I encountered on their own merits and not what anyone else might have to say about them. Rumors and speculation could be cruel. I'd learned firsthand that the official story wasn't always the correct one.

The page I'd been searching for flashed up on the screen just as Frankie burst through the rear wall, tie askew and fire in his eyes. "I've got Icepick Charlie and Suds out looking," he announced.

"How?" I knew Suds, the dead bank robber, liked to hang out

around my property. Icepick Charlie was a little scary. Not to mention stabby. I didn't like the idea of him floating around.

But Frankie was on a roll. "Brewer is grabbing guys as they hit the speakeasy. We'll go door-to-door and put the word out on the street. We'll bug every payphone in town—"

"No shooting," I warned.

"No *unnecessary* shooting," he conceded.

Okay, but Frankie thought all shooting was necessary.

"Look! There she is." Lottie gasped as an image flickered across my screen. "That's the face I saw!"

We all gathered to see. The photo from the 1956 Sugarland High senior class yearbook showed an impish young woman with a sparkle in her eye and mischief dancing across her wide smile. Her blonde curls spilled casually over one shoulder in a fashionably tousled manner, and the top few buttons of her blouse were left artfully undone to expose a glimpse of collarbone.

"It's a miracle," Ruth exhaled, looking at an equally astonished Lottie.

"It's Google," I told them.

"A picture ain't a location," Frankie bit out.

"Agreed." A few more taps and we had a start. "She lived at 238 Magnolia, which is just down the street from Ellis's house." It was an older neighborhood, with bungalows dating back to the 1940s. Young families had begun moving in, and many of the tidy houses had been painted in variations of robin's egg blue, sunshine yellow, and rose pink.

"Nice." Frankie gave a curt nod. "Take me out, and I'll get the guys. We'll surround the place and take it by force." He turned to go make it happen.

"I have a better idea," I said, typing again.

Frankie threw his hands up as if I were the problem. "Why do you always think your ideas are better?"

"Because they work," I said, keeping my eyes on the screen.

"They've also been known to backfire," he pointed out.

"Like your moonshine stills?" I asked.

"Look!" Ruth motioned Violet over as I pulled up a newspaper article from May 3, 1956.

LOCAL GIRL REPORTED MISSING

"That's Kitty's picture," Ruth said, pointing to the screen as Frankie nudged in around her.

The article showed a photo of Kitty Cunningham wearing pedal pushers and posing next to a 1950s Buick with tailfins.

"Give me a sec..." I pulled up another article from later that month, and more from one year, two years, a decade later. "It doesn't look like they ever found her."

"Well, she's certainly dead now," Lottie insisted.

"Last seen leaving the malt shop where she worked," Violet murmured, reading over my shoulder.

"Kitty claimed she was on her way to the Starlite Drive-In." I continued reading the article. "But did she ever make it there?"

The article didn't say.

Nor did the next one we pulled up.

Or the next one.

"Stop," Frankie ordered when I was ready to pull up yet another article. "No newspaper reporter is going to tell you where Kitty is when nobody's found her yet."

He had a point. "I'd say our best bet is the drive-in."

"Agreed." The gangster cracked his knuckles. "Get your keys. Let's head up there and ask around. If all else fails, we'll circle back to the malt shop."

"Let's all go," I said, looking up the address. Molly's friends were familiar with dark spirits, and we needed all the help we could get.

"I don't know if that's such a good idea," Ruth began.

"Oh, it's never a good idea," I assured her. The spiritual side of Sugarland could be dangerous even when we weren't hunting a dark ghost from a creepy cemetery who had possessed Frankie's girlfriend. Still, I didn't see where we had a choice.

Frankie drew the gun from his side holster. "What she means is we're running out of time. Every second we waste, we could be losing part of Molly."

My fingers froze on the keys. "How long do we have?"

"Days," he snapped. "No more than a week." He checked his gun for bullets. "But it's not going to take that long. I won't let it," he stated as if he could change it by will alone. "We'll find her tonight," he said, snapping the bullet chamber closed. "Now."

"It's not so simple," Ruth said, earning a withering look from the gangster.

Violet stepped between them. "She may not be at the drive-in or in the doll or at any of the places we've brought up so far. When you consider all the nooks and crannies that could attract the kind of dark spirit who would attempt possession—"

"Add in the ones we might not even know about," Lottie added. "Our search could go on forever."

"No, it can't," Frankie interjected.

"Okay, so we'll split up," I said, making an executive decision. "Violet, I think you should take the haunted doll."

"I'd rather Ruth handle that one," she said, looking at her friend. "She knows the most about it. I'll take the mine shaft down by the river."

"I'll take the entire Sugarland Hotel and focus on Room 13," Lottie volunteered. "We can meet up afterward at 238 Magnolia."

I nodded. If the owners of Kitty's old house didn't have a haunting yet, they would soon. "Frankie and I will take the drive-in."

Violet nodded. "Good luck."

"Same to you," I told her, powering down my computer as she and the girls faded away.

"I like it." Frankie nodded to himself sharply. "But we've got another problem."

"You're kidding," I said, pushing away from the table.

Frankie stared me down. "The Starlite is in rival mob territory. If they see me, I'll be shot on sight."

But we weren't starting a mob war. "Can't you just explain?"

Frankie snorted. "Yeah, gangsters love long chats." He holstered his gun and rubbed a hand over his chin. "I'll have to go in undercover. The Irish mob can't know it's me." He looked me square in the eye. "You too."

That hardly seemed necessary. "The Irish mob doesn't know who I am."

For that, I was grateful.

"If you want to keep it that way, you'll wear a disguise," Frankie said, leveling a finger at me. He adjusted his hat. "I'll be back ASAP. I don't care what it takes, I'm getting my girl back. And when I'm done, this Kitty is going to wish she never even saw my Molly."

I was all for it. "As long as one of us, meaning me, doesn't die in the process."

"Small price to pay," Frankie said, checking the bullets in his gun. "You have twenty minutes to get in disguise. Let's go."

Chapter Three

"A disguise?" I repeated, but the gangster was long gone.

Out the kitchen window, I could see that night had fallen.

I wasn't sure who else Frankie expected me to be. I was just a simple Southern girl with a ghost who courted trouble like fish jump at bait. And a friend needed me.

So I used the time to change from sandals to tennis shoes. Much better for running from potentially angry ghosts. Then I dialed up my sister, Melody, on my cell phone. She worked part-time at the library and was a whiz at research.

It rang twice before she answered, her voice echoing in the hushed serenity of the main reading room.

"I thought you'd be off work and heading home by now," I said, eyeing a few glittering stars out the window above my sink.

"I'm putting together a Cozy Crime & Punishment book promotion for adult readers," she gushed. "Each book is wrapped like a present, and the tag tells you five fun facts about that book's mystery sleuth."

"I like it," I said, wishing I had a bit less mystery in my life. "Listen," I said, leaning up against the kitchen island, "we've got a problem."

I filled her in on Molly's disappearance and how we didn't

have much time. I could hear the rustle of papers in the background, the click of a pen. Melody was always good in a crisis. "What do you need?" she asked, all business.

"I need you to dig up all you can on Kitty Cunningham. Also, the Starlite Drive-In. That's where Frankie and I are headed tonight."

"Is it safe?" she asked.

"Probably not," I admitted.

To her credit, she didn't push it.

"I can go with you," she offered.

"I'd rather you research." We needed to learn more about who —or what—we were up against. I shoved off the counter. "I've done a preliminary web search. It wasn't much. I just wanted to learn where Kitty Cunningham might be and what happened to her that made her target Molly."

"Verity—" she warned.

Yes, I knew seeking out a violent ghost wasn't the safest idea— not to mention digging up dirt on her life and afterlife.

I kept talking before she could stop me. "Try the old newspaper archives, family histories, anything you can find in the microfilm."

There was a pause, then a soft sigh. "I'll do my best, Verity. But be careful. Take Ellis."

"I would"—my handsome police officer boyfriend was always up for ghost adventures—"but he's knee-deep in family issues tonight."

"I don't suppose you can put it off?" Melody pressed.

"I would if I could."

"But you can't," she stated for me. My sister understood me better than anyone. "I'll call you as soon as I have anything," Melody promised. "And Verity?"

I knew what she was going to say next.

"Be careful."

I would and I always had.

Although sometimes, it wasn't enough.

A familiar scratching at the door yanked me from my thoughts. It wasn't Frankie. He never knocked. I opened the door, and Lucy burst in like a house on fire.

She spun in a circle and slid sideways toward me, her white-striped tail raised high like a proud flag.

"Am I glad to see you." I scooped her up, and Lucy nuzzled into my neck, her tiny body pulsing with warmth. "We're in trouble, girl." I held her closer, pressing a kiss to her head. "Or at least Molly is."

She licked my arm at the mention of the ghost. Lucy might not like Frankie, but she sure loved it when his girlfriend came to visit. They had a game where Lucy would chase Molly around the apple tree. You'd think one of them would get dizzy, but...no.

And just this fall, Molly had made up a game called "leaf tornado," where she'd whip up a swirl of foliage for Lucy to bat at and dance through. After one such session, I'd even caught Lucy napping in a sunbeam next to Molly, who couldn't resist stroking the air right above her fur.

I wouldn't sugarcoat it. "I'm worried," I said to Lucy, who looked up at me with big black eyes.

Then she jumped, and I did too as Frankie burst through the back wall, or should I say El Gato.

My poor skunk wriggled and began clawing to get down.

"Don't worry. We're doing everything we can," I said, lowering her to the floor. As soon as her paws touched, she made a mad dash for the stairs that led to our bedroom. At least one of us would get some rest tonight.

I turned back to Frankie. I'd never seen my housemate's alter ego before. I'd only heard the outrageous stories. El Gato stole the frame off the *Mona Lisa* just for fun. El Gato made Al Capone cry. El Gato seduced the wife of El Presidente with his sexy salsa dancing. And now I could see how the rumors might be true.

Gone were his usual suit and tie, replaced now by sleek black trousers, the material shimmering in the glow of my ghost. They clung to his form, accentuating his wiry strength. A white silk shirt, partially unbuttoned to reveal a hint of chest, added a dramatic splash I'd never seen from my housemate.

Who could honestly be quite stuffy.

His face was partially hidden behind a thick, well-groomed mustache, a stark contrast to his usually clean-shaven appearance. His hair, normally slicked back, hung loose and wild over his forehead and around his shoulders, adding to his outlaw persona.

Dangling from his fingers was a slim cigar, its smoke unfurling in languid coils. But it was the bamboo cane, a semblance of debonair elegance, that completed the transformation. It was no ordinary cane, though. Rumor had it that concealed within was a razor-sharp dagger, and the handle hid a lethal dose of poison.

The look in his eyes was equally deadly. Sharp and glittering, they held a steely resolve that left no room for argument. This was Frankie, but not as I knew him. This was El Gato, the flamboyant and deadly Cuban gangster, ready to infiltrate the murky underbelly of the Irish mob.

"You look fantastic," I said in all honesty.

"Why aren't you ready?" he demanded, his eyes bugging out. "We have to go."

"I put on my tennis shoes," I told him, holding up a foot. "Plus, I have Melody started on the research." I spotted my hemp purse on the counter by the sink. "Let me fetch my bag, and we're all set."

"No," he said, blocking my path to the door. "No...no, no, no."

I didn't get it. "Is that a Cuban thing?"

Frankie pinched his fingers to the bridge of his nose. "We're going into Irish mob territory," he said, his voice clipped. "You're wearing a pink flowered dress, a white headband with a bow on it, and your hair is screaming yellow blonde."

"Hey," I protested. I liked my hair, and it was far more corn-silk blonde than "yellow."

"You look like...only you do," he said, waving a hand up and down over my entire self. "Too many wiseguys know you're my sidekick. It's safer if they don't recognize us."

"Sidekick?" I asked. If anything, he was *my* sidekick.

"Focus," he told me. "If they see me, they'll shoot me. Which, I admit, won't feel like hugs and sunshine, but I'll wake up in an hour or so. They shoot you and you're dead. Forever."

His words sent a chill down my spine. Frankie was right. It wasn't like any of the ghosts could die again. I was the only one who could get truly hurt or killed if ghostly bullets started flying or if I drew the wrong sort of attention.

"I'll be right back." I darted to my room, not at all eager to think what the Irish mob might like to do to me. I focused on my outfit instead, which...could be complicated. I basically had one style—cute flowery dresses and sandals. Or tennis shoes. White jeans with colorful tops. Add a cheerful sweater if it gets cold. And well, that was it.

What can I say? It suited me.

"I'm not sure what else I can do," I said to Lucy, who sat on the bed, curled up on my pillow.

She flicked her tail as if to say, *You're the one who decided to get mixed up with a bunch of crazy ghosts.*

"This century!" Frankie called from downstairs.

"I'm hurrying," I promised. Molly needed us. Bad.

Then I remembered the costume I wore this past Halloween —a cowgirl outfit. It lay folded at the back of my closet, a bit dusty, but the checkered shirt, fringed suede vest, and red bandanna were still in good shape. Plus, the straw hat would cover my trademark blonde hair if I stuffed it all up inside. I paired it with a denim skirt and a pair of white cowboy boots and was downstairs a few minutes later.

"Let's go," I announced.

Frankie choked when he saw me. "What is that?"

"Something no Irish gangster has ever seen me in." I wasn't pretty, but I was proud. "Plus, it covers my hair."

Frankie opened his mouth, probably to argue, but his impatience made him bite back whatever he was going to say.

"Get your keys," he said, heading out. "If you get shot, it's on you."

What a reassuring thought.

I grabbed my bag from the countertop and made a quick stop in the parlor to retrieve Frankie's urn. We kept it next to the fireplace for safekeeping, along with my grandmother's favorite rosebush and the "Frankie" dirt I'd rescued from my garden. I couldn't always keep track of the gangster ghost, but at least I knew where his ashes were.

"*Acelera, mujer!*" Frankie whipped his bamboo cane up and brought it to rest on his shoulder.

"So, you can be obnoxious in two languages," I observed, slipping his urn into my hemp bag.

He was lucky he was dead.

"Don't test my talents," he warned.

"Don't test my patience." I strode past him for the door. I cared. I just wasn't going to get all dramatic about it. "Believe me, I want to find Molly as much as you do." She might be his girlfriend, but I considered her my friend as well, and I wouldn't let anything happen to her.

"*Un caballo, un caballo,*" Frankie muttered in my wake. "*Mi reino por un caballo.*"

"No more horses on the porch," I insisted, thankful for four years of high school Spanish as I locked the door behind us.

"You're killing me," he muttered.

As if that were possible.

Betsy Sue, the moonshine still, sputtered and chugged next to the pond, glowing a ghostly silver gray. Then she let off a pop that sounded like a firecracker.

I halted. "That thing had better not catch fire while we're gone—" I began. Then I gasped as Frankie whipped his ghostly power from me so fast it made my head clang and my ears ring.

"Why did you do that?" I bent to grasp my knees under the fringe of my skirt.

"No distractions," he warned.

Like explosions at my house.

"I told you she was going to blow sky-high," I insisted, trying to get my bearings as the remains of Frankie's powers crackled over my skin.

"Betsy Sue's fine. She's just settling," he insisted. "Besides, we have bigger things to worry about."

Unfortunately, he was right. At least on the latter point.

Chapter Four

The gangster made a beeline for the 1978 Cadillac parked at the back of the house, and I followed close on his tail. The land yacht had occupied the spot by the rose garden long before I'd inherited the avocado green relic from my grandmother, along with our family's antebellum home.

"Be honest. Do you actually speak Spanish?" I asked, sliding in on the driver's side and depositing the bag with Frankie's urn onto the bench seat next to me. I wouldn't put it past the gangster to memorize a few phrases and then fake the rest. At the same time, from my limited high school Spanish, he seemed to be making a bit of sense.

"You should never doubt me." He settled into the passenger side with his cane between his knees. "I take my crime very seriously."

I'd also been around him long enough to realize he didn't answer the question.

And that asking Frankie to be honest was like asking a cat to bark.

But I knew he loved Molly with all his heart, and that was the only thing that mattered right now.

I watched the gangster toss his unlit ghostly cigar into my car's ancient ashtray. "Tell me more about possession," I said, turning my key in the ignition. The engine gave a hard chug and a wheeze, but it started right up. "I'd like to know what we're up against."

Before it bit us in the behind.

Frankie dragged a hand down his face. "Possession is rare for a reason, and it can get real ugly, real fast." He dropped his hand out the closed window as we drove past the young peach orchard I'd planted in my front yard. "The first and only time I saw it happen was back when I was running hooch off the river near the old Southern Spirits distillery." He shifted in his seat and dug a silver cigarette case out of his back pocket. "I hadn't been dead long." He popped the case and whipped out a smoke, tucking a spare one behind his ear. "We had a guy named Scooter working for us. Real ace driver, could outrun any cop car." He planted a cigarette on his lower lip. "When he was alive, we used to give him a sticker on his car for every escape. He must have had a couple of dozen."

"Charming," I said as we neared the end of my neighborhood.

Scooter was lucky he didn't come up against my Ellis.

The gangster stashed his case and cupped a hand to light his smoke. "You'd have liked Scooter. He was fun. Unpredictable."

"Some of us like peace and quiet," I reminded him, taking a left onto Rural Route 7.

"No, you don't, or you wouldn't hang out with me," Frankie said as if I had a choice. Smoke trailed out of his nose. "Anyhow, out of the blue, ol' Scooter started acting strange." He took a hard drag. "We'd catch him talking to himself in different voices or forgetting how to work a gearshift. I figured he'd just had one too many nips of the good stuff."

I waved the ghostly smoke away from my face, never mind the fact that I couldn't actually smell it. Or make it go anywhere. "If the hooch Scooter drank was anything like what I saw you brewing out back, I'm surprised he didn't blind himself too."

The gangster took another hard drag. "I do have a blend called Blind Cat Biscuit," he mused. "Maybe I should make that next."

Oh, great. I was encouraging him.

I slowed. We were beyond the streetlights now.

Frankie glanced out the window. "Hang right." He pointed the hand cradling his smoke toward a narrow asphalt road that disappeared into the underbrush.

"You've got to be nuts." I edged the Cadillac to a stop on the grassy shoulder. The dim dashboard lights made the ghost appear watery in the moonless night.

He had his directions right. The abandoned drive-in stood off a lonely road past the civilized part of town. But there were nicer ways to get there, ones that didn't include a barely there dirt track through the woods.

"It's the most direct route," he said, tossing the stub of his abused cigarette out my window.

"But not the best one," I countered, watching him light up again. "Let's find an easier road so that we can also get out fast if we need to. There might be a better path off the new freeway past the truck stop." Unlike the gangster, I liked a plan. We didn't need to be making any escapes down dark, deserted back roads and risk getting turned around or trapped.

"El Gato knows best," he stated, pointing his cigarette at me, the smoke wisping around his fingers.

"El Gato doesn't exist," I reminded him.

He bugged his eyes like I was the crazy one. "Okay, let me put it another way. This route lets us sneak in the back way and draw a lot less attention."

"Now you're talking." I clicked on my brights and lurched back onto the uneven asphalt. Rarely did Frankie take the less dramatic way, and I'd go with him on this one.

My car's heavy frame jolted and rattled as we pushed its old suspension to the brink.

"Hurry up," Frankie groused, fiddling with his luxurious El Gato mustache.

"I'm doing my best," I vowed as my trusty land yacht bumped along the narrow forest path. Leafy limbs and half-dead greenery grasped at us from the encroaching shrubbery, scratching the sides of the car like ghostly fingers.

My headlights barely cut through the pitch black. I'd have to be careful not to get lost. I knew almost every inch of Sugarland except for what lay out here.

"You drive like a turtle on tranquilizers," he said, flinching as a particularly persistent branch snatched at the windshield wiper.

"I'm no hooch runner," I said, cringing as another bump elicited a foreboding crunch from below.

"Or drinker," he added.

"So what happened to Scooter?" I asked, squelching the argument.

The gangster's expression darkened. "We didn't realize he was possessed, not at first. We'd never seen it before." He took a deep drag and exhaled through his nose. "Then Scooter stopped talking in his own voice altogether, and we started to see these flashes of another face."

I inhaled sharply. "Like what happened to Molly."

"Yeah." Frankie turned away and tossed another ghostly cigarette butt out the window. I watched it disintegrate on the breeze. "It was bad by that point." He dug for another smoke. "He started calling himself Fast Eddie."

The road split in two. The path to the right led down to Johnson's Cave. A thick chain stretched over the entrance, blocking that wider, easier route. We took the narrower path, scarcely visible amid the trees and brush.

"Had you ever met this Eddie before?" I asked, slowing as Thumper's cousin darted across the road. "I mean, before he was in your friend?"

"No," Frankie said, lighting up again. "Never saw him before in our lives or afterlives." He ran a hand over his eyes. "Best we could figure, this Eddie was a wandering spirit. We couldn't peg how he got into Scooter." He shook his head. "I'll tell you, though, the longer it went, the more Scooter started taking risks. Big ones. He took home a guard dog as a pet. He hosted an illegal underground gambling parlor down at the church hall, right in the middle of dead-church-lady bingo. He dared Wyatt Earp to come to town for a shoot-out. That guy still locks people up in Tombstone."

"Yikes." I winced.

"Not that I didn't admire Scooter being creative and all," Frankie added, pausing for a drag. "But when he tried to pick-pocket me during a bank robbery over in Jackson, he crossed the line."

"You were at work." I nodded, trying to be sympathetic.

"Exactly. Plus, he palmed my lucky silver dollar. Almost made me fall out the window of the getaway car."

"Your days are never dull," I said, in the understatement of the year.

"Thanks," he said, blowing out a smoke ring.

I hadn't meant it as a compliment.

He pointed to a whisper of a path up on our left. "Turn there."

It was even narrower than our current non-road. There was a reason I hadn't been down this way since I'd met Frankie. That time, he'd been leading me to a creepy, abandoned haunted house.

The ghosts who tended to haunt the outskirts were often darker, tortured souls who would rather avoid attention.

I slowed and bounced over a bowling-ball-size hole.

"Did you try to get help for Scooter?" I asked.

Frankie fingered his cigarette. "We didn't realize how bad it was until it was too late," he said, taking a hard drag. "I mean, who doesn't like a guy who drives with his knees while counting cash?" His fingers shook as he gestured with the smoke. "Scooter just kept getting more erratic, though. Until he didn't want us to call him Scooter anymore. He was...Eddie."

How awful. "Where did Scooter go?"

He twirled the cigarette in his fingers, the paper crinkling softly. "I don't know. But soon his face was Eddie's face all the time. Eddie told us point-blank that he took over. Scooter was dead. For real this time."

It was unimaginable. "How could you be sure?" I pressed. "I mean, what if Eddie was lying and Scooter was in there somewhere?"

Frankie flexed his jaw. "Scooter would have given us a sign. We had a code."

"Did you stick around a while and give him a chance?" I pressed. Frankie tended to make snap decisions.

"Why are you blaming this on me?" he shot back.

"I'm not," I rushed to say. At least I didn't mean to.

He gripped the smoke so hard it bent. "The thing is, it's unnatural. You can't just take somebody's ghostly body. There's consequences. Eddie ate up his own energy fighting Scooter off so that he could keep possessing him. In a living person, you'd get booted at that point. In a ghost, it drains you until there's nothing left." Frankie's mustache twitched. "Scooter was a fighter. Once he was gone, Eddie wasn't far behind." His mouth formed a grim line. "They both bit it, for good and forever."

I was stunned. "They *both*...ceased to exist?"

"I watched it happen," he said, his voice stone-cold. "A fizzle and a pop, then..." He shook his head. "No trace of either soul ever again. Not on this plane, at least."

"What about the ether?" I managed. It was an in-between place ghosts could go to take a rest.

Not that I'd ever seen it.

"Not there." Frankie waved a hand helplessly. "We looked. And it's not like we watched either of them go to the light," he added, as if that were the most impossible choice of all for a wiseguy. "Scooter and his attacker vanished like they'd never existed."

"Oh, Frankie," I gasped. "It sounds like the worst permanent death imaginable." For both ghosts, but especially the one who was attacked.

"Thanks for the pep talk." He tossed his ruined cigarette out the window.

There was one thing I didn't get. "Why would any ghost attempt a possession when it will end both them and their victim?"

Frankie ran a hand down the side of his face. "I don't know. Desperation? Revenge? Maybe they think they hit on some big, grand idea and don't know the consequences."

"They couldn't possibly. Nobody would choose that." And to be on the receiving end... How awful. "And I can't imagine what it would be like to have your energy, your life force consumed like that."

He shot me a lethal look. "I can tell you it's not going to happen to Molly."

"It won't," I pledged.

We'd figure this out.

We'd make it right.

The alternative was unthinkable.

Chapter Five

It felt like we were entering another world as I caught sight of an abandoned gas station. The sign read *Tennessee Oil*. My headlights caught rusted pumps under an old tin awning. The narrow windows of the building at the back were dark and broken.

"This place hasn't changed much," I observed. It appeared just as it had the night I'd met Frankie, all those years ago.

"It's as shady as it's ever been." His gaze scanned the darkened windows as we passed an old diner, its white-tile exterior chipped and streaked with graffiti, its parking lot all but lost to weeds.

"The boys in high school used to dare each other to come out here," I said. I'd been too scared.

Now I realized it was sad, too. I'd read stories about disappearing rural towns, but never thought mine would be included.

"Unincorporated," Frankie said, "with a spotty police presence." He gazed out the front window with a faraway look. "The Irish had a hideout here long before the rest of this sprang up in the 1950s."

He cleared his throat as we passed a lump of a building completely overtaken by bushes and trees. "Left down this alley."

I did as he instructed, even though I could barely see it.

Crumbling brick walls rose on either side, dotted with festive iron stars bleeding rust.

No doubt someone had loved these places a long time ago like I loved Sugarland now. But the relic of a town didn't feel right.

Maybe I was merely unsettled about how easy it was to lose a home, a road, an entire community.

We drove until the asphalt road opened up into a field caged by a rusted chain-link fence. Brand-new silver razor wire wound along the top.

Someone had been here recently.

"Why would someone care about this old place?" I asked as my headlights caught the teetering sign outside the Starlite Drive-In. A kitschy nod to yesteryear's space age, its once-gleaming rocket red and cosmic blue were as faded as an old comic book left in the sun. The aluminum letters, meant to gleam like a constellation in the night sky, were now more like a half-remembered Morse code—some dangling, others gone AWOL.

"Kill your lights," he ordered, grabbing his cigar from my ashtray.

"Dang it, Frankie," I said, doing as he asked. He might be able to see, but I couldn't.

The last thing I wanted to do was be stuck out here in the dark.

"What part of sneaking don't you understand?" he muttered, producing a straw fedora hat and tipping the brim down to cover the bullet hole in his forehead. Then he passed straight out my car door.

"Plenty more than you do." Frankie was as subtle as a sledgehammer.

Rocks crunched under my tires as I parked behind the wooden explosion that sent a rocket up to the top of the sign, directed toward the great beyond.

I killed the engine and spotted the gray glow of the gangster as he skirted toward the gated front entrance. "Wait for me," I hissed.

I got that he was anxious to get going, but we had to work as a team.

"Frank?" I almost dropped my keys as his image disappeared entirely for an instant.

Maybe I'd blinked wrong.

But I'd never seen that before.

"Don't call me Frank," his disembodied voice grated in my ear.

Right. El Gato. "Well, hold up," I said, scrambling out of the land yacht and navigating the crumbling pavement in my rush to follow. I didn't like him getting too far ahead. First off because I wasn't crazy about being left alone in the dark outside an abandoned drive-in near an old mob hideout. And second, I didn't like what I'd just seen.

At all.

He'd been on edge and chain-smoking the entire ride out, which was understandable. But what if it had been worse than that?

I zeroed in on his image as he stalked the gate. "You're energetically connected to Molly," I murmured under my breath, wincing as I stepped on a rock that had somehow made it inside my cowboy boot.

"I'm not having this conversation," his disembodied voice hissed in my ear while I watched him light up.

"It's true, though, isn't it?" I murmured, yanking off my boot and shaking out the rock.

The gangster clandestinely checked the gun in his shoulder holster and the one stuffed in the back of his tight black pants.

Ever since he'd fallen for Molly, Frankie had drawn emotional energy from his relationship with the other ghost. It had made him stronger. Her too, most likely. And now, with her incapacitated...

I shoved my boot back on.

He paused to blow a few smoke rings as he strode, cane in

hand, toward the gate. At the same time, I caught him glancing through the bars to size up any threats.

This was it.

Go time.

I saw his energy flicker once more as I caught up to him and drew close enough to hiss in his ear, "How does Molly's possession affect you, Frankie?"

He stiffened, the harsh truth of it written in the resolve that flashed across his features. "It's not about me," he said, passing through the gate.

"Wow." I stopped cold. It was a phrase I never expected to hear from the hardened ghost.

The gangster could be in more danger than he was willing to admit.

"Irish at two o'clock," Frankie muttered in my ear, gliding ahead. "One more up in the booth."

He was going too fast.

And I couldn't see a thing. Not unless he tuned me in to the ghostly side.

Was there something he didn't want me to see?

I gave the gate a hearty tug. "It's locked." Or at least it sure felt like it. I dug out my iPhone and shone the flashlight on a thick winding chain secured by a shiny steel padlock.

"Bust it," he snapped.

Sure, let me grab the big hammer that I don't keep in my car. I felt my face grow hot. "I promised Ellis several ghost hunts ago that I wouldn't break and enter, much less damage property while breaking and entering."

"We don't have time for this," the ghost warned. "Ellis ain't here. Molly might be." He inhaled sharply. "And the Irish are everywhere."

He instinctively reached behind him for his gun.

"We need to be subtle," I urged, running my light over the sides of the gate, searching for an opening. I mean, it wasn't breaking and entering if they left it open for exploration, right?

I wouldn't think on that too much.

"While you dally, I'll eliminate the Irish," he gritted out. "Clear the way for our investigation."

That was not subtle. "What if the Irish know where Kitty is or what happened to her?" I hissed, running my light over the rusted fence to the left of the entrance.

"The Irish lie."

I didn't know about that, but I was fairly certain they'd notice three dead gangsters, and drawing that kind of attention wouldn't help us track down Molly.

"Just...hold up." I'd be able to help him make discreet inquiries or at least make it so that he wouldn't make a scene. People liked to talk to me.

People liked to shoot at Frankie.

"I got this," he said, leaving his gun holstered.

For now.

He stopped dead and glared down at something or someone that had to be ghostly because I didn't see a thing.

"El Gato," I snapped.

He didn't respond.

He merely pointed his cane at the threat he saw and began rattling something in Spanish that didn't even sound real to me. Then he whipped out a matador cape from thin air and twirled it before tossing it over his shoulders dramatically.

"Frankie!" I urged as quietly as I could.

He was going off half-cocked, and crazy didn't keep you from getting killed.

That would end my investigation really quick because, without his help, the only ghost I could see was him.

There had to be another way in, short of ramming the gate, which would not be healthy for the land yacht or me, and it certainly wouldn't help us stay under the radar.

I jogged along the rusted gate, scanning for holes or gaps in the shiny razor wire up top.

A large screen darkened the sky at the far end, its white paint peeling to reveal the wood skeleton underneath. Weathered holes dotted the fabric surface, which sagged heavily in the center. The old metal scaffolding holding it upright was rusted and bent, creaking softly in the night breeze. Beyond the dilapidated screen, at the top of a distant hill, I could see the glowing headlights of cars exiting the junction of Highway 63.

Inside the gate, the gangster gestured wildly.

Frankie wasn't known for his diplomacy.

At least he'd taken his hand off the gun. Although, come to think of it, that could get him killed quicker.

"El Gato," I demanded.

"You've got to see this," his disembodied voice crooned in my ear.

"What?" I asked, bending to try to pry the gate from the ground. I was fairly petite. Maybe I could crawl under.

Frankie's power hit me sideways, and I grabbed for the fence to steady myself. The unearthly energy sizzled over me, racing down my body. It felt like a thousand zaps of static electricity. Every nerve in my body crackled, and I could have sworn I saw stars.

I blinked hard, trying to adjust as the ghostly world came into view in shades of silvery gray. Only my situation was now worse because the fence outside the drive-in was no longer chain link, but plank wood at least ten feet high.

Tinny movie music floated from inside, along with dramatic voices from the big screen. *Look! you fools! You're in danger! Can't you see? They're after you! They're after all of us!*

"Hold on. I'm coming," I murmured, scanning the fence.

I hoped.

At least I could see better with Frankie's powers.

That was what did it because about ten feet down, I saw a break in the fence. The planks had been cut at the bottom, and the real-life chain-link fence didn't reach, either. I shoved my phone light into my bag and hurried to the break, dropping down and sliding under before I thought too much about who might have made the gap or why it existed on both planes.

Yes, it was suspicious.

No, I didn't like it.

But I needed to get in, and it was much better to focus on making sure I didn't touch any part of the ghostly fence. Contact with the other realm was cold and painful. Plus, my touch made ghostly objects fade and disappear entirely within a matter of minutes.

I'd rather not draw attention by zapping the fence.

Or myself.

So I crawled on my stomach with Frankie's urn rattling in the bag at my side. I kept a hand on my cowgirl hat and inched under and into the haunted drive-in.

Then I saw him. Frankie was backed against a ghostly glowing Chevy Bel Air by a massive ghost in a white shirt and black dress pants.

I popped up onto my elbows, then startled at the cold grip of a hand on my neck.

"Stop right there, kid."

Chapter Six

The touch of the ghost shocked me to the core. It felt wet and invasive and *wrong*.

I lurched away and retreated through the hole in the fence, cringing as the watery sensation oozed past my skin and burrowed down to my bones. Once I reached the other side, I kept going—straight into a patch of scraggly weeds.

A full-body shiver captured me, and I tried desperately to shake it off. I needed to be ready to defend myself, to run. I rolled onto my back and stared up at my captor with a gasp.

I knew her.

I hadn't seen her in over a decade, but she was unmistakable.

The ghost of my former Sunday school teacher peered at me through the hole in the fence, rubbing her arms as if she could scrub away the touch of the living.

"Miss Felicia?" I stammered, scarcely believing it.

"Verity Long." Her mouth opened and closed. Then slacked open again. She passed straight through the fence and loomed over me, no more than five feet tall, with short gray hair and piercing eyes.

Felicia Brightmore appeared exactly as I remembered. She even sported one of her trademark sweatshirts, this one with a cartoon cat clinging onto a branch for dear life, the words *Hang in there, purr-severance pays!* emblazoned beneath. She'd paired it with a long skirt and a comfortable pair of sneakers.

She stared at me for a second longer. "How's your mother?" she managed in the standard Sugarland greeting.

"Great," I said automatically. I struggled to my feet, backing up through the patchy weeds, trying to keep my distance without *looking* like I was keeping my distance. I realized I'd lost my cowgirl hat. I didn't think she'd hurt me, but she had touched me. Granted, she didn't appear exactly eager to make a second attempt, but better safe than sorry. "Mom and my stepdad are camped out at their favorite RV park down in Mississippi."

"Leaving you alone and itching for trouble," she concluded.

I'd expected to meet a mobster, not my moral compass.

"I'm grown and on my own," I said, wiping the dirt from my wobbly knees. "Please, I just need to dip through the fence for a minute," I said, trying to sound like I wasn't up to something when I clearly was.

"To see the movie?" she asked, arching a brow.

"No. Nothing like that," I said, trying to ease around her.

Frankie was in trouble. And now that I was tuned in to the other side, I could actually help. As soon as I made it past her and through the gap in the fence.

"In all my years..." She looked at me like I'd suggested we swap the communion wafers for fortune cookies. "I thought I taught you better."

I cringed as a gray glow spread from her chest down through her skirt. It radiated outward, blocking the hole entirely.

"I'd do this the right way if I could," I promised, halting before I got too close. "It's just that I'm alive, and besides, there's nobody in the ticket booth out front." At least I'd assumed there wasn't. Frankie had simply passed through the gate. Although I wouldn't put it past Frankie to sneak in. "It's not like I can buy a ticket."

She crossed her arms over her chest. "Excuses are like back

doors; they're always there if you're looking for a way out of trouble."

More like into trouble.

She had to understand. "My friend is a gangster, a dead one. He's already inside, and if he gets himself shot, we'll lose valuable time we need to save our friend who is currently possessed."

She dropped her arms. "That's a new one."

"It's true," I insisted, venturing closer, attempting to see past her. I sure hoped Frankie was all right in there. He hadn't exactly gone in with a clear head. "We're here trying to track down Kitty Cunningham. She's...very involved. Do you know where we might be able to find her?"

Miss Felicia's mouth thinned. "I don't gossip."

A location was hardly gossip unless Kitty was somewhere she shouldn't be. Now I really wanted to ask around inside.

"I still need to go rein in my gangster," I said. "Seriously. He could kill somebody. Or he could get whacked. It's happened before." More than once.

"Oh, I know all about the mobsters," she said, her eyes darting heavenward. "I invite them to Bible study every week. Brendan 'The Brick' Callahan is the only one who shows up, and he keeps trying to convince the group that making moonshine is in the tradition of turning water into wine and that the Ten Commandments are up for negotiation."

"I need a bingo card for every commandment my friend has broken," I joked.

Her eyes narrowed.

I was getting nowhere. Literally. I could try for a different hole in the fence—presuming I could find one—but I had a feeling Miss Felicia was onto me no matter where I went.

Unless I could convince her to give me a break.

I smoothed my denim skirt like a proper lady. "Pardon me for asking, but don't you have more important things to do?" She'd been in charge of at least six committees when she'd been alive, not to mention the rummage sale, the ladies' prayer circle, and the pastor's personal checkbook.

Her eyes softened. "You are important, Verity."

"I'd rather not be," I admitted. Not at this particular moment, at least.

Her lips twitched at my admission. "You never could stick to where you should be. I still remember the time you snuck out of my class." She clucked with fond reproach. "We found you up in the bell tower, trying to get a closer look at the pigeons."

I remembered. "I wanted to see if I could adopt one."

"You gave them all names." Her lips curved ever so slightly, and I jumped at the opportunity.

"So, I'm basically up in the bell tower again," I explained. "I'm not where I'm supposed to be, but I'm not doing any harm. I'm only here because I'm helping a friend."

She closed her eyes briefly, and I could feel her breaking, just like all the times we'd convinced her to let our class study outside.

"You can see for yourself," I insisted.

A small tilt of her head and her appraising eyes seemed to unravel me, thread by thread. "All right, but I'm going with you."

She backed off the hole, and my heart hammered fast as I clambered straight through.

I'd taken too long.

With any luck, my gun-happy gangster hadn't gotten too obnoxious with the Irish, or worse—gotten himself killed again.

My hat lay on the other side. I grabbed it, dusted it off, and stopped short when I saw the full glory of what had been the Starlite Drive-In.

Dramatic music sounded and cymbals clashed as a couple on the big screen fled through a narrow tunnel. The air was saturated with the scent of greasy burgers, sizzling hot dogs, and freshly popped popcorn. 1950s Fords, Chevys, and Packards lined up in neat rows, sporting fins and chrome. Ladies in pedal pushers and swishing skirts scurried between cars, their breathless chitchat and laughter punctuated by the sound of slamming car doors and the click-clack of shoes. A man in cuffed trousers waved to a man in jeans as they ferried popcorn and snacks past a man in a ten-gallon hat and his friend, who could have passed for Davy Crockett.

I glanced at the main screen. Were these guys dressing up for a Western movie?

If so, my checkered shirt and fringed jacket fit right in.

Then I saw Frankie.

He'd dropped his cane, his moustache had gone crooked, and he was pinned against a Chevy with painted flames down the side by a guy who looked like he'd stepped straight out of a James Dean movie. Broad shouldered with slicked-back hair and a leather jacket, he grabbed a fistful of Frankie's silk El Gato shirt and slammed him against the car.

I shoved my hat onto my head and rushed in to help, dodging a man balancing four hot dogs and two glass bottles of Coke. "Let him go," I demanded.

Frankie glared at me with wild eyes. "Bruja! I do not need your help," he insisted in a bad Cuban accent, flailing as the guy launched him back against the car once more.

Could have fooled me.

"I caught me a peeping Tom here," the rockabilly ghost growled. "Spying on me and my date."

A pretty blonde with ruby-red lips blinked up at me from the passenger side.

"It was an honest mistake," Frankie bristled once I made it to his side. "From behind, the guy is a dead ringer for Johnny O'Toole," he added, waving his hands. "I mean, check out that greasy hair." My housemate focused on me instead of the guy winding up to punch him.

"Watch out!" I warned.

"Bobby Rae O'Toole." Miss Felicia's voice bit like a bullet. "What would Jesus do?"

The rockabilly ghost froze mid-swing, his fist hovering inches from Frankie's face. He blinked, looking around like he'd just woken up from a dream. His eyes widened when they landed on Miss Felicia.

"Miss Felicia," Bobby Rae stuttered, lowering his fist. The hard-edged façade crumbled away. "We were only...talking." He eyed Frankie as the gangster edged off the car.

"Do I have to tell you-know-who you've been getting out of line?" Miss Felicia asked the tough guy, her voice softer now.

Bobby Rae shook his head, glancing down at his feet. "No, ma'am."

"Hello, Tina Louise." Miss Felicia leaned down for a look inside the car. "Are you staying six inches apart for Jesus?"

"Yes, ma'am," a sweet voice answered from inside.

Bobby Rae ran his hands through his slicked-back hair, appearing even more chastised.

"I know you are both good kids." Miss Felicia nodded, appearing pleased. She pivoted toward Frankie, who had tried to skulk off. "As for you," she interjected, halting him in his tracks, "I haven't seen your Johnny O'Toole since last night. He doesn't attend my classes, nor does he respect his elders as he should, but I can certainly help you locate him if you'd like."

"No, *gracias*." Frankie turned from her, straightening his moustache and retrieving his cane. He slicked back the sides of his El Gato coiffure and readjusted the straw fedora that concealed the bullet hole in his forehead. "If I can't shoot O'Toole, I'd like to avoid him, seeing as I'm the one who killed him."

"You should be ashamed," Miss Felicia gasped.

"He was in the way of my bullet," Frankie said as if he'd been helpless to stop it.

Miss Felicia wasn't buying it. Her lips pressed into a thin line, and her eyes—sharp as an eagle's and twice as penetrating—bored into the gangster. "Excuses are like belly buttons. Everybody's got one, and God's seen them all."

"Don't matter." Frankie shook his head. "While we've got you, you might as well know we're looking for someone."

"Well, don't expect me to help the mob." She drew a gold

cross out of her collar and smoothed it over her chest like a beacon. "This is a family establishment. Not like the den of sin that passes for a drive-in down in Mosbeysville."

Bobby materialized a few feet to her left. "What's that place called, Miss Felicia?"

"Never you mind." She waved him away.

"Is that what drew you?" I asked. "I'd have figured you'd be at church more."

She laughed. "Oh, I do keep an eye out. And I still sing with the women's choir every Sunday. But this place is special. Look at all the people who come here after they've died. They've chosen this particular slice of Sugarland. We have so many wonderful memories here." She smiled at an older couple arm in arm near the ticket booth.

Whoops—there was a ticket booth.

"My friend Mortimer likes to work the snack bar, and I keep an eye on the fence to catch kids sneaking in. I figure if they can't pay for a ticket, the least I can do is direct them over to Mortimer for a free Coke and popcorn." She sighed fondly. "This place can be heaven on earth as long as it remains pure and good. And if you avoid the problem souls."

That was the trick.

"We're only here briefly," I told her. "The last thing we want is trouble," I added, hoping Frankie would keep his mouth shut. "This is my housemate, Frankie. I wasn't lying when I said we're trying to help a friend who has been possessed."

"I...I don't think such a thing is possible," my teacher said, wringing her hands.

"It is." And I didn't have time to get into the specifics.

Frankie drew us aside to a darkened place away from the cars. "It's my girlfriend who's in danger," my housemate said, dropping the Cuban act. "Not that you should have told this lady my business," he added under his breath. "You need to break that habit."

I was trying.

Sort of.

In this case, it was the smart way to go about it. "This is not you helping a gangster; it's you helping us find a girl in trouble. We need to know if Molly is here," I said to Miss Felicia. "She's about five feet six with long black hair she wears in a bun."

"She's a raven-haired goddess," Frankie corrected, "with a cute button nose and a laugh bold as brass. She's got legs that go on forever, and—"

"Did you bring the locket she gave you?" I asked.

He drew it out of his pocket and flicked it open for Miss Felicia.

She studied it for a long moment before shaking her head. "I'm so sorry. I haven't seen that poor girl here or anywhere."

My heart sank. "We think she's possessed by the ghost of Kitty Cunningham."

My teacher drew a hand to her chest.

"I wasn't trying to gossip before," I explained. "We just need to figure out where Kitty might be. She was headed here when she disappeared on May 3, 1956. Maybe you've heard something —anything?"

She returned the locket to Frankie. "I remember when Kitty went missing. Her younger sister Patti was in my high school class."

"Where is Patti now?" I asked. "We'd like to talk with her."

The ghost adjusted her glasses. "Patti went to the light in 2008. She didn't stay one day. As for Kitty, I don't know anyone who's seen her since she left the malt shop."

My gangster friend stiffened. "We're drawing attention from the fuzz."

"Perfect," I said, following his gaze to a pair of officers standing near the snack bar. "They might be able to help." I gave them a wave.

The skinny one stood checking Frankie out. The senior officer lifted his radio to call something in.

"They're in tight with Chief McAvoy," Miss Felicia assured me. "Mac and Buzz are good men to know."

"Unless you have a couple of dozen warrants." Frankie harumphed in my ear.

He had a point. This could get sticky. But I didn't see where we had a choice. "The police are keeping an eye on the drive-in." That could only bode well for us. "And they might even be familiar with Kitty's case."

"Come on," Miss Felicia said. "I'll introduce you." She and I started over, but Frankie refused to budge.

"I'm not going to jail," he vowed. "Not today. Not when we need to find Molly."

"I'll do the talking," I assured him, trailing behind my old teacher.

"And say what?" Frankie demanded, catching up. "Sorry about robbing the evidence room during the annual police ball?"

"Please tell me you didn't," I hissed under my breath.

"They had my favorite gun."

Miss Felicia glanced at me over her shoulder. I wasn't sure if she'd heard Frankie, but I knew she'd heard me.

She kept her expression neutral and her tone light. "You should know, Kitty was a lot like you. She was never where she was supposed to be. She might have told people she was going to the movies, but she typically ended up somewhere else entirely. It gave her mother fits. I hear Mac and Buzz had to track Kitty down more than once."

"So they'd know her hangouts," I ventured.

"Stop walking," Frankie ordered. "We're headed right for them."

And we were learning things. "Okay, so if Kitty lied and said she would be at the drive-in, do you have any idea where she would go instead?"

Miss Felicia shrugged. "I don't want to tell unkind stories about the poor girl, but I can tell you my mother's sewing circle sure felt sorry for her mother. Although personally I figured it was probably her mother's fault."

Lovely.

"The police know more than I do," Miss Felicia assured me.

"You told her who I really am," Frankie said, his voice rising in my ear. "You told her Molly's name."

"You showed her the picture," I shot back under my breath.

Besides, she'd been my Sunday school teacher.

His voice rose more. "And now she's taking us straight to the cops."

"Let me handle it," I told him. "This is the best way to find Molly quickly."

This was the Sugarland PD. Ellis's department...just seventy or so years before his time.

"Mac," she said to the thin one with high cheekbones who fiddled with the handcuffs on his belt. "Buzz," she added to the older one with a super-short haircut. "I'd like you to meet a former student of mine. This is Verity, and she's here looking for Kitty Cunningham."

"Or this girl," I said, prompting Frankie to show them the picture from the locket. He hovered behind me, head down as he clicked it open.

"The living aren't welcome," Buzz said as if Miss Felicia had presented him with a dead fish instead of a live girl.

Mac stared past me, studying Frankie as if he were trying to place him. Or maybe it was the fact that Frankie was obviously hiding something.

"The sooner you help her, the sooner she'll be on her way," Miss Felicia reminded him.

Mac cleared his throat. "Word has it Kitty ran off with her boyfriend the night she disappeared. Nobody's seen her since."

"Do you know who she was dating?" I asked.

Buzz frowned. "Patrick O'Reilly."

"The Irish boss's son," Mac added.

Oh my. I heard a thud behind me and hoped Frankie hadn't fainted. "Is he here?" I asked.

"I haven't seen him," Mac said.

"He's around," Buzz confirmed. "Second in command under his father."

"Wonderful," I said, pasting on a smile. I glanced back at my gangster to find him headed in the other direction, cursing in Spanish and waving people out of the way with his bamboo cane. "Excuse me." I thanked the officers and Miss Felicia and rushed to catch up.

"Slow down," I said when I'd gotten close enough. "This is good. We're making terrific progress." The gangster was weaving between cars. I didn't think he even knew where he was headed. "Kitty ran off with Patrick. Patrick is here. There's a solid chance Kitty is somewhere as well." Sure, Miss Felicia hadn't seen her, but maybe she was somewhere Miss Felicia didn't go. "We just need to find Patrick O'Reilly."

"First the police and then the mob." He spun to face me. "We dressed like this to avoid talking to people like Patrick O'Reilly!"

"Plans change." He knew that better than anybody.

We both jumped when engines erupted behind Frankie.

"Drag race!" someone shouted.

"At a drive-in?" I'd never heard of such a thing.

The movie screen went dark. The overhead lights made popping noises as they turned on.

A pair of ghostly cars lined up on the far end by the fence. They spun their wheels, throwing off dust and making a terrible racket. Mac and Buzz dashed past us, straight for the spectacle, with Miss Felicia not far behind. The rest of the crowd took off that way as well. Couples hurried from cars. Families held back, watching.

"Come on!" Frankie said, heading for the thick of things.

Miss Felicia shrieked as the blur of a ghost shot straight through her and toward the action.

Frankie was already gone.

"I'm coming," I hollered, trying to catch up.

The loudspeakers crackled to life. "Gather round, ladies and gents," a sultry voice purred.

A lump formed in my throat. She sounded...unsettlingly familiar, yet different.

She giggled, then dropped straight back to sex kitten. "We're going to show you a *drop-dead* good time."

Chapter Seven

"Who's that on the loudspeaker?" Miss Felicia demanded. We hurried past the lineup of cars, toward the gap between the front row and the big screen.

"Who is it usually?" I asked, dodging a lady wearing a wide poodle skirt.

"I'm the only one allowed to use the loudspeaker!" My old teacher darted ahead of me, narrowing herself to pass through the crowd. "I don't understand," she said in a clipped tone. "No one would dare."

The movie halted, the screen blaring white.

The ghostly realm appeared as the most powerful ghost on a particular property saw it. The dominant ghost held it through superior energy or power or, at times, through sheer emotion. And now it seemed Miss Felicia had lost control to a sultry female with a penchant for fast cars.

The crowd halted at the edge of a dirt track carved into the dust. At the far end of the lot, a cherry-red '57 Chevy Bel Air and a turquoise '56 Ford Thunderbird revved their engines.

"Race! Race! Race!" the ghosts surrounding me began to chant.

I'd lost track of Frankie. Then I spotted him closing in on the two cars. He had his eyes trained on the spirit of a young woman. She strolled down the space between the Bel Air and the Thunderbird, whipping a handkerchief at her side with all the flair of a matador preparing for a fight. She wore a scandalously short skirt and had a dark ponytail down to her butt.

"Oh my." I froze. It could be Molly.

Frankie zipped up behind her. He spun her around, and I caught my breath.

I let it out in a whoosh. Her nose was too long and her cheeks too thin. The woman brushed him aside. Not Molly.

The gangster scarcely noticed. He backed off, furiously stroking his El Gato mustache as he scanned the fence line and crowd.

She had to be here somewhere.

This could be our chance to spot her, with everyone out of their cars and in one place.

"Help me look for the girl we showed you earlier," I said to Miss Felicia, craning my neck to see. The anticipation hung heavy in the air, thicker than the scent of buttered popcorn and sizzling hot dogs.

"All I see is sin," my old teacher replied, frowning at the girl in the daringly diminutive skirt.

She stood, knees stiff and arms outstretched, between the racers, the white handkerchief held high in one hand. The crowd counted down with her, "Three, two, one. Go!" She whipped the handkerchief down and spun to watch as the two classic cars shot forward with a roar, their engines echoing across the theater.

The '57 Chevy snagged an early lead, with the Thunderbird in hot pursuit. The crowd's roars filled my ears. They surged all around me, and I shuffled to the side to avoid touching anyone. The ground vibrated under my cowboy boots as the cars zoomed past, kicking up a storm of dust and exhaust.

Just as the Thunderbird seemed poised to pass, the Chevy rallied with a burst of speed, crossing the finish line with a triumphant surge of its engine. It swerved in a showy arc and came dangerously close to getting T-boned by the second-place Thunderbird.

The crowd clapped and whistled as the victor flung open the door and leaped out.

It was Molly!

Like I'd never seen her before. She wore a black leather catsuit that clung to her like she'd won the grand prize in a vacuum-seal competition. Her bangs were drawn up in a tight knot at the top of her head, leaving her long dark hair to flow over her shoulders. Her laughter rang out, a joyous sound that would have brought me to tears with relief if she hadn't immediately hopped up onto the car hood to pose like a calendar model.

"Molly!" I cried, waving frantically.

She didn't spare me a glance. She licked her lips and gave the crowd a sultry look before tossing her head back and letting out a loud *whoop!*

Oh, yes. Something had a hold of her.

Ghostly vapor churned around the car and Molly, and when she turned back in my direction, I saw Kitty's face instead of hers. My stomach flip-flopped as I registered Kitty's impish features and broad smile. Kitty's saucy wink.

"I need to get through," I said to the lady in front of me and the couple next to her. "This is an emergency."

Frankie sprinted toward Molly like a house on fire.

The people blocking my way ignored me. Same for the ones to the sides. And I couldn't touch them.

"Miss Felicia," I called as I swiveled my head. She could usher me through. Especially when I pointed out the ghost who had most likely taken over her drive-in. But my old teacher was nowhere to be seen.

"Go," I hollered as if Frankie needed me to tell him. I clapped my hands. "You've got it."

He was almost to her when an unseen force flung him back. He hit the ground and rolled twice before skidding to a halt, his mouth agape.

"El Gato!" I gasped. The smoke surrounding Molly and the car had thickened. That couldn't be a good sign.

The crowd churned all around me. I strained as close as I dared and watched him go for it again.

Frankie came within a breath of the car, but the second his hand and a foot disappeared into the ghostly cloud, it spit him back out again.

The crowd clapped and cheered, oblivious to Frankie's plight, caught up in the spectacle of victory. And no doubt because Molly appeared to be reenacting a White Snake video on the hood of the car.

And if that wasn't shocking enough, a gorgeous man in an impeccably tailored suit strolled right past Frankie, piercing the smoky haze. His dark hair was styled with a nonchalance that only accentuated his strikingly handsome features, and a hint of stubble shadowed his chiseled jaw.

He reached out a hand to Molly, cupped her chin, and drew her in for a hard kiss.

Frankie shrieked. The crowd cheered. Molly plastered herself against the handsome stranger and returned his kiss for all she was worth.

"Back off." Frankie drew his gun and fired a round aimed to knock the interloper to his knees. "Off, off, off!" he hollered, shooting three more times.

The bullets passed straight through and struck the ground, sending up puffs of dirt.

"Impossible," Frankie choked out.

The ethereal smoke around Molly shimmered and grew brighter. The handsome man kissed her like the ship was going down.

"Not with my girl." Frankie tossed the gun and leaped for the guy.

The gorgeous stranger lifted a hand and snapped his fingers. That instant, with a sudden pop, the entire scene disappeared.

The car, the stranger, Molly, the vapor—gone, like a television switching off.

Frankie stumbled into the void, fists raised and ready. "I'm here, Molly!"

He spun in a circle.

But he was a nanosecond too late.

The movie restarted on the big screen, the booming soundtrack reverberating across the lot. *Doctor! Will you tell these fools I'm not crazy? Make them listen to me while there's still time!*

I rushed to Frankie, wound up like a boxer, his face ashen. "What was that?" I asked.

He stared at me, slack-jawed. "My worst nightmare."

It was bad. I'd admit to that.

"At least we know Molly's here," I said, trying to look on the bright side. "She's okay."

For now.

One by one, the patrons dispersed for their cars or the snack bar.

Frankie dug a hand through his hair. "Did you see her? Kitty is too strong. She's taking over too fast. And I'm going to *kill* that guy."

He had every right to be upset. I was scared, too. But we had to think logically about this. "First things first. Let's figure out where she went."

Then, as if I'd conjured her from thin air, Molly appeared again at the far end of the lot near the fence. At least it appeared to be her—a girl in a skintight catsuit.

"Look!" I pointed. She walked alone at a brisk pace, arms crossed in front of her and shoulders hunched. The blaring movie cast a long shadow in front of her.

We both took off for her at full tilt.

We hadn't made it halfway when she turned and looked directly at Frankie, her eyes filled with fear.

"It's her!" I made a small leap. The real her. Molly, the girl who laughed too loud when she was nervous, who always had a kind word for everyone. The girl we'd been looking for. "Molly!" I called. "We're here to rescue you!"

"Help," her whispered voice sounded in my ear, so soft I almost wondered if I'd heard it at all.

Frankie shrank into an orb and zipped ahead of me just as a ghostly 1950s sedan materialized behind Molly, driving full speed.

"Watch out." I waved my arms.

But Molly didn't notice. She focused on Frankie alone, pleading with her eyes.

"I'm scared," she whispered as the sedan bore down on her in a blur of white. The front of the car was crystal clear, with a massive silver grille and large, round headlights. Kitty's face flashed over Molly's.

"Move!" I hollered, running for her, seeing the terror flash across Molly's face as she saw what was behind her.

She screamed and dodged out of the path of the sedan, but the massive grille swerved sharply, tires screeching as it aimed right for her once more.

Frankie zipped straight into the mist of the car.

I closed in on Molly, desperate to distract the car, to give Frankie more time, to somehow stop the disaster unfolding before me.

Only Frankie passed straight through the mist. He couldn't get a handle on it.

The headlights bore down on us.

Molly dodged again—too late.

She let out a panicked cry that was cut sickeningly short as the car slammed into her from behind, her figure dissolving into a cloud of mist as the vehicle passed straight through her. I threw myself sideways, hitting the dirt hard as the vehicle whooshed past, barely missing me.

I stared after it in horror, my heart pounding out of my chest.

The car screamed forward, passing straight through the gate, leaving no trace behind except for the echo of sirens in the distance.

Frankie crumpled to the ground. I rushed to help him, when out of nowhere a brute in pin-striped pants and a sweater shimmered into existence right in front of me, blocking my way.

"Who allowed this?" he asked in a deep Irish brogue.

He was built like a WWE wrestler, with slicked-back black hair and a stogie clenched between his teeth.

"He's talking to you, new girl," a harsh, lilted voice sounded behind me.

I'd been afraid of that.

Chapter Eight

I swallowed hard. I could handle the Irish mob. Maybe.

There didn't seem to be much choice in the matter.

"Did you see that?" I pressed. Someone had run down Molly in cold blood.

"I see you," the wiseguy growled.

I stared up at the gangster in front of me. His eyes, cold and unforgiving, were a piercing shade of gray, and his broad shoulders hunched as if ready for a fight. I glanced past the surly gangster to Frankie, where he'd collapsed on the ground in his El Gato getup.

My housemate took one look at the men who had me trapped and promptly disappeared.

Lovely. I tried to smile and ignore the way my stomach dropped.

"Let me guess. Johnny O'Toole?" I asked, trying to sound friendly, fighting a wince when my voice shook.

The wiseguy in front of me whipped the stogie out of his mouth and got right in my face. "How did you know my name?" I could smell his stale cigar breath, feel the chill of the ghost in front of me, not to mention his buddy at my back.

"Lucky guess," I said quickly. "I met Bobbie Rae earlier

tonight." In a manner of speaking. "You both have such pretty eyes. Very striking." In a lethal kind of way. Like a leopard ready to pounce. I tried to sound bubbly, friendly, as two more mobsters hemmed me in on both the right and the left.

Johnny O'Toole studied me like a bug under glass. "We have a certain obligation to keep order in our territory."

"Now the Cuban is back," the one behind me growled.

"The boss is unsettled," said the weasel-faced one to my right.

"I don't see why that's my fault," I insisted, raising my hands even though none of them had asked. "This is all a misunderstanding." I cleared my throat. "I'm here looking for Kitty Cunningham." They'd obviously been keeping an eye on the drive-in. "Perhaps you know where I can find her."

"Never," the guy at my back vowed.

"The cheek." Weasel Face cracked his knuckles.

"I don't see what the big deal is." I mean, sure, these guys wanted to kill Frankie, but a lot of people wanted to kill Frankie. And perhaps the Irish weren't overly friendly, but that didn't mean they couldn't answer a simple question.

"What are you up to?" O'Toole demanded.

"Nothing," I insisted as a cold wind whooshed over me. Goosebumps erupted from my chest and down my arms.

"We saw you with El Gato." His eyes narrowed. "We know the Cuban is behind tonight's power play. He thinks he can take over the drive-in. And everything else."

"I really don't think so," I said, wishing I could escape, feeling the icy chill of the ghost at my back as he drew within a hair's breadth of my shivering skin.

"Then why'd El Gato show up tonight after all these years?" O'Toole demanded.

"After what he pulled," the gangster behind me snarled.

"And why'd he go digging up the past?" growled the man to my left, his face a cloud of swirling gray.

Okay, that was creepy. I gave in to a small shudder and focused on the problem at hand. "Does anyone really know why El Gato does what he does?"

Seriously. It was a fair question.

The air grew positively icy as the four men left me no room to breathe. "What do *you* say, lassie?" O'Toole taunted.

"Me?" I asked, fresh goosebumps erupting over my skin.

O'Toole's lip curled in a sneer. "You're with the Cuban. You're alive and talking. So, talk."

I'd rather not.

"I'm just a friend of the family," I insisted, trying to keep my tone casual, my voice light. "Not El Gato's family. Never been to Cuba." I tried for a friendly chuckle, but it came out high-pitched and more than a little scared. "I'm trying to learn what happened to that poor woman we saw drag racing, the one who died."

The ghost at my back chuckled. "Looked to me like she was run down."

That was not what I'd meant, and he knew it. "Someone hit her," I insisted, looking O'Toole straight in the eyes. "I daresay it was on purpose. But who would do such a thing?"

"Somebody who thought she had it coming." O'Toole chortled, earning a round of guffaws from his comrades.

I ignored their lack of class. "Please. Let's be frank. Do you know Kitty Cunningham?"

The brute's smile disappeared.

"We're asking the questions, not you," O'Toole snarled.

"When Kitty was alive, she dated Patrick O'Reilly," I said, pleased when O'Toole flinched. "Now I believe Patrick is your gang's second in command." And since he was number two and the boss's son, he most certainly outranked Johnny O'Toole. "That was Patrick kissing her just now, wasn't it?"

O'Toole ground his jaw and glared at me.

"You all see him snap his fingers?" Weasel Face snickered. "He always snapped his fingers like that when they were off to the no-tell motel."

"How romantic," I said, pretending I knew the place he was

talking about. Surely, Frankie would have heard about it. It wasn't as if I could scandalize Miss Felicia with the question.

O'Toole silenced his comrade with a hard stare, then turned it on me. "You and the Cuban show up on the same night. Together. Him acting all crazy. You breathing and dressed like Annie Oakley."

"This is the style now," I insisted. "Haven't you been to town?"

He ignored me. "We figure maybe El Gato's seeking us out for help on a score. Maybe he's got some inside intel from a live girl." He took a hard drag on his stogie. "But then, instead of going through proper channels, instead of being polite, he's avoiding my guys and peeking around like he's up to somethin'." He tilted his head.

"He makes a big show of taking over the drive-in," the ghost to my left accused.

"El Gato's a nut," the ghost behind me insisted.

"Yeah, but he's always got a plan." O'Toole rolled his stogie in his fingers. "He's crazy like a fox. I mean, what was that insane car race we saw?" he added with a nod to where the ghostly scene had played out. "Why bring up Patrick's girl after all these years? What's gone is gone. What's he trying to prove?"

Wait. "She's been missing?" I gasped. "From your world, too?"

"Don't act dumb." O'Toole leveled the white-hot tip of the cigar at my cheek. "What's El Gato playing at?"

"Darned if I know," I insisted. "I'm just along for the ride."

He brought the tip of the cigar closer. "I highly doubt that." The glowing ash hovered over my cheek, so cold it burned. I could almost feel it kiss my skin.

Then a gut-wrenching blast tore through the night. Orange and yellow fire exploded up from the lot outside the theater, past the snack bar. It lit up the sky.

For a heart-stopping moment, the world seemed to freeze, and the air held a stunned silence. Then the reality of the explosion shattered the stillness.

People began running and screaming.

"This way," O'Toole ordered his men, abandoning me as they zipped to the source of the blaze.

I didn't know if I should run or stay. I mean, my car was in that lot. I wouldn't be able to avoid the melee—or any gangsters —if I did try to escape.

And Molly needed me here. She'd asked for my help, and I couldn't just run.

"What were you doing with the Irish?" a voice behind me demanded.

I turned and came face-to-face with my roommate turned Cuban gangster turned Benedict Arnold. "You disappeared and gave me to the Irish mob. Four of them. Is my cheek red?"

That lit cigar had come scary close.

"El Gato needed you to face your fears," Frankie said, like some deranged pop psychologist.

I shot him a level look. "In that case, I fear I might leave your urn at the snack bar and go home."

He lost the smirk. "Stop messing around. Molly's needs come first, and I can't afford to get shot."

And I could? I beckoned him closer. "The Irish accused me of being in cahoots with El Gato."

"You are," he said, smoothing his mustache.

To my everlasting regret.

I glanced toward the parking lot. "They've been watching us since we got here."

"I'd be insulted if they didn't." He made a quick visual check of the immediate area as if one of the Irish might spring straight out of the ground behind me.

"Something big is happening out there, but at least they're distracted." At least we had a second to think.

"Yeah, I blew up the boss's car," Frankie said.

"You what?" I gaped at him. "Why?" So much for working

with the Irish mob now. Provided they figured it out. "You were the one who said we needed to keep a low profile."

"We do," he insisted. "But don't forget, El Gato is crazy. He gets urges. He can't help himself."

I felt my teeth clench. "El Gato is made up."

"Exactly." Frankie planted his cane in the dirt. "And luckily for us, he's much better at disappearing than you." He whipped his cane up to his shoulder. "Now that I've saved you, we need to stop wasting time."

I didn't argue, only because he was right on his last point. "According to the Irish, Kitty was kissing Patrick O'Reilly back there."

Frankie's eyes bugged out. "He's seven years old!"

"In 1938 when you died."

Frankie scrubbed a hand over his jaw. "I'm not going to ask how you knew that."

"Lucky guess." And I knew how easy it could be to lose track of other people's kids as they grew. Now for the bad news. "The weasel-faced mobster said that when Patrick snaps his fingers, it means he's headed to the no-tell motel with Kitty."

Frankie's fingers tightened into a fist. "I'm going to kill him." He spun and took off toward the rear of the drive-in.

"First we're going to save her," I said, hot on his heels. "So I gather you're familiar with the place."

"It rents by the hour," he ground out.

"In Sugarland?" I blurted. I could hardly believe it.

"Not everything's so sweet about your Sugarland," Frankie snarled.

We'd agree to disagree.

"Shouldn't we head out to my car?" I rushed to keep pace.

"I know a shortcut."

Wow. "To the no-tell motel?" I called after him. "I never pegged you for the type."

Frankie had always been a bit of a prude, at least around me.

"It was after my time," he snapped. "But I can get to the place."

The gangster moved swiftly with me right on his heels. He was on edge, his shoulders tight as he glanced behind us.

"What do you see?" I asked, his nerves contagious as I snuck a peek. We had a big enough problem as it was.

Most of the movie crowd had crammed into the parking lot to witness the fire. We appeared to be all alone.

"We're being watched." He drew a cigar out of his pocket. He gripped the Cuban in his teeth while checking the gun in his belt holster.

"Is it the Irish?" I asked, my breath going shallow as I scanned the abandoned cars, many with their doors hanging open. A smattering of souls lingered by the snack bar.

He struck a match and lit up. "The Irish are more direct, shoot-you-in-the-kneecaps, toss-you-off-a-bridge type of guys."

Maybe I'd rather not run into them again. "They're also pretty busy with their boss's exploding car."

"You're welcome." He nodded.

I hadn't meant it as a compliment.

We passed under the movie screen and entered a shadowy area that felt unsettlingly desolate. A wooden fence stood in the distance, a solid barrier that marked the edge of the drive-in.

I caught a shadow out of the corner of my eye.

"El Gato," I whispered and pointed.

As quickly as I'd seen it, it vanished.

"Stick close. Move fast." The tip of his cigar glowed bright in the gloom.

He didn't have to tell me twice.

The stretch behind the screen was a no-man's-land, a dark, foreboding expanse. Like many of Frankie's escapades, this didn't seem like a good idea.

"There's got to be a better way." I kept my voice low.

"If there is, I can't think of it," he ground out.

That was the problem.

I gritted my teeth and kept pace with the gangster.

"I've been thinking about what we saw tonight," he said, moving swiftly. "Some ghosts don't have the flair I do. Some are nothing more than a memory."

"I realize that." Some days, I wished Frankie could be more like them.

"That flashback to the drag race, and after—" he said, glancing back at me.

"Her death," I finished for him.

I was still trying to process what we'd witnessed tonight. A sedan had run down a young Kitty Cunningham. She'd been so scared.

"I'm starting to think Kitty was pulling up a memory. She was showing us her death."

Or perhaps the killer was calling the shots, tormenting the girl for daring to revisit the crime scene by forcing her to relive the nightmare. "It would have been nice if we could have seen who did it." Or at least the make and model of the car. A license plate. *Something.*

"Maybe she doesn't know. Maybe she was drawing her killer out. Maybe he's following us so he can find Kitty."

I glanced back, unable to pick up anything in the shadows that surrounded us. "Then we should stop. We should keep him away from Kitty and Molly."

"I'm not about to leave Patrick O'Reilly alone with Molly."

"This could be bad either way."

"Then don't go." Frankie reached the fence.

"El Gato!" I protested as his hand disappeared into the shadows, followed by his foot and his torso—

Any second, he could slip away to the other side.

My stomach clenched. If he dared leave me here, with whomever or *what*ever was stalking us...

Then I saw where he'd opened a door in the fence, a door I'd had no chance of spotting until I was almost on top of it.

"Ever consider a vow of silence?" Frankie hissed, stepping through the opening.

"I'm a cowgirl, not a nun," I said, slipping inside. The door clanged shut behind us.

We stood at the threshold of a long, narrow passageway—a corridor walled in by fences on both sides. The path was tight, the fences close enough to touch, their metal links cold and unyielding. Shadows clung to every surface, swallowing any light that dared enter this lifeless place.

"This just went from bad to worse," I whispered, my voice echoing eerily against the fence walls. It was the kind of claustrophobic tunnel I'd avoid at all costs, one that promised no escape should things go sideways.

Frankie glided ahead, his flickering gray form the only illumination against the pitch black. "I told you, this ain't about us."

"True." I pushed forward, my pulse jackhammering. We needed to find Molly fast. Before Patrick and Kitty got any ideas.

With each step, the fences seemed to close in tighter, the shadows deepening around us. I could feel malevolence pressing down, almost hear the echoes of past victims screaming out a warning. But we had no choice except to keep going, plunged into the cold dark heart of this godforsaken place.

Still, Molly would want us to be smart about this and not lead something bad right to her.

The hair on my neck prickled as we walked, certain something lurked just out of sight. I imagined hungry eyes tracking our every movement. The shadows skittered and shifted like ghostly insects crawling a breath beyond the edge of our vision. An icy breeze chilled my back, carrying the faint sound of disembodied whispers.

Goosebumps skittered up my spine.

There was no room to maneuver in here. Nowhere to go but forward.

Leave it to Frankie to take the risk. And to me to storm in after him.

I swallowed hard, clutching my fringed jacket tighter around me as we hurried deeper into the narrow passageway, the darkness closing in behind us like a heavy curtain. As we moved farther away from the drive-in, the sounds of the movie faded, replaced by the lonely crunch of my boots on crushed gravel.

Frankie's voice floated to me in the dark. "What did the Irish want with you?"

I snorted. "Same thing they wanted from you before you disappeared and left me with them."

"Nah. They wanted to hang *me* by my thumbs until I told them where El Gato parked the gambling boat he stole from them."

"You what?" I nearly tripped.

Maybe Johnny O'Toole did have a legitimate beef with my housemate.

"I didn't know the boss's daughter was on board."

"Of course not." Frankie didn't tend to be big on planning.

"Or that Ice Pick Charlie would fall in love and talk her into eloping."

I fought the urge to bang my head against the fence. "They didn't mention any of that." Some days, I wasn't surprised at all that Frankie had been shot between the eyes. Other days, I wondered why it had taken so long for it to happen. "They asked me why you were sneaking around."

Frankie stopped, and I nearly ran into the back of him. "What'd you tell them?"

"The truth," I said. "Go." I waved him forward. The sooner we got out of here, the better. "I have no idea why you do what you do." At least they hadn't suspected his real identity. "You need to keep a lower profile around these guys."

Frankie ran a hand through his hair. "You're right," he said in a rare concession. I felt myself soften toward him. "I can't afford to screw this up."

"You won't." He really was trying. He was doing everything

he could to find his girl. When it came down to it, I didn't have to agree with his choices in order to support my friend.

"I already am." He winced. "El Gato would have slid into the car next to each lady, waxed poetic about her beauty, and made her fall in love with him while he disarmed her lover."

And we were back to Frankie being Frankie. "You are not the most interesting man in the world," I informed him.

"Even the *Mona Lisa* doesn't appeal to everyone," he reasoned, slowing as we came up to the end of the tunnel.

Now was not the time to stop.

"What are you doing?" I hissed, slipping past him as he lolly-gagged, his fingers lingering on the edge of the fence.

"Making sure it's behind us," he said in my ear.

"Why on earth—?" Had he gone completely crazy?

The gangster brought a finger to his lips as his voice sounded in my ear once more. "The tunnel was a test to see what we've got on our tail. It would've nailed us if it wanted to."

What a horrible thought.

Frankie stepped out into the night. "Logically, you would be the first to bite it," he continued, ignoring my gasp. "Being in the rear and all. But it didn't attack you, which is good."

"It would have been nice to let me in on the plan," I said under my breath, wishing I could sic it on him. Then it hit me what he'd been doing. "If it didn't attack, it must need us for something."

The gangster gave a faint nod. "I think it's using us to get to Kitty."

Chapter Nine

The Hideaway Motor Inn loomed behind a grouping of scraggly bushes. Its 1940s architecture rose starkly from the rugged, desolate terrain. If there had been any other buildings close by, they'd crumbled years ago. This one had been built to last.

"It would be nice to know what room Kitty and Patrick liked," I said.

Frankie winced. "This way," he said, making his way toward the motel.

I took one last glance behind us at the darkened tunnel. "What about our tail?"

"El Gato has a plan," he assured me.

"Truly?" Because Frankie usually didn't.

The buildings appeared the same in the real world as they did on the ghostly plane, and as I took it in, I realized it was more of a complex than a single building. A break in the bushes led to a front office that looked more like a way station than a lobby.

On the ghostly side, the brick buildings glowed like beacons in the night. Windows spilled pools of light, illuminating the motel's sweeping curves and distinctive pyramid-shaped glass blocks, and a neon sign flickered outside the lobby entrance, humming like a bug zapper.

"Follow my lead," Frankie urged.

"Only if you hold the door," I countered, glad when he obliged instead of simply passing through. It hurt me to touch ghostly items, and I avoided it when at all possible. Not to mention, my touch had a way of making ghostly things disappear.

That never went over well.

We made our way to the motel's postage-stamp-size lobby. The warm glow of a vintage lamp bathed the checkerboard floor in a soft light, casting long shadows across the glossy surface. Doris Day's voice drifted from the radio. "*Que sera, sera...*whatever will be, will be..."

Behind the brick counter, a lone figure sat, absorbed in a newspaper. He was an older man, dressed in a white shirt and rumpled vest, his bald head gleaming under the overhead lights. His glasses perched precariously on the tip of his nose, magnifying his squinting eyes as he scanned the daily crossword puzzle.

He looked up as we approached, his gaze flickering over us with a practiced indifference. "Evening," he said, his voice gravelly with age. "Twelve dollars per night, or two dollars an hour." His voice slowed as he etched a word onto his puzzle. "Cash only, paid up front. Three-hour minimum. Don't matter whether you stay the whole time or not."

Frankie drew the cigar out of his mouth and leaned an elbow on the table, breaking into a charming El Gato grin. "We're looking to join Miss Kitty Cunningham," he said with an engaging Spanish lilt to his voice.

"Are you now?" The man's brows lifted a fraction before his gaze hardened almost imperceptibly. He folded his newspaper and laid it aside, steepling his fingers on the wood. "I'm not saying I saw her or didn't see her. Because, either way, I didn't see her." He met Frankie's gaze. "I don't see nobody."

I smiled, bright as I could. "We understand. It's just that I'm her best friend, and she asked me to meet her here."

"Then she would have told you where to go." He reached up and rested a finger on a switch on the wall. "I flash the porch lights and the cops are here in under a minute. Now, do you two want a room, or are you here to cause trouble?"

"We'd like a room," I said before Frankie could pick the second option.

The man smirked.

Frankie glared at me.

I gave him my most innocent look. "Pay the man, sweetie. A full three hours." I winked at our granite-faced host. "I go wild for Cuban men. We'll need every minute."

Frankie grumbled under his breath, but he didn't argue.

This time.

Instead, my housemate shoved a hand into his pocket and yanked out a roll of cash the size of my fist. He peeled a bill off the top and slammed it onto the counter.

"Look at you, acting all gangster." I fluttered my eyes at Frankie. "I didn't know we'd be role-playing right away."

Frankie looked like he'd swallowed a bug.

Our host didn't bat an eye. He merely shook his head and made change while Frankie probably thought of a dozen mob-approved ways to string me up.

"Room twelve," the man said, easing open a drawer and retrieving the key. I tried to see what other keys were in there and which ones were missing, but he was too fast. He slid the key across the counter. "Second row, down near the end."

"*Gracias*," I said while Frankie barged out ahead of me. "I learned that from him." I giggled, trailing after him.

I barely made it out the door, which he slammed behind me, before the gangster turned on me. "What was that about?" he demanded. "We don't need a room. And for you to suggest El Gato would be with...you!"

I was plenty cute, but that wasn't the point. I put a finger to my lips and glanced into the lobby, but the man behind the counter was already absorbed in his newspaper again.

"Chalk it up to El Gato being outrageous," I said to the gangster. "Besides, in most normal 1950s motels, he would have taken a key off a rack. That would have shown us what keys are missing and, therefore, what rooms are occupied."

"Right," Frankie said as if he'd known all along.

Too bad this was not your typical roadside inn. "At least now we have an excuse to be on the property." I pointed to the key in his hand. "We'll just be really bad at finding room twelve."

"And fast at finding Molly." Frankie gripped the key hard.

The yellow glow of the hotel porch light shone straight through his head as he adjusted his silk shirt and glanced toward the entity that may or may not have still been lurking in the tunnel.

"Room seventeen," he said loudly, in attempt to throw off our uninvited guest. "And you had a little too much fun back there," he added to me, clutching the plastic fob.

"You know I'd do anything for Molly." Besides, he'd driven me crazy plenty of times for no reason at all. At least my ruse could give us a chance at finding her.

The last thing we needed was a suspicious manager warning Kitty about our interest. It could scare her off. Or worse, make her try to take over Molly faster.

I skirted away from the light along the rounded corner of the lobby. A gap in the manicured hedge surrounding the building offered passage toward a wider main road. On the other side stood the first row of rooms. Each one resembled a quaint little cottage, complete with a private garage. The rooms were laid out in two rows, with the rear of the buildings forming a long alleyway.

I braced myself. "Hurry. Maybe we can lose whatever's tailing us." I hadn't spotted it since the tunnel, but I knew better than to think it had left us alone.

A police cruiser slowly patrolled the perimeter of the motel, its headlights casting long shadows across the honey-glazed brick buildings.

The manager hadn't been lying about backup.

I shared a glance with Frankie. "Funny how interested the police are in this place."

"It's not good." Frankie stiffened.

"We're just looking for our hotel room," I insisted. "They have no reason to mess with us."

"Speak for yourself. I just blew up the Irish boss's car," Frankie countered.

"You simply had to cause trouble," I ground out.

"It's part of El Gato's charm."

We ducked behind the ghostly hedgerow, waist-high and perfectly pruned on the ghostly side.

The hedge was stone-cold dead in the real world, and I had no trouble seeing through it as the patrol car passed.

"Room twelve. Go!" My housemate zipped straight through the hedge.

"Watch the fuzz!" I hissed, popping my head up to get a clear view of Frankie, but he was gone.

The headlights of the police cruiser cut across the night, nearing the end of the alley. They'd missed him!

So had I. And there was no way he was heading to our room.

I skirted as far as I could along the hedgerow, trying to see.

The cruiser turned right and disappeared down the far row.

That left me with one choice, and I hoped Frankie had made the same one. I clutched my purse strap in both hands and made a break for the shadowy alley between the quaint cottages.

There, about a third of the way down, I spotted the glow of my ghost.

"Took you long enough," he grumbled.

"You know, maybe you should go back to being Frankie so we don't have to worry about the police arresting you." And possibly me. I was now a known associate of El Gato.

Frankie scoffed. "I have more warrants out than El Gato," he said as if it were a point of pride.

He had to do everything the hard way.

"You're missing your left leg," I told him. It had vanished from the knee down.

"That's the least of our problems," my housemate concluded.

It was still an ominous sign. These days, my gangster buddy brimmed with energy, fueled by the power he gained from his bond with Molly.

Now? He was running on empty.

Of course, he was worried sick for her. That alone could be draining his reserves. And heaven knew tuning me in depleted his power. How terrible to think I actually hoped his frazzled nerves were the problem. I hated to think it could be anything more nefarious.

The rear garage doors, lined like sentinels, stood tall, their roofs almost touching the starlit sky above. I didn't see any porch-lights back here, only the gray glow of the buildings. They appeared mostly the same in the real world as they did on the ghostly side. Maybe a few weeds or chips in the brick, but overall, the place was well-preserved.

"I don't know how we're going to know which room she might be in," I said, my fingertips grazing the shiny brick blocks.

"Leave it to me," Frankie said, sticking his head through the nearest wall.

That was one way to do it.

I heard a faint scream. Frankie emerged a second later, horror written over his features.

"Is it her?" I pressed.

"No," he said. "It's a pillow fight. The guy has a whole fort built. The woman's launching throw pillows like missiles, and there's a little dog jumping up and catching them."

"Did they see you?"

"No." He shook his head. "I hardly saw *them* with all the feathers flying."

We'd have to be careful.

"Try the next one," I urged. "And keep a lower profile this time," I added, knowing it would be an impossible task.

We'd get caught eventually. It was inevitable when a person went sticking their head through walls. But with any luck, we'd save Molly first.

I kept to the unbroken blacktop, stepping light, doing my best to keep my boots from making too much noise. There were no room numbers back here. No way to tell who was coming or going.

Frankie popped his head into a garage this time.

At least he'd chosen to be more subtle.

"Okay, that's good," I said. Then his entire body stiffened. Oh no. "What did you see?"

He yanked his head back. "My short-lived marriage." He shook off the memory. "A couple in a car, arguing about where to eat tonight." He looked to the garage. "The guy wants a burger, BBQ, anything while the lady shoots down every idea and then says she doesn't care where they go. Looks like they've been going at it for decades."

I'd been down that road before, and it could feel like decades.

Suddenly, Frankie held up his hand. A pair of ghostly head-lights turned down our alley.

"It's the fuzz!" he ground out. At the same moment, I saw the police lights on top of the car.

"Run." Only running was a bad idea because they'd see us.

I pressed my back to the wall. There was nowhere to hide, at least for me.

"Where do we go?" I demanded as Frankie passed straight into the garage of the next building.

I hated it when he did that!

I dashed to the garage where Frankie had disappeared, spun in a circle, and tried to spot somewhere to hide. But there was no vegetation. No cars in the alley.

Then Frankie's head popped out of the garage next to me and scared me half to death. "Get in here!" he demanded.

"I'm not a ghost," I hissed as the patrol car drew near. "I can't glide through a garage door. Just stay in there, and I'll hang out by the door and act casual and hope they don't grill me like the Irish did." Or try to stick me in the back of a ghostly cruiser.

"It's unlocked," he said like I was some kind of nervous Nelly.

I reached behind me and gripped the door handle in the real world. It ground hard as I turned it, but it gave. Oh wow, good. I yanked the door upward, cringing as the springs squealed.

Please let that racket be on my side of the veil.

I lifted it about a foot and rolled underneath faster than you could say Great Escape.

I popped up triumphantly, realizing a split second too late that I'd neglected to close the door behind me. Any second, the patrol car's lights would shine underneath, right on our ankles and feet. I looked in horror at Frankie, who had just finished lowering the door on the ghostly plane. It closed with a light snick.

I let out a huge exhale of relief. "Thanks, buddy."

The gangster stood stone-faced, and we waited for the engine outside to stop, for the car to halt. For the police to tell us to open up.

We tensed as the purring patrol car engine passed us by without incident.

I sighed again while Frankie remained silent. Of course, he couldn't even breathe.

I glanced at my housemate and couldn't help but grin. "Look at us, evading the police."

He didn't appear as happy as I'd expected. "When you're done joking around, look behind you."

Chapter Ten

I turned to see the outline of a car parked under a dusty old covering. It was as real as I was, yet a ghostly gray glowed from underneath the tarp. "Oh wow." I bent down and spotted a tire wrapped in cobwebs thick as cotton. "What do you make of that?"

Frankie stood rigid, his eyes narrowed to slits. "I don't like it."

I brushed a hand over decades of grit, leaving streaks in the gray film. "I admit it's strange." I lifted the corner of the tarp, and years of dust rising in a cloud made me sneeze. I rubbed my nose and rolled the cover back to reveal the wide trunk and chrome tail fins of a 1950s cruiser bathed in an eerie ghostly glow.

Underneath, I could just make out the same car in the real world, cloaked in a shroud of decades-old dust and dirt. The chrome bumper, now rusted and pitted, bore silent witness to the passage of time, while the back windshield, veiled with cobwebs, guarded the sedan's secrets.

My stomach knotted. Frankie had been right to suspect trouble. The car looked a lot like the ghostly cruiser from the hit-and-run we'd witnessed. Same boxy shape, same imposing size.

Frankie's jaw tightened. "I know trouble when I see it."

We also had a knack for finding it.

Still, the body of the car we'd seen earlier had been half-mist. There was only one part I'd made out crystal clear. "Let's check the front." I'd recognize those big, round headlamps anywhere— the ones that had lit up Kitty's face with fear an instant before the car mowed her down.

I rounded the cruiser, my footfalls sounding loud in the quiet garage. I grasped the filthy canvas cover and whipped it up and away, stirring up a dust cloud that tickled my nose and made my eyes gritty. But I didn't care because I was too busy staring at the huge, round headlights. Exactly as I remembered.

That wasn't the worst of it.

The right one had shattered, in our world and the ghostly realm. Glass shards clung to the ruined headlight, smeared with—

"Blood," I stated flatly. I'd been on enough cases to recognize dried blood when I saw it.

On the ghostly side, the blood shone fresh and wet.

My stomach lurched at the sight.

The hood was a crumpled mess on both sides of the veil. The imposing grille caved in. Rusty bloodstains splattered across the crushed metal and smeared across the fractured windshield.

"This was the car that killed Kitty," Frankie said flatly.

The violence of the scene was palpable, echoing from the twisted metal and broken glass. I could almost hear the horrifying crunch of the impact, the panicked screech of tires on asphalt. And I'd never forget the terrified expression that raced across Kitty's features the second before impact.

I blinked hard.

Focus.

We had to do this right. "Technically, we don't know for sure this is the car," I said, my voice hoarse. I ignored the groan from my housemate. "Let's think this through." I had to be as thorough as Ellis would be, because he'd taught me well and he wasn't here. "Think about it. Why run a teenager down in cold blood and then leave the murder weapon in a motel garage for decades?"

Frankie let out a snort. "I wouldn't. I only kill crooks who have it coming, and I know where all the bodies are buried."

"Charming."

"In any case, it looks like they got what they wanted. She's dead, and nobody found the car."

Until us.

The gangster began to pace.

I adjusted my bag, feeling the clank of Frankie's urn against my side. "It still seems like too much of a risk for a killer to take. Unless maybe they panicked."

If so, why didn't they return for the evidence?

Frankie glided to the driver's side and stuck his head through the window. "Maybe whoever whacked her got whacked." He made a quick visual inspection of the inside of the car. "It happens more often than you think."

"Maybe." I rolled the canvas cover all the way over the smashed-in windshield, but it was so damaged, it was hard to make out the inside of the car.

I pushed past the ghostly image and examined the interior of the car as it appeared in my world. Broken glass scattered like snowflakes over a crushed pack of Djarum Black cigarettes in the front seat on the driver's side.

Dust lay thick across the glass, the cigarette pack, and the moldering bench seat.

"Doesn't even look like they cleaned up after themselves." I couldn't make sense of it. Unless Frankie was right and we were looking at a double homicide.

Meanwhile, the tarp caught and tried to roll down again. I shoved it back, pushing it up and over. I gasped when I saw what had snagged the fabric.

Mounted on the roof was an old-fashioned police dome light. The red and blue spinning bulbs dark and still.

"It's a police car." I froze. "She got hit by a police car."

"Wow. I mean, yeah. I mean, see?" Frankie choked out. "Never trust the fuzz."

I edged past him to the driver's side. "Give me space." I pushed the tarp up over the door to reveal the faded emblem of the Sugarland PD.

"Damn," Frankie said over my shoulder.

I let the tarp drop. "I don't believe it."

But there was no mistaking it. Ellis's department logo was clearly visible through the thick layer of grime, its once vibrant white and blue paint dulled to a lifeless hue. It glowed sickeningly clear in the ghostly realm as well.

Frankie was at my side in a second. "You talked to the cops back at the drive-in." He brought his hands to his head. "Two of 'em. You told two of them our business."

"They're the police," I shot back, guilt churning in my stomach. They'd seemed nice enough at the time. "You're supposed to trust the police." I mean, that was how I'd grown up. That was Sugarland.

He threw his hands into the air. "The problem with you is that you refuse to think the worst until it happens."

I was bad? "You think murder is a hobby."

He reared back. "More like a messy last resort. Or sweet revenge," he added thoughtfully. "Brewing hooch, robbing banks, stealing pretty diamonds. Those are hobbies."

"You know what?" I held up a finger. "Maybe the police didn't do anything bad."

The gangster wrinkled his nose. "You want to take another look at that car?"

"Hear me out," I said, wagging my finger one too many times. "Maybe someone stole the police car."

"And the police never found it?" Frankie balked. "In their own town?"

"What if a crazy criminal like your buddy Scooter stole it?" It could happen. I'd heard stories. From Frankie himself.

"Okay. Yeah, sure. I'd love to steal one myself, but I wouldn't get to keep it. The cops would be on me like ducks on a June bug until they got it back. And this is Sugarland. You would have heard all about it before anyone found it in a garage seventy years later."

He had a point. "Okay, why would they hide it in a garage?" I pressed.

"Why would the police kill Kitty?" Frankie countered.

None of it made sense.

I stepped away from him and stared at the garage wall to think. "Maybe it was a single officer with a vendetta against Kitty," I conceded. Still, I couldn't imagine how or why a pretty young teen could become a target like that.

"She was dating the mob boss's son," Frankie said, joining me. "The Irish are vicious."

"I admit it wasn't fun meeting them." At the same time... "Surely, Patrick O'Reilly would protect her."

A tinkle of laughter echoed from the other side of the wall. Frankie held up a hand, and I spun around.

"You hear that?" he hissed.

We both froze and listened as hard as we could. The garage had gone silent once more.

Then I heard it again, coming from the hotel room off the garage.

There's someone inside.

The gangster and I exchanged a glance as we stepped closer to the door to Room 7. It had been white years ago. Now it was more of a dull gray, with a simple tarnished gold knob in the center. It did not glow ghostly gray, which scared me more than I wanted to admit. I'd rather not run into any live people in this forgotten place. The dead were scary enough.

"Hellllo?" a sweet voice singsonged.

My mouth went dry. It didn't sound like Molly.

If there was a living person on the other side of that door, it was a sure bet they were up to no good. And if they wanted me to go inside, that couldn't be good for me, either.

Worse, I'd be completely on my own. No one knew I was out

here except for my sister, Melody, and I'd told her I'd be at the drive-in.

"Maybe we should call the police now," I whispered, reaching into my bag for my cell phone. The Sugarland PD would be here in a flash to rescue us.

Ellis wouldn't be far behind.

Then they'd take the car and the evidence, and that would be the end of this part of our investigation.

They wouldn't even want a statement about the ghostly crime we'd witnessed.

"Shh...!" Frankie's voice sounded in my ear. "For all we know, it's Kitty's voice. Molly might be in there."

"No glowing door," I pointed out.

"You really think a ghost has to haunt every stinking inch of a place?"

I'd give him that. Although I would have preferred a ghostly hint.

Hand shaking, I reached for the plain handle on the center of the door and twisted. It creaked softly in response as it yielded to my feeble push, revealing a short hallway. The air inside was stale and oppressive, a fair match for the dread I felt.

The room beyond flickered pale gray.

A muffled whisper rolled through the darkness, echoing off the walls.

Frankie drew his gun. I kept my breath steady and my wits about me. My heart pounded as we crept down the hallway and turned a small corner.

There it was—the source of our mysterious laughter. A ghostly television set housed in an artsy wood box on skinny legs. It faced the bed, flickering gray light and faint peals of laughter.

I could see the end of a bed. It appeared empty. An ancient mahogany desk stood beneath a solitary window. The rays of moonlight slowly creeping through the glass illuminated an old-fashioned telephone receiver with a tarnished metal dial affixed.

A light voice from around the corner *tsked*. "Took you long enough."

A woman's voice.

I stepped inside the room, and my heart stuttered. "Molly!"

She lounged in an armchair near the head of the bed, her long hair draping over her shoulders, wearing the same black leather catsuit we'd seen earlier. The zipper plunged daringly low, flirting with the laws of physics.

At the sight of me, she jolted upright in her seat.

"Babe!" Frankie rushed toward her, arms extended.

Molly let out a shriek, launching herself across the bed away from him. "Who are you?"

"We're here to rescue you!" He reached out to embrace her. He couldn't help himself.

She threw out a hand, and an invisible force slammed into Frankie, knocking him straight through the wall in a burst of drywall.

"Whoa!" I almost stepped between them, then thought better of it. "I promise he's here to help. We both are."

Molly's jaw went slack, her eyes glazing over. Her features shifted until Kitty stared back at me, the sweet face from the photograph now sinister.

The temperature plunged, my breath puffing out in icy clouds. Goosebumps rippled up my arms as Kitty's face contorted with rage.

"Get out!" she shrieked.

Frankie burst back through the wall, lips curled in a snarl. "You get out!"

Kitty gave a shrill cry and scrabbled against the headboard.

"This is your last chance, sweetheart." He leveled his revolver at her. "Let Molly go, or I'll make your afterlife hell."

Kitty glared at him defiantly. Then her eyes flooded with tears.

"You're scaring her, Frank." If he wanted action, this wasn't the way to get it.

My housemate didn't budge. "She's got Molly hostage, and don't call me Frank."

Okay, but Kitty was also a high school girl, a Sugarland kid. Call me crazy, but mob tactics might not work. I took a tentative step toward her.

Sure, bad people could come in all shapes and sizes, and I'd met plenty of scary ghosts. But there was evil and there was desperation, and sometimes they looked a lot alike.

"What's going on?" I asked gently, careful not to frighten the quivering teenager.

Her gaze darted from Frankie to me and then back to Frankie.

I inched closer, palms raised unthreateningly. "Why are you doing this?"

She swallowed hard.

I stopped just out of her reach. "You're not a bad person," I said. "I know you're not."

Frankie's knuckles whitened on the gun. "Yes, she is."

Kitty flinched at his harsh tone, shrinking away.

"Frank," I snipped. He wasn't helping. I turned back to Kitty. "He's just worried about Molly. We all are. Let us help you."

"I'll shoot her anyway," he vowed. "Don't think I won't."

"Nobody is shooting anybody," I insisted. First, because I doubted Frankie could pull the trigger on Molly, even if she was possessed. And second, shooting Kitty wouldn't solve our problem. It would only leave her dead on the floor for a few hours, which would make everything worse.

We needed to get to know her, to talk her into doing the right thing.

"Lower the gun," I urged.

Frankie hesitated, but he didn't say no.

For once in his life, the gangster needed to trust me enough to take my advice. And with Molly's afterlife on the line, he might just do it.

But in that split second when his attention wavered, she hit him with a burst of energy that knocked him off his feet.

"Frankie!" I warned. Too late.

He slammed to the floor, his gun spinning out of his hand, coming to rest against the wall behind him. His eyes rolled back, his mouth slack. He lay utterly still.

Oh, my word. He'd better not be dead.

Then she started coming for me.

Panic bubbled up inside me. This was not how it was supposed to go.

"I know this is overwhelming," I said, trying to keep my voice steady and my tone light, even though I'd rather scream and run, but *somebody has to be the adult around here.*

Kitty was more mist than human now. Tendrils of fog curled around her, obscuring the sweet face of the teenager I knew she was.

"Remember. You're good," I urged, stumbling backward, pulse hammering in my ears. I'd seen how lovingly she'd looked at her boyfriend. How happy she'd been to win the race. Only now there was only coldness in her eyes. Anger etched across her petite features.

"You have no idea who I am," she snarled. "Or what I can do to people who get in my way."

My knees wobbled, and I threw out a hand, bracing myself against the wall.

My terrified gaze darted to Frankie's gun. The icy metal glowed just out of reach. I recoiled at the thought of touching the ghostly weapon. It would be cold and wet and awful, and I'd been right when I told Frankie it wasn't the solution.

But it was my best, last, and only line of defense if Kitty truly meant to hurt me.

My mind scrambled for another way.

Kitty loomed closer, and I shuddered. I had to do something. Frankie was down. Molly was trapped in her own spiritual body. It was up to me now.

So I pushed myself off the wall, stiffened my spine, and

ignored the way Kitty drew back her hand the same way she had right before she'd struck down Frankie.

"I'm not leaving," I insisted, not at all heartened at the way my voice cracked. "You seem like a nice girl." Wild, but I could respect that. "I really do care about you and what happens to you."

She rolled her eyes. "Why does every old fogie say they care about me?"

I let that one go. "Because this is Sugarland, and we watch out for each other," I reminded her. "I'm here because I also care about Molly, and I absolutely will not let you control her." I ignored the way her fists clenched at the mention of the woman she'd hurt. "I care about Patrick O'Reilly," I added, "who seems quite smitten with you." At least from the way he'd kissed her on the hood of that car.

From the way her cheeks flushed gray, she might have been thinking the same thing.

"This guy here," I said, gesturing to the gangster she'd knocked out cold, "he's known Patrick since your boyfriend was in kindergarten, and you zapped him to the floor."

She bit her lip. "He's not dead. I mean, not from me."

It still didn't make it right. Sure, she seemed to have had a wild streak going in her youth, but she also grew up on Magnolia Street and in Sugarland to boot, which meant I expected better. "What would your mother say?"

Chapter Eleven

My heart pounded as I scanned the room, grasping for a solution. But I came up blank. I was on my own.

Kitty glared at me, and her delicate features twisted with fury, her glossed lips pressed thin. She turned away, a veil of ebony hair shielding her face. But I saw the explosion coming.

I notched my chin up and stood my ground, for better or for worse.

Then her sculpted features crumpled like tissue paper. Her slender shoulders slumped. "It's hopeless!" she wailed, collapsing onto the bed. "I don't know what to do. I haven't seen my mom since I left for the malt shop."

"The night you died," I ventured, more than a little shocked at the turn of events.

Kitty inhaled sharply, her breath hitching on a sob. "I was her honey pie, her little miss, and I didn't even say goodbye. I just *left*." Tears filled her eyes as she stared blindly at the ceiling.

"Oh, sweetie." She was little more than a child.

I screwed up my courage and perched on the edge of the bed, wishing I could pat her shaking hand or at least offer her a bit of comfort.

She swiped at her eyes, smudging mascara across her cheeks. "I just want to go home," she whimpered.

"I know," I soothed. This was too much for everyone involved. But if there was one thing I could do for her, it was this. "I can guide you to a better place. Let me help you find the light."

Or at least point her in the right direction.

It was the best I could do. I wasn't a spirit. I couldn't see the light. Although, I couldn't help but feel a twinge of guilt at the idea of sending her off and hoping for the best. I chewed my lip. It was clear the poor girl hadn't found peace on her own or a way home.

She jolted upright. "My mom must be worried sick." Tears streaked her cheeks. "My little sister, too. I promised I'd bake sugar cookies with her. Instead, I've been trapped in the dark for years and years." She collapsed back onto the bed, tossing an arm over her face as sobs racked her slight frame.

I hesitated, choosing my words with care. "You may have passed on, but that doesn't mean there aren't still possibilities. Maybe you can leave Molly and go find your mother or your sister." Perhaps her mother's spirit lingered nearby. Her sister might carry fond memories. "We can go to your old house," I offered, screwing up my courage and scooting a little closer.

She jerked away, mascara pooling under her reddened eyes. "You just want to get rid of me," she said, her voice going cold. "You want me out of your friend, no matter what. Even if I get buried again."

"I—" The words died in my throat because, to my shame, she'd hit too close to the truth. But I had to think of Molly first. "I'd be glad to help you afterward."

"You should be gone!" she shrieked. I leaped up from the bed as she pounded her fists against the mattress, working herself into a frenzy. "What's wrong with me? I can't even scare the living!"

Truly, that should not be a life goal. Or an afterlife goal in this case.

"Maybe it's because deep down, you're a good person," I insisted. "This anger and fear? It's not you. It's this terrible situation you're trapped in."

She froze, staring up at me with those lost, haunted eyes. In their depths, I saw a flicker of the girl she'd once been.

She swiped at her ruined mascara. "You need to go. I'm waiting for Patrick."

Ah, yes. Her boyfriend. I remembered their passionate embrace on the car hood. "He seems quite taken with you."

She let out a stuttering sigh. "He should be here by now." She stood and attempted to straighten the tousled bedsheets. "He always pays for the room. He talks to the desk clerk so I don't have to feel embarrassed. He does everything for me." She smoothed her hair back over her shoulders. "He loves me."

Frankie groaned from the floor. "That doesn't mean you need to kiss him."

My housemate looked like he'd been through the wringer. "You hanging in there?" I asked.

"No," he grumbled, kneading his temples. Tufts of hair protruded wildly from his scalp.

Kitty whirled on him, eyes ablaze. "You don't get a say in who I kiss!" She held her chin high. "I'm eighteen. I could get married tomorrow if I pleased."

The gangster hauled himself to his feet. "Not while you're traipsing around in my girlfriend's body, you won't."

"Frankie—" I warned as he stalked past me and straight for her.

"Get out." He leveled a finger at her. "Now."

"I can't!" she cried.

"Well, you got in there, didn't you?" He grabbed Molly's face between his hands, peering intently into her eyes. "Molly, are you in there?"

Kitty slapped his hands away. "Stop it! Get away from me!" She retreated to the wall by the bed. "You think I wanted to be trapped in this body? I mean, look at me." She wrinkled her nose. "I'm a brunette. Patrick prefers blondes."

Frankie's hands formed into fists. "Molly. Is. Beautiful!"

"I possessed this body so I could meet Patrick here. Tonight. Right now, and now you're ruining everything!"

"You don't even know pain, lady." Frankie closed in on her.

She flung out a hand and zapped him like a bug. I felt the energy from where I stood, sizzling up my arms.

"Okay, let's calm down," I hollered, although nobody was listening to me.

He went for her again, and I saw he was missing both his legs now.

"Frankie, stop it. Look at yourself!"

He ignored me.

She sizzled him.

The force of it rang in my ears. Dang it. "Ow!"

She dropped him to his knees.

"Frankie, wait—" I warned, but he was already rising unsteadily, gun clenched in his hand.

Was I the only sane one in this room?

"It hurts!" Kitty wailed, zapping him again.

Frankie jittered like a live wire. His gun vanished along with his entire hand and wrist.

"Stop it!" I ordered, panic rising. She was sapping his power. And hers. She was draining them both before my very eyes. "How do you do that?"

The electricity between them sizzled the air.

Kitty held her wrist in her hand, lower lip trembling. Frankie bent over, his face creased with pain, staring at the stump where his hand had been.

"There's an energy between us." She trembled, standing straighter. Practically glowing. "It's a lot to feel all at once, but then I get so much power from it."

"By using the love between him and Molly," I said as I realized what was happening with dawning horror. Kitty wasn't feeding off Molly's energy alone. She was killing him, too. "You're using their connection to drain away Frankie's power and use it for yourself."

"I'm not *trying* to," she protested, shaking out her hand.

"You're not fighting it, either," I said. She was using it as a weapon, zapping him whenever he got too close.

I felt bad for her. I did. But I wouldn't lose my friend and my roommate to her.

Kitty brought a hand to her mouth. "I'm sorry."

"Are you?" I asked. "Look at what you're doing. You have to stop before you destroy Frankie completely." I gestured to my housemate, who lay facedown on the bed. That last struggle had taken even more out of him than I'd realized. He'd lost his body clear up to the waist.

Kitty's shoulders slumped. "I don't have a choice," she whispered.

I refused to believe that.

I strolled toward the chair by the television to give us all some space. She hovered in the far corner.

"Why did you stage that scene tonight with Patrick?" I asked.

Longing filled her eyes. "I haven't seen him since I died. I needed to get his attention somehow. I thought it worked—he kissed me." Her voice broke.

Then he'd disappeared, and we hadn't seen him since.

"What about after Patrick left you tonight? The car that came up behind you. Your...death."

Fear flickered across her features. "I didn't plan that at all. It was awful." She smoothed her hair. "I wanted to remind Patrick of the good times." She ventured forward, trailing her fingers along the wall. "What happened later, how I died. I don't like to think about it."

"But it did happen that way," I clarified.

She nodded.

Either she'd got emotional and brought up a memory or someone else had.

She stopped at the window. "You know what? It's fine." She pasted on a bright smile. "Everything's going to be great now. The drive-in was our spot. I knew it would make Patrick remember, and it worked." She glanced out the window as if she'd spot him strolling down the road outside. "He's going to be here any second."

I shook my head sadly. He would have been here by now. "Ghosts can appear in a familiar place with a thought." I hated to break it to her, but... "If Patrick was coming, he'd be here already."

"That's not true," she insisted.

"How did you get here?" I asked. "With a thought, right?"

Her face fell.

"Frankie and I found you the old-fashioned way, and we didn't even know where we were going," I pointed out.

She stiffened, her hands closing into fists. "Molly zapped me out of our kiss. Maybe this is her fault."

That got a rise out of Frankie. He pointed a finger at Kitty. "It's Molly's body. You can't make her kiss someone else."

Kitty's bottom lip trembled. "I promise I'll give her body back once I'm done with it."

Frankie shoved himself up. "You don't understand how this works, do you?"

Kitty twisted her hands together as a flicker of doubt crossed her features. "Patrick and I were supposed to get married. He finally had the money." She touched the diamond band on her finger. "We were eloping to Las Vegas like Rita Hayworth and Dick Haymes." She stood over Frankie as he struggled to sit. "I'm sorry. I have to figure out what went wrong."

Frankie glared up at her. "If you don't get out of her soon, you both die."

"Stop trying to scare me." A tear rolled down her cheek as she raised her hand to—

Oh no.

"Enough." I cut them off. I was starting to think we wouldn't be able to force Kitty out of Molly. And she'd never believe us and leave on her own unless we somehow gained her trust. I rested my hands on my hips, trying to think. "When was the last time you saw Patrick when you were alive?"

"Here," she said, gesturing around the room. "He gave me my beautiful ring. He said he was about to make our dreams come true and that I needed to meet him at the fence in an hour and not to tell a soul." Her expression darkened. "That's when I was hit by the car."

Frankie tilted his head. "Who hit you? We didn't see the driver."

Kitty shuddered. "I never saw the driver, either. It was dark. The drive-in was closed. I only caught a glimpse of the car. Just the headlights speeding toward me. Chasing me down."

I knew the feeling. "We have reason to believe you were hit and killed by a Sugarland Police Department cruiser."

Kitty's expression shattered into shock. "You're lying. No, the police wouldn't..."

"We found a damaged Sugarland PD cruiser hidden in the garage attached to this very hotel room," I said. "You can see for yourself. It looks like it hit someone."

Kitty blinked hard.

She disappeared in a flash and was back just as quickly. "You're not lying."

Frankie shoved himself off the bed and went to lean against the wall. "We're not lying about anything, sweet cheeks."

I still didn't get it. Why run a teenager down in cold blood and then leave the murder weapon in a motel garage for decades?

"Did you have any bad dealings with the police?"

"Never." Kitty backed away, trembling. "Police Chief McAvoy lived two doors down from me. I babysat his daughters." She sat down on a chair by the door. "So nobody knows who killed me?"

My heart broke for her. But she deserved the truth after all this time. "You were considered a missing person."

She still was, after all these years.

We'd fix that.

Kitty shook her head. "The last thing I remember was those headlights speeding toward me. Then I was trapped without a body in that awful cemetery. I cried for years, knowing Patrick must be looking for me, that he might never know what happened to me or where to find me."

I paced, trying to think. "He might not have even known you were dead."

Her gaze turned inward. "Or he might be feeling guilty because he knows who killed me."

I frowned. "Why would you say that?"

"He was in the mob, which sounds sexy—"

"It is sexy," Frankie cut in.

She smoothed her hair back with a wan smile. "Too bad his dad hated me. They all did. Patrick protected me, but I caused problems for him sometimes." Regret flickered across her face. "I've had a lot of time to think about it, and I recognize that now." A smile ghosted her features. "I liked surprising Patrick, showing up at their club unannounced."

I leaned forward. "Did you walk in on anything private?"

"Probably," Kitty said with a stunning lack of hesitation. "If I did, I didn't care. I just wanted to see my boyfriend." Her face fell. "Maybe they killed Patrick too. He didn't look any older tonight than when I last saw him alive."

Ghosts always appeared the same age as when they died.

Kitty twisted her hands in her lap. "For years I hoped Patrick would find me and rescue me from that cemetery, or at least bury me somewhere nice. He could've helped me understand why I don't have a spiritual body. I mean, most everybody else has one. But he never came, not once. I thought maybe he abandoned me, that he decided he didn't love me after all."

"He came earlier tonight," I offered. That had to mean something, even if he hadn't shown up at their special spot.

Kitty looked at Frankie. "I'm sorry about your girlfriend. But I can't let go of my connection with Patrick until I know what happened between us. If there's a chance we could still be together, I have to take it."

Frankie shook his head. "Yeah, but it's not working out that way, is it? I mean, where is he? He's not showing up."

"Maybe he can't," I suggested. "Maybe he's as lost as she is."

Kitty sniffled and wiped her nose on her sleeve. "I can't go until I know what happened to him. To us. I mean, I was his one and only girl, right?" She looked at me as if I should know.

"If we knew who killed you, we might learn what happened to Patrick," I ventured.

"No." Frankie cut me off. "We are not solving a mystery. We are saving Molly. That means Kitty needs to leave and go float around somewhere, and Molly will be free."

Kitty's face crumpled. "I'll never have a body again. What happened to my body? What happened to me?"

"I don't know," Frankie snapped. "There are plenty of wailing, bodyless ghosts around. Maybe you can go to England and find a nice castle. I'm sure that's not all bad. In any case, it's not our problem. We're here to save my girl."

I shot him a startled look.

"What?" He shrugged a shoulder. "I'm all for love," Frankie said. "I am. But there are limits."

I hated to think it, but I agreed.

Frankie glided toward us with no legs, a missing hand, and an ear that had gone AWOL. "You're killing me here. And you're draining the life out of Molly."

I nodded. "You're being harmful, and you need to leave."

Kitty's face crumpled. "I'm sorry."

"You could kill her, Kitty," I said gently.

She squeezed her eyes shut. "If I leave, I'm nothing again. Maybe I'm nowhere." She opened her eyes and looked at me pleadingly. "I'll be lost and alone, and nobody will know me or love me ever again."

"If you stay, the spirit body you're in will die. It will cease to exist and so will you. Do you understand?" I pleaded.

Kitty cried harder.

"You'll be gone forever," I urged. "Lost. You'll be well and truly dead."

Her misty form flickered, her petite shoulders slumping. A spasm rocked through her slender frame. "I—I'm too scared to let go."

Molly's face surfaced, her warm brown eyes fighting to focus. She clutched at her temples as if trying to hold back pain.

"Frankie?" Molly choked out in a hoarse whisper. She reached toward him tremulously.

I backed off as Frankie rushed to her and took her hand in his. "Molly?" he gasped. "Is that you?"

With a tender smile, Molly drew their clutched hands up and drew a heart over her chest.

Relief broke across Frankie's face. He grasped her hand like a lifeline. "Babe," he breathed, bringing her fingers to his lips.

Molly's smile faded, replaced by urgency. "I know you want to save me. I want that too." She squeezed his hand weakly. "But we can't abandon this sad girl to drift alone forever."

"Yes, we can," Frankie said without hesitation. "She's killing you. And me."

I felt the revelation rock through my chest. "I knew it. I knew there was something wrong with you."

I just hadn't known it was that bad.

Molly and Frankie were locked in a determined gaze.

Molly clasped Frankie's hands. "I've been in this body with her long enough to see she's not evil. She's scared. She's alone. And she's so, so young." She broke a hand away and caressed his cheek. "You and I? We have a chance to save her and her afterlife. I don't think I could live with myself if we didn't try."

Frankie closed his eyes tightly.

She cupped his chin and ran a loving finger along the indent under his bottom lip. "Are you in, babe? Please tell me you are because we have to act fast."

Frankie lifted their joined hands and kissed hers fiercely. "I love you, but this is insane."

"So are you," she said with a wink that made him melt.

Too bad for her that it didn't work on me. "This is incredibly risky. We could lose you both and still not help Kitty. Maybe she should leave your body first, and then we'll figure this out."

Molly shook her head. "We don't know where she'd end up. She has no body and no way of moving around in your world or in the spiritual plane. She can lurk, like she did in the corner of our cellar, but not much else."

I chewed at my lip. Curse it. She knew how to make me all sad and soft.

"Add that to the fact that Kitty was intimately connected to the Irish mob," Molly said. "We have to figure out what she might have known that got her killed."

Frankie gritted his jaw. "I do know the Irish mob went down in 1956. At least here in Sugarland." He glanced at Molly. "Police raid. Killed the lot of them."

Molly drew a hand to her chest. "Kitty didn't know." Then her eyes lit up. "You realize this is not a coincidence. We need to know what happened that night." She glanced meaningfully at me. Frankie's girlfriend loved a good mystery. "I'm guessing that's why Kitty was run down."

"I can find out more," Frankie pledged. "I'll talk to my guys."

He'd know all about it by breakfast time. The gangsters I'd met gossiped like sorority girls.

"Find out what triggered the raid," I suggested. "If Kitty knew the police chief and was in with the mob boss's son, she could have been the trigger. Maybe that's why she was killed."

"That's where I was going, too," Molly said. "Even if we discover something different, I don't think we're going to flush out Kitty's killer or bring her the peace of knowing what really happened without her help."

"Just because it makes sense doesn't mean we should do it." Frankie sighed. "Admit it, doll. This is too risky."

Molly squeezed his hands. "I believe in us. In you." She kissed him lightly on the cheek, on the forehead, on the lips. "There's no one I trust more."

Frankie leaned into her touch with a soft expression I'd never seen before. I suddenly felt as if I were intruding on something very intimate.

Molly glanced at me. "I wouldn't risk this without you either, Verity. You always figure things out."

Frankie closed his eyes, touching his forehead to her cheek. "Verity takes too long, and she talks too much."

Molly ruffled his hair with a coy smile. "You two make a great team. And I hate to admit it, but so do Kitty and I. She's a good person, I can feel it. And she's the type who's willing to do the hard things. We'll be with you every step of the way."

Kitty's voice spoke next. "You'd really help me? After everything?"

Frankie startled and drew back.

Molly smiled warmly. "You were sad and alone. I know how that feels."

Frankie squeezed Molly's hands. "I'd do anything for my girl."

Kitty let out a small squeak. "I haven't had friends in so long."

"I only have one rule," Molly instructed. "No more kissing other boys."

Kitty nodded, smiling shyly. "Once I know Patrick loves me, I can go. He'll be my anchor. My rock. My love." Her smile faltered. "Unless he was the one who killed me."

"There's no need to borrow trouble," I cautioned.

We had enough as it was.

Molly straightened with renewed urgency. "Let's be quick about it, then. We've burned a lot of energy tonight, and we don't have it to spare." She touched Frankie's cheek. "I'm sorry you're feeling it, babe. I want to sever our connection so you can stay strong."

Frankie drew her to her feet and held her to him. "Don't you dare." He kissed her on the head. "I'm strong because of you."

She melted into him. "I don't know what I'd do without you."

"Good," he snarked. "Because you'll never have to find out."

Chapter Twelve

Flashing lights sliced through the darkened motel room.

Frankie's eyes widened. "It's the fuzz. They found us!"

He should know.

I dropped to my knees as the stark beams raked over the dingy curtains. "I'm not surprised they're keeping an eye on this room, considering what's in the garage out back."

And if they figured out we were in here, we'd be in trouble.

Heart fluttering in my chest, I scrambled beneath the window and pressed myself flat to the faded floral wallpaper.

"You brought them here!" Kitty's panicked shriek pierced the tense silence. "You brought my killers right to me!"

Boy, I hoped she was wrong.

"Let's all stay calm." I risked a furtive peek over the windowsill. Gravel crunched under tires, and I caught the outline of spinning lights as a patrol cruiser crept past our unit, the headlights scanning the row of rooms. "They don't know we're here," I said, relaxing a little. "They're probably not even looking for us." I gave a little chuckle.

Until the car stopped right outside.

"I'll handle them," Frankie drew his revolver and planted his back on the wall between the window and the door.

"Put the gun away," I ordered. We couldn't risk a shoot-out. Not here, not now. And especially not against the police.

"You got a better idea?" he asked.

Not exactly.

"Maybe the police cruiser is in the real world." I hoped. Then we'd only be in trouble for trespassing. Maybe some mild breaking and entering.

I strained to see if the police lights had the color of the living world or if they were black and white, but it was impossible to see without pulling back the curtains, and I wasn't at all sure I wanted to give myself away like that.

If it was the ghostly police, we were screwed, even if they weren't after Kitty. I mean, here we were in the room right off the garage where they'd hidden the car that killed her. There was no way we could pretend we didn't see it.

I wasn't even sure I'd replaced the cover. Although anyone with eyes would still be able to see it had been disturbed.

Kitty hovered next to Frankie, pale and trembling. "What if they are after me again?" Her warbling voice held a note of despair. "Or Patrick?"

"I'll shoot 'em first," Frankie promised.

Kitty bit her lip, not at all soothed by the idea. "Five minutes ago, you wanted to shoot me."

"You don't have to take it so personally," Frankie said, double-checking the bullets in his gun.

"Maybe I truly am lost," she whispered.

Then she vanished once more.

"Noooo!" Frankie reached for the empty space where she'd stood, fingertips grasping air.

"Oh, Kitty." A heavy weight settled in my chest. If she decided to run from us, we might never save Molly in time.

"We got to find her," Frankie said, panic rising.

We had to do more than that. Kitty needed to know she could trust us, that she could work with us. "We've got to make some noise on this case. Solve this murder. Or at least reunite her with

Patrick. We have to help her find peace with her old life. Then we can help send her to a better place."

It was our only hope if we wanted her to work with us and to give up Molly.

Frankie gaped at me. "Damn. I think you're right."

"I usually am," I told him.

Horror dawned on his face. "I might even need your help."

He always did.

"Luckily for you, I'm glad to give it."

A gruff rap at the door made us both jump. Frankie slammed the chamber closed and steadied his grip on the revolver. I clambered to my feet.

This was it. "What do you think?" I hissed. "Ghost or real?"

"Your guess is as good as mine," Frankie muttered, taking aim.

The sharp rap came again, more insistent. "Police. Open up!"

I recognized that voice. "Ellis!" I launched myself off the wall and hurried past Frankie to open the door.

"You positive?" Frankie demanded. "I can't afford for you to get shot."

"Your concern is touching," I said, twisting the knob and opening it a crack, just to be sure.

Backlit by the flashing lights of his squad car stood my tall, handsome boyfriend, Deputy Ellis Wydell. His crisp uniform accented his broad shoulders. His chiseled features were drawn in hard lines, tension radiating from his imposing form.

When his gaze met mine, his expression melted into relief as well. "You sure know how to make a guy's heart beat faster."

His gravelly voice sent a shiver up my spine, and a nervous laugh burst from my lips. I launched myself into his arms, pressing close and breathing deep of his woodsy scent. After the night I'd had, being near him was like curling up in a warm blanket on a rainy day.

His embrace tightened around me. "Not that I'm complaining," he added, and his breath tickled my ear.

"How did you know I was in here?" I asked with my cheek against his shirt.

"I didn't. I saw a flashlight through the window."

Whoops.

"You want to tell me what you're doing?"

I nestled against the solid heat of him, tension draining from my body. No one made me feel as safe as my Ellis. "You're never going to believe it."

"Probably not," he teased, pressing a quick kiss to my hair. "But try me."

"Well." I drew a lock of hair out of my eyes. "It's really scary. Molly has been possessed by a ghost of a girl named Kitty who disappeared from the malt shop back in 1956. We tracked Kitty to the abandoned drive-in, and then Kitty led us out here trying to find her old boyfriend."

"Fiancé," Frankie corrected. "Get your facts straight. Molly's afterlife could depend on it."

"Fiancé," I corrected. "They met here on the night they were supposed to run away to get married. Then Kitty freaked when you showed up," I said to Ellis, "and she just disappeared. To be fair, she's had a pretty traumatic night."

Ellis's brow furrowed, but my story also had him nodding because he took my ghost hunting as seriously as I did. "Why was she scared of a living person?"

"It was your police lights," I said.

"Show him the car," Frankie urged.

"In a second," I told him. I wanted to approach this in order. "The thing is, Kitty didn't run away like the Sugarland PD reported in 1956."

Ellis furrowed his brow. "You just said she was running away to get married." Then his eyes widened. "Wait. Are you talking about the missing Cunningham girl? The police closed that case. I'm sure they had evidence."

Or someone was lying. "Were there any shady officers in the Sugarland PD then?"

Ellis rubbed the back of his neck. "There were a couple of officers arrested in '56 for working with the Irish mob."

"Oh, my word." My hands flew to my mouth.

His expression darkened. "You know them, Frankie?"

"I'll ask around," he vowed.

"That was after his time," I said.

"That's not our only problem." Ellis drew me closer. "The gate on the north end of the drive-in is broken. You might have run into some live criminals tonight."

"The thought hadn't even occurred to me," I said, probably being a little too honest.

"I figured that and so did Melody. She's the one who told me you came out here tonight. When I didn't find you at the drive-in, I figured I'd do a sweep of this old motel, just in case." He glanced back at his squad car, the flashing lights screaming in the dark. He stepped into the time capsule of a room. "I was worried about you." His gaze swept the dingy interior. "This place is a magnet for drifters and criminals—so centrally located right off the freeway. They use the old, abandoned garages out back to drop off and pick up drug stashes."

My nose wrinkled. "Here in Sugarland?"

"It was. Now, technically, this is unincorporated," he admitted.

"Thank goodness." But still, I didn't like thinking about how the evil in this world could creep into my comfortable small town.

Ellis wrapped an arm around my shoulders. "That's why I do what I do, honey. To keep the people I care about safe."

I nodded, glad all over to have a person like him in my life.

"Bleck," Frankie said. "Less lovey-dovey. More investigating."

"Give me a sec," I told him. It wasn't as if the car was going anywhere.

Then Frankie's face lit up. "Actually, I'm going to go see if Kitty is still in the area. Let her know Ellis is on her side. That'll get her back working with us."

"That's a great idea," I said. "I wish I'd have thought of it."

My ghostly housemate would be able to find Kitty quicker and easier if he wasn't dragging me around. I just hoped she wouldn't be too hard to find.

We needed Kitty's help, and keeping track of her meant keeping track of Molly as well.

"Someone's got to be the crack investigator," Frankie said, disappearing in a blink.

Someone, indeed.

Although I had to admit my gangster buddy had come a long way.

I let Ellis in on the plan and then couldn't help but add, "I thought you'd be with your parents tonight."

He winced. "I took this shift to get my mind off things. After trying to referee another battle between those two, I would have volunteered to stake out my own driveway if the chief had asked."

My heart sank. "So it didn't go well?"

"My parents are insane," Ellis ground out.

I wouldn't argue it. "That bad?"

"Let's just say I'm glad for the distraction."

Poor babe.

"Then I've got something really big to show you." I wound a hand in Ellis's and gently tugged him toward the door to the garage. "Come on."

I felt him stiffen beside me, muscles tensing. "Hold up." His hand dropped mine and drifted toward his holstered gun. "I hear someone outside."

My heartbeat quickened. "Like a live someone?"

It had to be.

We froze, every sense straining. Then...*BOOM!* The unmistakable blast of a shotgun shattered the quiet night.

Ellis snapped into action. In one smooth motion, he drew his weapon, stepping in front of me. "Get down!"

I dropped into a crouch behind him as he took a shooter's stance by the window, gun leveled in a steady two-handed grip.

"Police!" he bellowed, voice ringing with authority. "Drop your weapon immediately!"

We waited, nerves singing.

Then a rusty voice broke through the dark. "Ellis Wydell, is that you?"

"Maisie?" Ellis called out, poised and ready.

"Want me to shoot again so you can be sure?" She cackled.

"Not on your life," Ellis said, reholstering his firearm.

He ducked out the doorway with me right behind him.

Outside, lit by the whirling police lights, stood an elderly woman clutching her smoking shotgun like an Old West gunslinger. Maisie was rail-thin, with flyaway white hair escaping from a long braid trailing down her back.

She squinted in momentary confusion. Then a gap-toothed grin lit up her weathered face. "Why, Ellis *and* Verity. What are you two doing at the no-tell motel?"

Ellis ignored the question and strode out toward her. "You can't just discharge your weapon like that, Maisie."

"Sure I can," she said. Then she caught herself and waved a hand airily. "My apologies, darlin'."

I wasn't sure if she was talking to me or him.

She had a soft spot for Ellis. He made it a point to check on her since she lived alone on a remote farm. He also helped her out with house repairs and such.

Ellis sighed. "What brings you out here with a shotgun anyway?"

Maisie gripped the weapon possessively. "I was aiming for a big old turkey," she said, not fooling anybody.

"At midnight?" Ellis challenged.

"That's when the big ones come out," she insisted.

I spoke up. "Ellis caught me inside the hotel. Investigating." Maybe I could distract him and let her off the hook.

Maisie lowered the shotgun, keeping it out of Ellis's reach. "You looking for ghosts?"

"Already found a few," I told her. Maisie and I went way back to my first case. Frankie and I had let ourselves into the old, abandoned haunted house on the hill, which happened to be on Maisie's land. She'd pulled a shotgun on me then, as well.

But then I'd helped her find some money her late husband had buried. After that, we'd become much more friendly.

She nodded sagely. "Well, be careful. I had to run off an intruder last night."

"Inside the drive-in?" Ellis asked.

"Out behind the old Irish bar." She frowned. "It's been getting worse."

"Hence my patrol," Ellis pointed out.

"I saw the lights from my house up yonder," Maisie insisted. "Sometimes when you flush out the hooligans, they come running toward my property." The corner of her mouth ticked up. "Thought I'd head them off and make them think twice about coming into my backyard, even though this here should also be my backyard."

"How so?" I asked.

Ellis lowered his eyes. "This all would have been Maisie's if my parents hadn't swindled her out of it."

Oh wow. "The inheritance." It had been two years since we found proof that Maisie was a long-lost Wydell relative and the rightful heir to a portion of the sizable fortune Ellis's parents now controlled. But Ellis was the only honest one among them, and his urging to give Maisie her due had fallen on deaf ears.

"I had big plans for this plot of land," she said, planting the butt of her shotgun in the dirt next to her. "I was gonna fix it up. Open a flea market to start. That would liven things up." She shook her head. "Now all I can do is keep other folks from destroying what's left."

My heart ached for her.

Her mouth formed a thin line. "No offense, Ellis, but your parents have done nothing good for this place."

"No offense taken," he said, shaking his head. "This slice of land isn't sexy. It's not new. They've ignored it for years, and now look what it's become. A haven for drifters and thieves." He shook his head ruefully. "My parents like to pretend they are the keepers of our town's heritage, but here they are letting a historic part of old Sugarland rot."

I looked from him to Maisie. "Isn't there any way you can talk them into giving it to her?" I asked. After all, they weren't doing anything with it. And it should be hers anyway.

"If I had the land and just a fraction of that cash, I could open up the drive-in again," Maisie said. "Maybe rebuild that old mob bar and let somebody open up a restaurant in there."

"That would be amazing," I said. To return this property from the ruins. To bring back a part of our history.

Too bad she'd have to get past Ellis's parents first.

Ellis ran a hand over the back of his neck. "Sorry to say my dad is keeping this property in the divorce. He wants to tear everything down."

No. "Even the drive-in?" I protested. It was still mostly sort of standing.

"Especially the drive-in." Ellis sighed. "That's why Dad's in town—he's putting the final touches on a deal that will raze this place to the ground."

"But it's historical," I said, knowing the Wydells wouldn't care. "It's also a haven for ghosts." Would it be the same for Miss Felicia and the rest of them if Leland Wydell ripped down their happy place?

"My dad's determined," Ellis said grimly. "He's been here getting permits to build a distribution warehouse on this land."

"So he's not also here to see your mom?" That seemed a bit cold as well.

Ellis's face darkened. "Dad's saying goodbye in his own way." He shook his head bitterly. "Mom and Dad used to go to the drive-in every Friday night when they were dating. It was one of their special places." His jaw tightened. "Now he wants to destroy it to spite her."

"That's awful." I rarely felt sympathy for Virginia Wydell, but I did at that moment. His father was just being petty.

"There's no talking him out of it. Believe me, I've tried," Ellis said, turning to Maisie. "He's dead set on total destruction."

She reached out to pat his arm. "This is hard on all of us," she conceded.

"Well, I might have some information that could throw a wrench in things," I said, drawing the attention of both of them. "You'll have to see it for yourself," I added to Ellis.

I led Ellis and Maisie into the garage.

Ellis watched uneasily, and Maisie cradled her shotgun as I rolled the tarp off the old police cruiser.

"I remember these," Maisie exclaimed at the sight of it, the Sugarland PD emblem unmistakable.

Ellis snapped into cop mode. He squatted to get a closer look at the blood on the front grille of the car. "You found this as part of your ghost hunt tonight?"

I nodded. "Kitty Cunningham didn't run away back in 1956. She was struck and killed. And I'm pretty sure this is the car."

He stared at me for a long moment. Then with a sharp nod, he snapped out of it.

"There's only one way to find out," Ellis said, reaching for the police radio on his belt. "Stand back," he told us both.

"Wait." Maisie looked from Ellis to me. "What does this mean?"

I watched Ellis call it in. "It means he's about to reopen a cold case."

Chapter Thirteen

Dawn broke the next morning with a harsh, unforgiving light, which was just as well because I'd hardly slept a wink. Ellis had spent most of the night working the crime scene I'd uncovered. He'd messaged me at half past four to let me know he was heading home at last. Not like he could tell me anything.

But that wasn't what had kept me tossing and turning. Not entirely.

From what I could tell, Frankie hadn't made it home. I hadn't seen him since Kitty fled the motel and he'd left to find her.

It worried me more than I'd like to admit.

I nudged my feet into a pair of slippers. I mean, I'd known Ellis would be working hard to secure the scene. Frankie's absence was unexpected.

Not that the gangster wouldn't move heaven and earth to track down the ghost who'd taken his girlfriend. But it was more like he couldn't. He shouldn't be able to disappear like that. He should have been ripped out of whatever he was doing the second I left the motel property.

It was for that reason alone I'd stuck around longer than I should have—until Ellis's investigator buddies had arrived and basically kicked me out.

Even then, I'd stalled.

I'd done everything I could to make sure my housemate had all the time he needed to make a thorough search, provided Kitty hadn't fled far. But when I'd taken my leave, there was no grumpy gangster in my passenger seat. No put-upon housemate ready to strategize in my kitchen and scare my skunk.

I shrugged on a robe. Frankie always made it home with me. It was part of the deal. He went where his urn went, which, at the moment, was nestled in the purse next to my bed.

Only Frankie was nowhere to be found.

A cold dread curled in my stomach. I was afraid something had gone terribly wrong.

"Come on, sweetie," I said to a joyful, scampering Lucy. Her small, black-and-white body bounced eagerly down the stairs, her tail fanning out behind her like a plume of smoke. "At least one of us had a good time last night," I added as her tiny paws pitter-pattered against the wooden steps.

When I wasn't tossing and turning, I'd flipped on the light and played a bit of tug-of-war with Lucy and her stuffed banana. It had cheered me a little, or at least taken my mind off things. And naturally, Lucy had been more than ready for some attention after my evening absence.

I set the coffee to brewing and made my way out into the yard, past Lucy's obstacle course. Frankie's moonshine still lingered in a hulking heap by the pond, bathed in the soft glow of dawn. The copper coils gleamed in shades of orange and pink, reflecting the breaking dawn, while the entire structure cast a long, lopsided shadow over the placid water.

Despite my feelings for the monstrosity, the ramshackle still brought a pang of fondness. It stood there, a stark reminder of my friend in all of his gangster glory. Each dent, every rusted pipe, felt like a piece of him. So did the shed by my pond.

I rapped on the door. "Frankie?" I called, pushing it open.

The interior lay bare. The smooth wooden planks, both walls and floor, held a hint of the fresh scent of the hardware store, their grains still vivid and unweathered. Dust motes pirouetted in the shafts of morning light.

I was still tuned in to his powers, so I expected to see the remnants of Frankie's life. An overstuffed armchair where he'd sit and scheme. A worn poker table, a testament to countless late-night games. The lamp with the garish, peacock-feathered shade —a trophy from the "best bet he ever made."

But there was none of that. The room lay barren, the silence deafening.

Frankie wasn't there.

I returned to the kitchen, my dread gnawing a dark pit in my stomach. Surely, he was fine. I mean, I still had his powers, or else I wouldn't have been able to see the moonshine still. So if his energy was still flowing to me, he had to be around...somewhere.

"He's fine," I said to Lucy, who'd followed me back inside. She typically liked to spend the dawn romping in the yard, but she was worried about me.

"Frankie can take care of himself," I reassured her, and myself, with a determined finality. She spun a lazy circle and sat looking up at me.

At least I'd had the sense to text my sister, Melody, last night to let her know I'd made it back home safe. I wouldn't want her to worry about me like I was about Frankie.

I grabbed an egg out of the fridge and whipped it up with a dash of chopped red pepper and a bit of cheese.

"I know what you're thinking," I said to my skunk. "You're thinking Frankie is off moping in the ether, that maybe he doesn't want to see either one of us right now."

It was a distinct possibility. Still, I had to think Frankie would want to talk to me about last night's events if only to make a plan to move forward.

It wasn't as if we had a lot of time.

"The trick is, I don't think he'd disappear by choice," I said, adding some spinach to the mix before cooking up an omelet. "Not when there's so much at stake."

Lucy licked her chops.

The avocado green telephone fixed on the wall by the laundry room punctuated the morning quiet with a shrill *ring-a-ling*. I clapped a lid on the pan and headed to answer it.

"Verity." My sister's voice, warm like freshly baked bread, came over the line. "I was hoping you'd be up."

"I couldn't sleep," I confessed, meandering over to the fridge while wrestling with the telephone cord's seemingly eternal tangle. "Frankie went to track down the ghost who took Molly, and he still isn't back."

"I'm sure he's fine. He's a gangster."

"Which is how he died the first time."

There was a pause at the other end of the line before Melody changed the subject. "Alec told me about the police car you found." Melody was newly engaged to Ellis's close friend on the force.

"It was vintage Sugarland PD," I told her. "The plate was something like V, H..." My words trailed off as I tried to recall.

"VHJ-1932," my sister supplied effortlessly.

"Wow," I said, retrieving a dish from the fridge. "How'd you know?" I was sure I hadn't texted that.

"There was a picture of the car on Ovis Dupree's blog this morning. He photographed the investigation from a distance."

"Of course he did." Ovis was Sugarland's most intrepid reporter and had been for the last fifty years. I kept thinking he'd retire, but he only seemed to get wilier with age.

"I was curious," Melody said, "so I popped into the library just now and cross-referenced the license plate number with photos from our Sugarland history collection."

"Oh, my word, you are brilliant," I interjected.

"Thanks," she said cheerily. Melody was nothing if not thorough. "Anyhow, guess what? The car you found belonged to Police Chief McAvoy."

I stood for a moment, stunned. "The chief?"

Police Chief McAvoy was the Sugarland version of Andy

Taylor from *The Andy Griffith Show*—a small-town officer whom everyone loved and looked up to. He had a park named after him, as well as the high school auditorium, and his picture still hung in the VFW Hall.

"It's his car," she said, her voice tinged with excitement. "Or at least it was the one he drove in the Homecoming Parade every year."

"Wow." I whooshed out a breath. "I wonder if it's a setup." It was the only explanation. "Although, if it was a setup, nobody would believe it."

"If it was a setup, why hide the car?" Melody challenged.

I gripped the phone tighter. "Are we sure about this?"

"I confirmed my information with Alec right before I called you. Although he was a little miffed, I knew."

"He'll get over it," I said, unconcerned about the uptight officer's feelings.

"He's sweet that way," Melody agreed, which hadn't at all been what I'd meant.

"Ellis told me last night that the police had a problem with corruption in the 1950s. They caught a couple of officers conspiring with the Irish mob, but I have a hard time believing McAvoy was involved. First off, because Grandma thought he moved heaven and earth." And she was a great judge of character. "But more because he gave his entire estate, minus the house, to start the After-School Kids Club downtown."

"I'll give you that," Melody said. "His gift was generous, but he didn't have crazy money. A lot of other people have donated over the years."

I wound the phone cord around my wrist, thinking. "It would be nice if I could talk to the chief." Get the real story. Or at least get a feel for his side of things.

"Okay, let's figure that out," Melody said as if she could produce him for me.

"Too bad he wasn't anywhere near his car last night." He might not be haunting Sugarland. Not everyone came back. "I wonder if Ellis would let me wander around the station house a bit."

There was no telling what I could find.

"McAvoy's son, Steve, still lives in the family home," Melody supplied. "He's a retired police officer and even served for a while under his dad."

I ran a hand over my chin. It was a start. Plus, Steve might know more about the steps his dad had taken to address corruption in the force. "Do you have the address?" I asked.

Because it was Melody.

"Sure do," she said, "and I'm going with you."

"I usually go alone," I hedged. Well, with Frankie.

"Not always," she reminded me.

Melody had been instrumental in helping me solve a series of murders on a haunted pirate island.

"You were a pretty stellar partner on Phantom Island," I admitted.

Although she hadn't yet developed a healthy fear for her own hide.

"Then it's settled," she concluded. "I'll be there in twenty minutes."

Chapter Fourteen

That gave me about ten minutes to shower and dress. First, I finished cooking Lucy's omelet. Then I served her a helping of Skunky Sweet Bread with raisins that I'd whipped up at two o'clock in the morning, hoping it would help me relax and sleep.

Spoiler alert: it hadn't.

But Lucy seemed to relish her breakfast as I hurried upstairs to get ready.

I had just looped my hair into a casual ponytail and was adding a swipe of pink lip gloss when Melody's knock echoed from downstairs.

"Hello!" she called, her voice muffled by the heavy oak door. I headed down the stairs as the knob turned and she let herself in.

My sister gave me a friendly wave from the entryway, her blonde hair styled in a loose boho updo. She wore a pair of distressed jeans that somehow managed to look both lived in and high end. Tucked into these was a sweater in a soft peach hue that complemented her glowing complexion.

"I brought you breakfast," she announced, her eyes sparkling with an infectious energy.

"Ooo...mine," I said, speeding down the last few steps to

retrieve the white paper bag and an insulated cup. The aroma of fresh coffee perked me right up.

My stomach gave a low rumble, reminding me that I had been so preoccupied with making Lucy's breakfast that I had forgotten to prepare anything for myself.

"I about had to wrestle Fred Nary for the last Super Berry Crunch muffin," she said as I withdrew a masterpiece, a scrumptious jumble of blueberries and cranberries bursting from the golden crust. A sprinkle of oats and a fine dusting of sugar crystals adorned the top, giving it a delightful crunch.

"You think of everything," I said, taking a big bite.

"Who can forget the bakery case at Coffee Cartel?" she asked as if daring me to try. Melody bent to stroke Lucy, who swooshed her tail with delight. "Now you eat, and I'll drive."

"Deal," I said, breaking off a piece of muffin and feeding Lucy a little nibble before we headed out the door. After the night I'd had, it felt comforting to be taken care of. "Be good," I called to my skunk, who was already waddling over to the parlor couch for her morning nap.

Melody had parked out front. As I slid into the passenger seat of her red Toyota Prius, I was greeted by the familiar scent of her vanilla air freshener. With a wink and a grin, she shifted the car into drive, her enormous rock of an engagement ring glittering in the morning sunlight.

"I'm glad to see you haven't blinded yourself yet," I teased as she steered down the tree-lined road that led from my house toward the highway, her ring hand resting on the top of the steering wheel.

"You're lucky I stopped staring at it long enough to pick you up," she grinned.

Alec had acquired the ring while helping me dodge pirate ghosts on Phantom Island, and he'd proposed to Melody with the help of his French bulldog, Arlo. They hadn't set a date yet. Knowing my sister, I half-expected her to elope.

"So, tell me what happened last night," she pressed. "I heard

Alec's version, who heard it from Ellis, but neither of them mentioned that Frankie is missing."

"That's because they don't know yet." I shifted in my seat. "I left his urn at home in case he's somewhere on the property or maybe in the ether." That was a place ghosts went to rest and recover. "Still, it's not like Frankie to disappear on me."

My sister shot me a long look.

"Okay," I relented, "It's not like Frankie to disappear and not return at all. Or stay gone overnight. Plus, I brought his urn home. That should have compelled him to return to my property. I don't understand it." And it worried me more than I'd like to admit.

This case was unlike any we'd tackled before. Frankie had never had to deal with a friend in mortal danger, much less the love of his afterlife. Plus, the power drain he was experiencing was scary. I understood that he wanted to go all out, all the time. That was Frankie. It was part of his charm, and also why he drove me a little nuts. But if he didn't watch it, he might not have the strength to save her.

And worse—Frankie's energy was linked to Molly's. If Kitty could drain Molly down to nothing, could she do the same to Frankie?

I explained it all to Melody, along with the details of what had transpired the night before. I watched as her eyebrows furrowed the lines of worry etched across her forehead. She remained silent as she turned off toward Main Street, her hands gripping the wheel tightly. She was all too familiar with the dangers associated with ghost hunting, having stood by my side during our last hair-raising adventure.

"This is bad," she said, taking a left down Third Street toward one of the oldest residential neighborhoods in Sugarland. "I mean it was bad enough when my research on Kitty drew a big blank last night. I mean... Me. Researching."

"It's unthinkable." Melody could find anything on anyone.

Good thing I'd met Kitty in the meantime.

Melody drummed her fingers on the steering wheel. "What are we missing?"

I wish I knew. "Now you know why I couldn't sleep," I said as we passed the first of several streets of tidy bungalows dating back to the 1940s.

The houses here were quaint, their postage-stamp-size front yards adorned with coneflowers and purple horsemint and graced with mature trees. Each one bore unique touches—a weathervane here, a stained-glass window there. Many of the families had opted to paint their homes in vibrant hues like sky blue, daffodil yellow, and blush pink. On any other day, I would have been admiring each one of them. Today, I held my breath as we came up to Kitty's former home, 238 Magnolia.

Ivy crept up the sides of the charming pink bungalow.

"Stop here for a second," I said to my sister.

Melody had barely parked the car before I was out and rushing toward the white-painted front door. If Kitty was here, and Frankie had tracked her down... Well, that would solve two of my problems.

And probably create more.

I knocked, my knuckles rapping against the solid wood, but got no answer. After a second, more insistent knock, I attempted to peek through the gauzy white curtains of the large picture window out front.

"There you are!" declared a voice behind me.

Molly's friend Violet walked straight through the door, nearly giving me a heart attack. I jumped back, but she took no notice. Lottie and Ruth piled out after her.

"Thank goodness," Lottie exclaimed, shoving an errant corkscrew curl out of her face.

"Where were you?" Ruth's eyes darted anxiously. "You were supposed to meet us here right after you checked out the drive-in."

I hadn't been thinking. So much had happened. "I'm sorry. I

was delayed." A bit overwhelmed, and more than a little frightened.

"Did you find something?" Ruth asked. "Our searches were a bust," she admitted.

"Where's Frankie?" Violet asked, her angular features drawn tight. She looked past me as Melody made her way up the stairs.

"We found Kitty at the drive-in," I announced. "Then later at a motel nearby. We talked to her a bit. We even got to see Molly. But then Kitty fled. Frankie is chasing her."

"Where?" Lottie demanded.

"I don't know," I confessed. "I was hoping you might."

"They didn't come back here." Lottie looked to Violet.

"Nobody is haunting Kitty's house as far as we can tell," Violet added.

"Well, except for us now," Ruth chimed in.

I explained more about the events of last night, as well as the current issue of Frankie's disappearance. "Do you know why he wouldn't be at my house when I have his urn?"

Lottie fiddled with the cameo necklace at her throat. "He shouldn't be able to disappear like that." She glanced once more at Violet, who frowned.

"Something is very wrong," she agreed.

The silence that followed was deafening.

Ruth was the first to speak. "He could be too weak to manifest," she said, glancing at the others. "You still have his power, so that means he's somewhere." Her voice was firm, but I could see the worry in her eyes.

"We'll look for him," Violet pledged. "We can go places you can't."

"And quicker," Ruth added.

"We'll track him down," Lottie promised.

"You follow up on the clues from last night," Violet urged.

"We're already on it," I said with a glance at Melody. "Come by my house when you have news."

"Your place will be the first one we check," Violet said before all three women disappeared.

"That leaves us investigating McAvoy," Melody said.

It always amazed me how much both my sister and Ellis could get from half of a conversation. It wasn't like they could see the ghosts. But my sister knew me better than anyone, and she understood what we were up against.

"No need to park again," my sister added as we set off down the stairs. "It's a short walk to 242 Magnolia."

"Let's just hope Steve McAvoy is home," I added as we turned west toward the home of Kitty's former neighbor.

The story-and-a-half bungalow was painted a light blue-gray, with stained wood trim around the windows and along the roofline. A large pin oak tree dropped deep red leaves in the front yard, and holly hedges lined the front walk.

I didn't see a car in the driveway, but the blacktop drive extended to a large free-standing garage out back.

We ventured to the front door, the crunch of fallen leaves under our feet echoing in the crisp morning air. Melody stood back as I knocked.

The door swung open to reveal a tall, fit man, probably in his early sixties. He had expressive, deep-blue eyes. His salt-and-pepper hair was impeccably groomed, and I could have sworn I'd met him before.

Given this was Sugarland, I was probably right.

"Hi," I said, extending a hand. "My name is Verity Long, and this is my sister, Melody."

Recognition flashed in his eyes. "I remember both of you," he said, his handshake firm. "How's your mother?"

A grin spread across Melody's face. "She's at the Great Mississippi River Balloon Race down in Natchez with our stepdad."

Steve's expression brightened. "I've always wanted to do that."

"It was on her bucket list, too," I chimed in. These days, if my mom and stepdad had a hankering for adventure, they simply packed up the RV, and off they went.

"We're wondering if you have time to talk," Melody added, getting down to business. "I found some historical pictures of your dad in our library collection and have a few questions."

"Sure." Steve stepped back and gestured us inside. "Come on in. I was just brewing up some maple pecan coffee."

As we entered, we were immediately enveloped by the enticing aroma, a heady blend of sweet maple and nutty pecan, with a hint of espresso. A large picture window filled the room with ample natural light, casting a soft glow on the polished hardwood floors.

"Make yourselves at home. I'll be right back with the coffee," Steve said, disappearing into the adjoining kitchen.

A stylish, angular sofa upholstered in rich, dark leather dominated the sitting room, its clean lines mirrored in the sleek, hand-hewn wood coffee table in front of it. A pair of matching leather armchairs flanked the sofa, their masculinity softened by a plush, patterned rug in shades of gray and cream.

Melody strolled over to a colorful, woven tapestry carefully framed and hung on the wall above the couch. "Gorgeous," she said on an exhale, more to herself than to me. She studied the vivid patterns. "I'll bet it's from Peru."

I was more interested in the sturdy wooden bookshelf on the near wall. The titles ranged from Agatha Christie to modern thrillers, with a generous smattering of historical biographies. Among the neatly arranged books were travel mementos—an ornately painted Russian matryoshka doll, a skillfully carved Kenyan wooden statue, and a meticulously detailed Swiss cuckoo clock.

But it was the framed family photos that caught my eye. Steve and his dad hiking up a mountain pass, an older woman baking cookies while a younger Steve laughingly tried to steal one, snapshots of him in uniform with his colleagues on the force.

Then it clicked. "I knew I recognized Steve," I said to Melody.

"He came to our school every year for the safety assembly. He was Safety Steve!"

"Buckle up and make it snug," Melody quipped, recalling one of Steve's old safety slogans.

"And have yourself a seatbelt hug," I added. We resisted the urge to high-five. Barely.

"Oh, and remember when he gave out coupons for a free cone at Scoopty Doo?" Melody asked.

Steve reappeared then, carrying a tray laden with steaming mugs of coffee. "I think I still have a stack of those coupons tucked away somewhere," he joked.

"I was racking my brain trying to place you," I admitted.

"In your defense, I did have a lot more hair back then," Steve countered, placing the tray on the sturdy wood table in front of the couch. "I also met you briefly a few years ago. I was working the murder of Reggie Thompson."

Found dead in the vault at the First Bank of Sugarland. "That was one of my first ghost-hunting cases."

He handed me a steaming mug. "It was my last case before retiring," he said. "I have to say I was impressed with how you helped solve it."

"Thanks," I said, grateful he'd noticed. That case had helped build my reputation.

I noticed a small, wooden Maori totem from New Zealand near a photograph of Steve with the stunning backdrop of the Milford Sound behind him. "It seems like you're enjoying retirement."

His grin was broad. "Some people like fancy cars. I prefer discovering new places." Steve cleared his throat. "You mentioned you have some pictures of my dad?"

"Yes," Melody said as we moved to sit. She and I took the couch while he flanked us on one of the chairs. I took a sip of coffee, pleased it tasted as good as it smelled, while Melody retrieved an envelope from her bag and handed it to him. "These are part of our Sugarland Heritage collection. They show your dad driving a squad car in the Homecoming parade in 1954 and 1955."

"Right behind the Roan's float, just like every year," he said, carefully extracting the black-and-white photos. His eyes softened as he looked at the images. "That's the old '54 Plymouth Savoy. Dad loved that car. He used to say it had more personality than he did."

I hardly believed that. "Everyone loved your dad."

"He could never figure out why." He chuckled, lost in the memory. "One time, he rigged up a makeshift PA system and used it to play Elvis Presley songs during his patrol. Nearly gave Mrs. Henderson a heart attack."

Melody laughed, then got right back down to business. "Since the license plate is the same in both pictures," she continued, "I'm assuming that this was his squad car?"

Steve's jovial demeanor faltered. His gaze returned to the pictures. This time, with more discernment. "Yes," he confirmed quietly. "This was his squad car, and that's the right plate." He placed the photos down on the coffee table, his gaze still fixed on them. Then he looked up at Melody. "Why do you ask?"

"I'm not sure if you've heard about what happened last night," I ventured.

"I'm afraid not," he said, shaking his head. "A tree limb messed up one of my windowsills last night. I read a book and went to bed early so I could get an early start out in the wood-working shed this morning."

"I was out ghost hunting," I told him, meeting his puzzled gaze with a steady one of my own. "Trying to learn more about the death of Kitty Cunningham back in 1956."

"Kitty was fine in '56," he corrected swiftly. "I'm not sure what's happened to her since, but I know that for sure."

I hated to be the bearer of bad news, but... "She died on May 3, 1956. She told me all about it."

His jaw dropped. "I—suppose you would know."

"I also witnessed a replay of her death," I pressed on. People deserved to know the truth. "She was run over and killed by a police car."

The color drained from his face. "That's impossible," he said, his voice barely more than a strangled whisper. He drew a hand to his chin and accidentally knocked the historical photos off the table. "It just... It can't be."

"I'm sorry to be the one to tell you." I held his gaze. Meanwhile, Melody retrieved the historical photographs from the floor. "I found the car that killed her in a garage at the Hideaway Motor Inn," I stated, my voice steady despite the gravity of what I was sharing. "It was your dad's police cruiser."

"Same model. Same plates," Melody said, slipping the photographs back into the envelope.

Steve ran a hand through his hair, trying to process the bombshell we'd dropped on him. "So that's what happened to Dad's car," he murmured, more to himself than to us. "Sorry. This is...a lot to take in."

"Wait." My heart skipped a beat. "You knew the car was missing?"

He nodded, his gaze distant. "Dad did." He returned his attention to me. "You have to understand, all of this was before my time. Literally. I was the surprise baby, born in 1960." He leaned forward, elbows on his knees. "Still, Dad and I used to talk about all his old cases. We were tight. And that was a huge one. I mean, that was the night my dad took down the Irish mob."

Melody turned to me, surprised. "I didn't realize. Did you? I'm sure we have records at the library."

I'd had no idea. "Kitty didn't tell me." And it had been after Frankie's time.

Steve folded his hands together, elbows resting on his knees. "The Irish mob ran a bar near the state highway, not far from the drive-in," he explained. "It was a prime location for shuttling stolen goods. They mainly dealt in cigarettes and counterfeit Rolexes. Then they made a big score—something different, huge. Dad caught whispers about it, but nothing specific. And they never kept goods at the bar except to ship them out." His fingers curled into loose fists. "Then Dad received a tip that they were planning to move their prime score out that night from the bar. This was his chance to catch them red-handed."

Melody leaned forward, matching his stance. "Did it work?"

Steve's lips curved into a smile, the corners of his eyes crinkling with pride. "It was the biggest takedown of Dad's career." His fists loosened. "But get this. Just as everything was about to unfold, I mean, right on the brink, Dad had his officers encircling the place. They were awaiting the signal. Dad dashed back to relay final instructions to one of his lieutenants and noticed his cruiser wasn't where he'd left it. It was a big deal because he'd parked it in a good position in case he had to give chase. His initial thought was that someone had moved it, but later he realized it had been stolen."

"Stolen?" I asked. "In the middle of a stakeout that was about to escalate into a raid?" The audacity of such a move was astounding. Not even Frankie would be that bold.

Oh, who was I kidding?

Frankie would have stolen it, driven a loopty-loo around the stakeout, and then tried to impersonate a cop with it.

Steve leaned back in his chair. "None of Dad's men had any inkling where his car had gone. Which is weird, right? Needless to say, it was a bit of an embarrassment." His hands spread in a helpless gesture. "So they kind of swept it under the rug. Dad reported it as totaled in the raid. I mean, technically, he did lose a car."

"In a very broad sense." Broad as a barn door.

"Two officers were arrested in 1956 for conspiring with the Irish mob," I said. "It could have been one of them."

"You did your research," Steve said. "You're talking about Mac and Buzz. They were partners. And they were dirty. Dad had them arrested shortly after the raid." He clasped his hands together." But it wasn't Mac or Buzz who took the car. Dad had them watched the entire night. He was feeding them false information while he built his case."

Frankie had been right not to trust them. And I'd paid the price. It wasn't long after I talked to the officers that I'd been accosted by the Irish mob.

There was one more thing I didn't understand. "Why didn't your dad report his car stolen?"

Steve took a deep breath and looked at me warily. "Because Dad knew who stole it."

Chapter Fifteen

"Wait," I broke in, my mind racing to understand. "You said none of the police officers saw what happened. So how did the chief know who stole his car?"

Steve leaned forward, his hands clasped together. "Dad knew in his gut who did it, and Dad's gut was never wrong." He glanced down at his hands, then back to me. "You see, Dad had an informant on the inside who was planning to skip town right before the raid went down."

"Patrick," I said. The pieces were beginning to fit together in a dreadfully coherent puzzle.

"Exactly," Steve said, locking eyes with mine. "Son of the ruthless Irish mobster Seamus 'The Galway Ghost' O'Reilly. Seamus was the head of the local Irish crime family. Word had it Patrick was being groomed to take over the business one day."

"But Patrick fell for Kitty," I finished.

A heavy sigh escaped him. "My dad had known Kitty all her life. He'd watched her grow up. He was beside himself, shocked that a good girl like Kitty could get mixed up with a gangster." He ran a hand through his hair. "Her parents were livid. Within an hour, the entire block was buzzing with the news, and the neighborhood mothers started piecing together evidence. It seemed she'd been sneaking out at night."

"Poor Mrs. Cunningham," I said, knowing my mom would have been mortified to find something out that way.

"I mean, I used to sneak out at night," Melody reasoned. When we both looked at her, she added, "I'm just saying it's not rare."

"You weren't meeting a gangster," I said. Just the cute drummer in the high school band. "And mom knew. She was just too much of a hippie to mention it."

Not that we could get up to too much trouble in Sugarland.

Although Kitty certainly had.

Steve rubbed the back of his neck, as if secretly glad he'd never had children. When it was clear Melody and I were finished, he continued, "Kitty was one of a kind. That was part of her charm. My dad knew she was a good kid deep down, but she was definitely a handful. Her parents were trying to keep her busy with shifts at the malt shop and babysitting gigs, and she had a small army of protective neighbors on the block looking out for her."

"But if the whole neighborhood was keeping an eye out for her, wouldn't that protect her, too?" Melody asked. "Most criminals don't like drawing attention to themselves."

"Have you *met* Frankie?" I asked.

"Not technically," she replied.

"Kitty mentioned she'd shown up in places she shouldn't," I said. "I asked her if she'd seen anything that would get her into trouble. I mean, she'd been inside the Irish operation by the drive-in. She'd shown up uninvited at their gatherings."

"And?" Steve asked, perking up in anticipation.

"She can't recall anything unusual." I shook my head, disappointment creeping into my voice. "Maybe something will come to her."

"Ask her again," Steve advised, his eyebrows knitting together. "Specifically, ask Kitty what she might have seen that might have made the Irish mob turn on her."

"Wait. What?" Melody blurted, her jaw dropping.

"What do you mean when you say the Irish mob turned on her?" I echoed, my mind racing to process this new information.

"I doubt this is in your library," he said, nodding at my sister, "but you'll find it in police records. And if you're serious about investigating this case, I think it's important that you know." He directed his gaze at me. "Shortly before what everyone believed to be Kitty's disappearance, Seamus O'Reilly put a hit out on her."

"A hit?" I stammered, taken aback. "On a high schooler? I—" Wow. "Seamus was a monster."

Steve's jaw tightened. "They were all monsters. That's why my dad cleaned up the town."

For the first time, I was glad Frankie wasn't around to have a word.

"Wait." Melody raised a hand, then stilled it in midair as she pointed a finger at Steve. "Nobody ever considered that Kitty might have been murdered on the night she disappeared?"

"No," Steve said grimly. "One of the reasons Dad went after Seamus and his ilk so fast was to protect her, and he believed he had." He looked from Melody to me. "Only her family and the police knew about the hit."

And every single one of the mobsters. Any one of them could have done the job.

Steve sat back in his chair to think. "When Dad learned of the hit, he told her parents, who dropped the hammer and told her she'd never see Patrick again." He paused for a moment, his gaze distant. "Dad also assigned officers to watch over Kitty twenty-four seven."

"A teenager's worst nightmare," I said, wondering why Kitty hadn't mentioned it.

"Yes, well, it didn't work," Steve said. "Two days later, she slipped out of the malt shop and ran off to Vegas with Patrick." He cleared his throat. "At least that's where we heard she was going."

"And none of the police followed her out of the malt shop?" Melody asked.

"Not when she said she was going to the bathroom," he said. "She climbed out the window," he added as if he'd never encountered a wily teen before.

Okay, so Kitty was on her own, not realizing the danger she was in. The mob and the police knew about the hit. And the police had let her escape. My stomach danced. There was no good way to say this. "Maybe there were other corrupt officers besides Buzz and Mac," I suggested. It pained me to say it, but... "Maybe your dad missed one."

Steve didn't blink. "Dad was very thorough," he said, brooking no argument. "He took the corruption on the force personally and dedicated every resource he had to ensure it never happened again. And as far as Kitty's protection went, I'm sure my dad assigned officers he trusted to keep Kitty safe."

That was all fine and good, but had Chief McAvoy been one hundred percent correct about whom he could trust?

I got up from my seat and strolled toward the bookcase. My fingers brushed against the spines of the books as I walked. I mean, even if every one of the police officers guarding Kitty had been a straight-up Boy Scout, there was still one thing I didn't understand. "Surely Patrick would have protected her. He would have gone to his father."

"He did," Steve said, his gaze following me as I paced. "Patrick got his dad to call off the hit, but the whole thing shook him badly. His dad wanted him to prove himself by going all in on that big job they were pulling. Patrick used that to his advantage. He went to my dad and worked out a deal for a more subtle form of police protection in exchange for information."

"The kind that led to the raid," Melody said.

"And the downfall of the Irish mob," Steve added.

I stopped at the end of the bookcase and turned to face him. "But your dad had already taken steps to protect Kitty before he ever made the deal with Patrick."

"He did," Steve said with pride. "I think that's one of the reasons Patrick trusted him. He knew my dad was a stand-up guy and had Kitty's best interests at heart." Steve ran a hand over his chin. "Don't get me wrong. Dad was tough, hard when he had to be. But he was doing it to protect our town and its people."

He glanced down at his hands, his fingers absently tracing the buttery leather of the armchair. "Not to mention Kitty was practically part of the family. She babysat my sisters all the time. Dad was really torn up about the whole thing. He thought he should have seen the signs she'd gotten in with the wrong crowd. He blamed himself for always thinking the best of people. And Kitty was a mess. She told him how upset she was about the police guard and how stressed she felt at home at night with her parents. So Dad paid Kitty to come over under the guise of babysitting while he protected her. He had a patrol car out front, watching."

Oh, my word. "She was supposed to be under his protection the night of the raid. Babysitting!"

Steve's gaze fell, his face shadowed by a frown. "But she left the malt shop early. Then she canceled on Dad. She said she was going away for a while, and Dad feared the worst, but he didn't know where she was. He assigned the patrol to find her, but they didn't have any luck."

Melody placed a hand on the arm of his chair. "I'm sure your dad did all he could."

Steve nodded, his hands tightening into fists. "Dad was setting up for the raid when he learned she'd made a big show, drag racing at the drive-in. He sent two officers over, but by the time they got there, she was gone." He raised his hands in a helpless gesture. "Dad jogged over. Patrick had her holed up somewhere, but he wouldn't tell Dad where. Only that they were getting out of town before the raid went down." He dropped his hands. "When the car was missing afterward, Dad figured Patrick and Kitty had used it to run away. That's why Dad was okay with Patrick stealing his car. It was all for the good of those kids and for Sugarland. He was taking down the mob and giving Patrick and Kitty a fresh start."

"I suppose he never heard from them again," Melody said.

"Why would he?" Steve asked. "That would be dangerous. Plus, they were free and happy. He had no reason to think they didn't make it."

"But why not at least report a missing patrol car?" I asked. There was no way anyone could get away with that today.

Steve shrugged. "Out of loyalty to Kitty and to keep his sources quiet. You need to protect the people who help you or else all of your sources will dry up. Informants need to know they can trust you."

A tremor ran through me, the magnitude of the story sinking in. "It's hard to imagine all this went down in Sugarland." I mean, this was the peaceful, picturesque town I knew and loved—a place where people took care of each other. Up until a few years ago, I hadn't even bothered to lock my doors.

Steve gave a small smile as if he understood. "Dad worked hard back then to make Sugarland what it is for you today."

He had. Hadn't he?

With a thoughtful hum, I leaned against the bookcase and tried to piece together the events that had transpired. "Okay, so somehow Patrick stole a police car from under the noses of the Sugarland PD." I couldn't help but think how proud Frankie would be of that. "Kitty was waiting for him at the motel and then went to meet him by the fence at the drive-in. So did Patrick kill Kitty?"

Steve's brows furrowed. "It's always possible," he said, his voice strained. "But why would he betray his family to protect her, only to kill her himself?"

"Unless he betrayed his family for a different reason entirely," I suggested, although I couldn't think what that might be. "But that implies he killed Kitty in cold blood." Remembering the way he'd kissed her, I found it hard to imagine.

Melody, her eyes bright and calculating, chimed in. "The only other option is that someone intercepted Patrick, stole the car, and killed her. It could have been Seamus. Maybe he followed Patrick."

"Past the police?" Steve asked. "I know my dad looks bad getting his car stolen, but he was a fine officer. So were the rest of the men working the raid that night." Steve glanced at Melody. "Plus, Seamus would have also had to sneak back into the Irish bar while the police had it surrounded."

I nodded slowly, mulling over the possibilities. "I still say Seamus would have needed a reason to want to hurt Kitty."

Steve gave a curt nod. "I grant you this. By the time the police had the place surrounded, it would have been pretty clear to the mobsters that my dad had someone on the inside. Why else would he show up on the night they were supposed to move their big score? I'd say it's more likely one of the mobsters must have escaped and killed Patrick and Kitty."

Meanwhile, Melody had been engrossed in her phone. "According to what I'm seeing, Seamus's body was never recovered after the raid."

Steve seemed taken a bit off guard at that. He opened his mouth, then closed it before answering. "There was a fire. A lot of the bodies burned. Dad was pretty sure they got Seamus."

"But maybe they didn't." She glanced up at Steve. "Maybe he snuck out to go after Patrick and never made it back in. Maybe he ran over Kitty."

"Then why wouldn't he keep the police car and use it to skip town?" I asked.

"It's hard to lie low in a police cruiser with a smashed and bloody front grille," Melody replied.

I had to admit, she had a point. "The front window was pretty busted up too. It would have been hard to drive."

Melody looked back down at her phone, her fingers scrolling quickly. "It says here that there were rumors afterward. Sightings of Seamus O'Reilly in Las Vegas in the years after the raid."

I straightened, pushing myself off the bookcase. "I'd like to try to track Seamus down."

Melody raised a brow. "In Vegas?"

"I'll start with the Irish bar," I said. Frankie would get a kick out of that.

If and when I found him.

Melody tapped a finger against her phone, her gaze thoughtful. "Are your sisters still in town, Steve? Do they remember any of this?"

He shook his head. "They retired to Florida about ten years ago. They were too young at the time to understand what was happening, but they always liked Kitty. They were sad when she left town..." He cleared his throat, the sound echoing in the silent room. "Well, now we know she died." His gaze grew distant as if lost in a memory. "I'm going to hate breaking that to them, even after all these years."

"I'm sorry," Melody said.

So was I. But another thought had captured me. "What about your dad?" I wondered aloud. "This was his house, right?" At Steve's nod, I continued, "Do you mind if I take a quick look and see if he's still around?"

It would be invaluable to hear the chief's perspective on the events. If he still believed Seamus had died in the raid. Now that he'd crossed over, he might have had the chance to investigate further. Plus, I'd like to know more about the cigarettes I'd spotted on the front seat of the wrecked police cruiser—were they his or the killer's?

"Sure." Steve forced a quick smile. "Take a look. Sometimes I swear I feel him here." He brushed his lap off and stood. "It would be nice to know if he's still knocking around. I tell you, he would have had plenty of ideas for the windowsill I've been fixing."

I excused myself and made my way to the kitchen at the rear of the house.

It was a cozy space, smelling of the coffee and biscuits Steve had made for breakfast.

The countertops were polished granite, the natural design of the stone providing a striking contrast to the modern white cabinetry. A sleek, single-handle faucet sat atop a deep, farmhouse-style sink. Black appliances gleamed under the warm glow of recessed lighting. Steve did have a talent.

The attached dining area was similarly well-kept. I edged past a hand-hewn wooden table and looked out the window over the large deck leading out to the backyard. There was no sign of the chief outside or through the open doors of the workshop out back.

A staircase divided the space between the kitchen and the front sitting room. I could hear Melody and Steve in the front room. They talked quietly as they looked through family albums, studiously ignoring me, giving me the space I needed to work.

Pleased, I ascended the staircase that divided the kitchen from the front room, my hand tracing the smooth, varnished banister. The hallway at the top was narrower than the one in my friend Lauralee's historical bungalow. Yet this one, like hers, was adorned with family photos going back decades.

A small guest bedroom stood at the top of the hall, and another farther down. Both rooms were small, tastefully decorated, and empty.

Across the hall stood the master bedroom. I'd saved it for last because it was such a personal room and because the door was closed.

Yet Steve had given me permission to examine the house.

With that in mind, I pushed open the dark-stained wood-paneled door that appeared to have been made by Steve himself. Or perhaps his dad.

As soon as I did, the scent of smoke wafted toward me. It was sharp and sweet, a blend of spicy cloves and rich tobacco.

Steve didn't smoke. Did he?

I hadn't smelled it on him. Or this scent.

I kept my wits about me.

The room was spacious, dominated by a plush king-size bed with a stylish tufted headboard. A sleek armoire stood against the wall, its polished exterior reflecting the room. The carpet was a soft, neutral color, and the walls were painted a soothing shade of white.

In one corner of the room sat a shimmering gray chair, well-worn and in an ugly striped pattern. On closer inspection, it appeared to be an armchair, its upholstery a faded pattern of leaves and vines.

"Chief McAvoy?" I called.

The room lay silent.

A simple wood table stood next to the chair. In my realm, it displayed a very healthy-looking jade plant. On a ghostly table, the same table, a glowing gray ashtray held a lit cigarette. The smoke curled upward, the scent of cloves filling the room.

It was as if someone had only stepped out for a moment. I examined the pack lying next to the ashtray—Djarum Black. The same brand I'd found in the wrecked cruiser.

"Chief McAvoy?" I ventured to the bathroom door, hoping I wasn't about to invade the ghost's privacy. I knocked twice. "My name is Verity, and I'd love to chat with you."

I pushed the door open on an empty room.

"Hello?" I turned back to the chair. The seat sagged with a well-worn indent.

It seemed he'd been here recently. At least I had to think it was McAvoy. Which meant I could meet him. If I could only find him.

"I'm going to leave you a note," I said, glad I'd kept my purse on me. I jotted down a quick request on the back of a Finer Diner receipt:

Dear Chief McAvoy,

I'm not quite sure how to say this, but Kitty Cunningham did not run away on the night of May 3, 1956. She was murdered, and I have proof. Please contact me at #1 Peach Orchard Lane. Your friend, Verity Long (granddaughter of Delia Marchcamp Long)

"There," I said, tucking it next to the ghostly ashtray.

With any luck, I'd soon have the police knocking at my door.

Chapter Sixteen

"You wrote the ghost a note," Melody deadpanned as she steered the car toward Rural Route 7 and home.

I didn't see what the big deal was. "It wasn't as if I could leave him a voicemail," I pointed out.

A breeze blew through the open windows, tousling my hair. Outside, treetops blazed in a riot of reds and oranges.

My sister leaned an elbow out the door through the open window. "So if the long-dead Chief McAvoy is around, you think he's just going to drop by your house."

"Like any good neighbor would," I agreed, waving to Jeanette Strohm, who was out manning her fruit stand. "I mean, I found his missing cruiser. I have answers he's waited years—and the entirety of his afterlife—to learn." The chief struck me as a man of action. "I half-expect him to be on the back porch when we get home."

"Fingers crossed, then." Melody giggled as she made the gesture.

"Hey, I'm serious," I told her.

Truth be told, I was hoping for a lot more than a visit from McAvoy.

With any luck, I'd find Frankie at my place along with the

chief. I needed to know my gangster buddy was safe, even if he wouldn't appreciate me extending an invitation to the fuzz.

We'd just have to agree to disagree.

I was also very eager to learn what had happened to my housemate while he was out looking for Kitty and if he'd learned anything new.

"It just strikes me funny," Melody said, tucking a flyaway lock of hair behind her ear as she steered the car along the ribbon of country road, nearing the turn-off to my place. "I mean, what would we have said five years ago to you hoping for a ghost on your porch?"

I felt the shadow of a grin quirk on my lips. "What would I have said last week?" Typically, ghosts on my porch brought nothing but trouble.

Worry niggled the back of my mind. It was one thing to plan a rendezvous with a ghost, quite another to face the reality of it. Ghosts could be as unpredictable as live people—and far more dangerous.

Still, there was no avoiding it. I blew out a breath and wiggled some of the tension out of my shoulders. I'd do the best I could like I always had.

Melody navigated the car along the gravel driveway beside my house and parked near the rose garden in the back. The car ground to a halt, and the engine's hum faded, replaced by the chirping of birds.

"Do you see the chief?" Melody asked, peering toward the white-painted porch, her gaze darting between columns and shadows as if she could somehow spot the ghost.

"Not yet." I slipped out of the car, squinting against the midday sun.

The last of the summer bees buzzed with a lazy sort of urgency around the pots of mums on my back steps, and a sunbeam caught the porch swing in a golden spotlight.

But there was no chief, no Frankie. My heart sank. "I don't see either one of them."

A crisp breeze swept through the yard, rustling the leaves of the large tree by the pond. Its branches, sagging under the weight of ripe apples, were a stark contrast against the blue sky. The surface of the pond nearby was a mirror, peaceful and serene.

It would have been beautiful if I hadn't been so disappointed. And a little scared.

If I had Frankie's urn on my property, that meant he was here. He was *always* here. And not always in a fun way.

But now?

My sister walked with me to the shed next to the pond and watched me creak open the door to discover an empty, ordinary shed. There were no whiskey-swilling gangsters, no poker game going on from the night before. Not even Frankie polishing his second-favorite gun. I let the door bang shut.

"Something must have gone terribly wrong last night," I said, trying to imagine what could have severed Frankie's tie to my property.

Fearing the worst.

"Are you going to be all right?" Melody asked.

"Yes." I mustered a half-smile. "No sense borrowing trouble." It found me on its own. Besides, conjuring up worst-case scenarios wouldn't help. I had to look on the bright side. "At least McAvoy isn't out there wrestling Frankie to the ground, ready to cuff him over that eyesore of a moonshine still."

My ghost might be missing, but Betsy Sue the Third hadn't gone anywhere.

I took that to be a good sign. A butt-ugly beacon of hope.

The twisted copper coils and beat-up drum were a monument to the absurdity that had become my life, and I'd completely forgotten about it until now.

How crazy was that?

I turned to Melody. "Thanks so much for your help this morning. I really couldn't have done it without you."

"You would have found a way," she assured me. All the same, she beamed at my appreciation. "Anyhow"—her eyes twinkled with a hint of mischief—"if you don't mind, I'm going to head back to the library and return those historical photos. Technically, they shouldn't have left the building."

Reason number four hundred and twelve why I loved my sister. "I promise I won't tell Duranja you're a rule breaker," I said, hugging her goodbye.

Her boyfriend was the most by-the-book police officer I'd ever encountered.

He was going to have his hands full with my sister.

"He knows," she said, more amused than she ought to be.

Yes, Duranja was in trouble for sure, I decided as she waved and drove away.

But what about Frankie?

I turned back toward the moonshine still. It stood silent and dead, as it had since Frankie disappeared.

My backyard was bathed in the golden light of the late morning sun. It cast long, playful shadows that danced on the ground. Birds chirped. Squirrels chased each other across the yard and up tree trunks. It was a classic Tennessee autumn day, one that would have made me want to grab a steaming mug of vanilla spice coffee and sit on the porch swing to soak it all in. Now, the utter peace felt wrong. Absurd.

So I watched and waited.

For Frankie to come home. For McAvoy to appear. For Molly's friends to drop by with news.

I took a break and let Lucy out. I could always count on her for a greeting and a snuggle. She did her business quickly and then took to chasing butterflies by the pond. I planted my rear on the bottom step of the porch and waited some more.

My biggest concern was Frankie. It was unprecedented for him to be off-property without me. Something big had changed. And since he hadn't returned yet, I had a feeling it was bad.

"Come on, Frank," I said to no one in particular. "You should be here."

Meanwhile, Lucy had tired of her game and decided to curl

up under the apple tree. A butterfly landed on her head, but she was too relaxed to care.

Oh, to be a skunk, I sighed. Then I caught a subtle, metallic rattle coming from Betsy Sue the Third.

Lucy leaped up and dashed for her favorite hiding spot under the porch.

"Frankie?" I called, hurrying toward the beast. Was he brewing up a new batch? Fiddling with the metallic monstrosity? A dewy condensation had formed over the coils, and the bottom drum leaked a putrid ooze onto my grass. It was beautiful. Perfect. "You're here, aren't you?" Whatever else was wrong, we could fix it. "Give me another sign." I reached out, hesitating to touch the ghostly object. Instead, I hovered a hand over the dented old oil drum and felt the otherworldly chill. "Please tell me this is you."

"I'm not *in* the still," the gangster snarked.

"Frankie!" I whooshed out. He was back. He made it! "It's so good to hear your voice." I swiveled my head to locate him. "Where are you?"

"I'm right here," he said, each word dropping like a stone. Frankie kept himself invisible. I could only hear his voice. And lucky me—he sounded annoyed. "I've been here since you dragged me home last night. I was here today when you left. I was trapped here because you. Didn't. Take. My. Urn."

"Oh, that's wonderful," I exclaimed, ten kinds of relief washing over me. He hadn't been held prisoner somewhere. He hadn't been lost or powerless or cut off from me. The rules hadn't changed. The world made sense again.

"You want to take another crack at that apology?"

"No time." I waved him off. And it wouldn't appease him anyway. "I didn't know where you were. I assumed you were gone."

"Like I can go anywhere without you," he groused.

"I couldn't see you," I explained, glancing back at the still, half expecting him to materialize there. "In fact, I still can't," I added, a niggle of worry creeping back in. We had to get back to work. "Stop playing games."

"Behind you," he managed.

I whirled around, and there he was, a misty semblance of the gangster I knew and sometimes wished I didn't.

His head and torso hung limply in the air, weak and almost entirely transparent.

The rest of him was flat-out gone.

"Oh, Frankie," I managed. My poor friend. This was bad. "You look terrible."

He scowled at my words and vanished.

"Frankie!" Panic edged my voice as I reached out to him without thinking, my fingers slicing through the chilly morning air.

"You made me feel bad," his voice intoned from near my left shoulder. "And when I feel bad, it gets worse."

"I'm sorry." I hadn't meant it. If there was ever a time he needed me, it was now. "You're sooo good-looking," I said, turning toward him, hoping a little levity might help him feel better.

"I know that," he bristled. "I don't need you to tell me that." But his form flickered back into view, clearer this time.

Although still missing way too many body parts.

"What's happening, Frankie?" I asked, drawing as close as I dared. "Why are you fading so quickly? Did Kitty do this to you?" We had to find a way to fix it.

The mere mention of her name made him fade again. Only his eyes glowed. "I caught up to her at her death spot. She was freaking out, worried the police had arrested Patrick. That kind of emotion made her drain Molly fast. Scary fast. So I cornered Kitty and told her I'd shoot her if she didn't calm down."

"And?" I asked. Terrified for Molly, knowing this wouldn't turn out well.

"Kitty freaked out more," he said as if it were inconceivable. "She was sucking Molly down quicker than I could ever have imagined. It was so bad I thought I might lose her then and there. I gave Molly everything I could, and Kitty took it all. I mean, look at me!" He flickered with rage. "Molly talked her down, helped her get a handle on it. Then I passed out." He cursed in frustration. "When I came to, I was back at your place, on the ground with my arms missing and popcorn in my hair—too weak to manifest or to even get you to listen to me."

"Okay, calm down for a second," I said. I needed to think. And he needed to save his strength.

"I can't calm down," he shot back. "Kitty is draining Molly faster than I can help her."

It was horrifying. And I was making it worse. I was still tuned in, draining what little power he had left. "You can't afford to be giving your energy to me, too. Not when you're like this. You should have cut me off."

He looked at me as if I'd suggested he eat snails. "Not a chance. You were investigating."

"Well, cut me off now," I insisted. I didn't care if McAvoy showed up. We'd find another way.

Frankie gave a slight nod, and with a motion that was more of a weary withdrawal than a deliberate action, he reclaimed his power.

I braced myself for the icy-cold zap that usually left me bent over, clutching my knees and shivering. But this time, only a small, weak breeze fluttered through me. "Is that it?" I asked. "Did you do it already?"

Frankie squeezed his eyes shut. "You've already helped drain me. You don't need to insult me, too." He opened his eyes to glare at me. "I wasn't kidding when I told you we're running out of time."

Chapter Seventeen

"We need a plan," I said, trying to get a handle on the situation. Because Frankie was right—we were running out of time.

"Come on." I led him up toward the porch swing while I filled him in on the events of the morning, in particular, what we'd learned from Steve about the night Kitty was killed. How Patrick had betrayed his father and the Irish to save Kitty. And about the raid that had brought down Seamus O'Reilly and his crew. Frankie's form tensed, his jaw setting in a hard line as he took in every word.

"Good," he said to himself as he settled down into the swing. "Good."

"You're feeling better?" I'd hoped a little rest would help.

"No." He paused, gazing past me. "I'm wondering why McAvoy raided the Irish on that night, of all nights."

"Oh," I said, deflated. "They were moving a new kind of shipment, something big." I joined him on the swing. "The entire Irish mob was there."

"Says the police," Frankie scoffed.

"I trust the police," I informed him. "At least, I trust the motives of the chief."

"I don't," he said, with a sardonic twist of his mouth. "Even your boyfriend Ellis said some of the cops back then were dirty."

"It was Mac and Buzz. McAvoy was building a case against them. He arrested them after the raid."

"I told you they were bad news," Frankie snapped. "And it usually doesn't stop there. Maybe McAvoy could spot a crooked cop because he was one. What if McAvoy wasn't there to take down the mob, but to take their big score?"

I clasped my hands in my lap and forced myself to consider the idea. Only I couldn't quite make it add up. "For one thing, McAvoy lived a comfortable, but modest life in the same three-bedroom bungalow for his entire life." That didn't sound like a guy going after a mob score. "For another, taking down the mob was one of his biggest accomplishments, a career highlight."

"I'd like to give him a highlight he'll never forget," Frankie snarled.

"Focus," I told him.

Then, wonder upon wonder, Lucy toddled up the porch steps.

Frankie froze for a second, and so did I as she paused to give him a once-over.

"This is new," he muttered as she approached him on purpose and slipped under the porch swing where he sat. "What's she doing?" he asked, stiffening.

I took a peek. "Aww... She's curling up to rest, right underneath you."

The gangster appeared almost frightened at the thought. "I must really be on death's door."

That ship had passed.

But I caught the shadow of a grin, and his form grew stronger.

"She knows you don't feel good," I said simply.

"Huh," he grunted, staring out into the yard.

I sat with him in silence for a bit, mulling over his distrust of the chief. Then again, Frankie didn't like any police. He even liked to assign nefarious intentions to my boyfriend from time to time.

I glanced at my gangster buddy, then straight through the slats of the porch swing to my therapy skunk. She'd snuggled into a little ball, her tail twitching. "Like it or not, people still talk about Chief McAvoy and all the good he did."

Frankie gave me the side-eye. "Fair enough. But that don't mean he was some crusader taking down a bunch of hardworking criminals trying to make a dishonest living," he gritted out. "Maybe he had a beef with Patrick for getting Kitty into trouble, and a mob takedown was a convenient excuse for murder."

"But if Patrick was dead, who took the chief's car?"

"Maybe the chief used it to run Patrick down, and he hit Kitty by mistake," Frankie said.

"It sure looked like whoever hit her did it on purpose." I'd watched her try to dodge the oncoming vehicle.

"Then the chief hid his own car," Frankie continued as if facts didn't matter.

"You always think the worst of people," I said. It wouldn't hurt him to work on that.

"You're just mad because I have a point," he countered.

It was a far-fetched theory, and it certainly wasn't the only explanation.

"It's impossible to say," I admitted, more bothered than I'd like to admit.

"But it is possible," he pressed. The gangster fixed me with a look that could have cut glass. "It's also possible that the dirty dead chief could have been listening to everything you told his son."

Yikes. "I hadn't considered that."

"And now he's coming to our house." The gangster's words hit me hard.

"If we're lucky," I said, earning a frown. "Are you just angry because I didn't take you with me this morning?"

His eyes narrowed. "Oh, I'm spitting nails, sweetheart. You left the one guy at home who knows how criminals think."

"What's done is done." I couldn't change it. Or escape his

opinion now. "Still, I have to consider any chance to meet the chief as a good thing." If we could swing it. But that would require power Frankie couldn't afford. "We need to figure this out fast. We need to give Kitty her closure—and hopefully reunite her with Patrick—so that she can move on and leave Molly be. And you."

"I don't know how much longer I can hold out," he admitted.

"I know." Frankie looked sunken, like he'd aged twenty years in the ten minutes he'd been talking to me. Lucy jumped up and settled into the space between me and Frankie. He barely looked at her. "Tell me. How dangerous is this...thing with your energy?" I asked, the words catching in my throat as I considered the very real fact that Frankie was fading away, piece by piece.

If we didn't stop it soon, there might be nothing left.

Frankie gave a small sigh. "It's like the time I drove an overloaded rumrunner down a winding switchback in Colorado only to figure out halfway through that the brakes went out."

"So it's both dangerous and stupid," I concluded.

"It's what I do best," he said with an air of finality.

"Frankie—" My words earlier had come out sharper than I'd intended, a thin veil for my worry. I ran a hand over my eyes. I knew Frankie could be a reckless idiot, but he was my reckless idiot, and it would kill me to watch him immolate himself when there had to be a better way. "I'm asking you as a friend. Please. Save your strength."

He let out a sound halfway between a scoff and a choke. "I don't care about my strength. I care about Molly's."

"Well, I care," I snapped back. We couldn't delay this investigation a minute more. I stood, leaving the swing to rock. "Let me handle this. I'll go to the Irish bar and see what I can learn without you."

"You're bonkers," he said as I pulled out my phone and leaned on the porch rail to send a quick text to Ellis. "You need my power if you're going to talk to Seamus."

"Maybe I can do this without Seamus," I said, typing. "I

didn't need your power at McAvoy's. I learned a lot without you."
He didn't have to do everything. "There's a real-world solution to
this. There are witnesses left in my world. The wrecked police
cruiser was left here in my world. That means more real evidence
could be here, too."

"We don't have time for you not to find everything you can,"
Frankie insisted. "Without my power, you wouldn't have known
McAvoy was still at his house. You wouldn't have left him the
note that's going to bring him here to possibly kill you."

"Don't say that." I'd be offended if I weren't kind of worried.
"Number one," I said, pointing my phone at him, "that's a
terrible assumption. Besides, my power's off now, and even if you
turned it back on, I'd hope you'd cut it off again before anybody
hurt me."

"Turn it on, turn it off..." Frankie mumbled in a poor imita-
tion of my admittedly perky manner.

Lucy turned a circle and settled back onto the bench with her
back to me, swishing her furry tail.

She might not have to listen to this, but Frankie did.

"Number two, we don't know if McAvoy will see the note.
And number three, you're going to see that the note is more brilliant than dangerous." I sent my text to Ellis and dug in, ready to
stand my ground. "You know I'm good at this. You just save your
strength and count on me."

He looked at me like I'd asked him to dance the Macarena.
"You are not in charge of this investigation."

"I am when you make yourself so weak I couldn't find you
this morning." It was a low blow, but I was serious. "Save your
strength for when we really need you. You know this investigation
is in good hands with me." He'd seen my knack for untangling
mysteries firsthand. "I've solved every case I've tackled."

"You thought I'd escaped the yard," he shot back.

"I can talk to anybody," I insisted.

"You can't talk to Molly's friends without me."

"I'm a whiz at putting clues together."

"You won't know the whole truth until you talk to the Irish," he warned.

It pained me to think he might have a point. I felt it like a lead ball in my stomach. "Let me check it out in my world first." The bar had been abandoned since that night. "I can see if there's any evidence still there."

"Because gangsters love to leave evidence around," he said dryly.

He'd be surprised. "Well, you can't go anyway. The Irish would shoot you on sight." Then he'd be out of commission for several hours, or longer, given his current shaky form.

"They unmasked me as El Gato," he grumbled.

I wasn't exactly shocked. It had been a flimsy disguise at best. "When did that happen?" I pressed.

"Suds told me this morning. It seems I lost my hat and my accent right after I blew up the boss's car."

"Well, that would do it."

"It doesn't matter." He squared his shoulders like a soldier facing battle. "I'll go in as myself. I'd walk through hell for Molly."

I hated to point it out, but... "You don't even have legs anymore."

He rose from the bench. "I'm not letting you leave me behind," he insisted, his voice firm, like he could will himself solid with sheer stubbornness and pride.

"Even if it kills you?" I asked. He had to see reason.

"Even then," he said grimly.

Lucy leaped off the swing and stood between us, flicking her tail.

I pinched the bridge of my nose between my fingers, feeling a headache coming on. His recklessness and pride could be the end of him—permanently. And I wasn't about to let that happen. Letting out a slow breath, I dropped my hand and stared him dead in the eye. "Here's another suggestion. Why don't you just trust me? Trust me to handle it. Trust me that I'll come get you if you truly are the only man for the job."

Frankie shifted uncomfortably, the uncharacteristic hesitance making him look almost out of place in his own translucent skin. "Do you know how crazy you sound?" he asked, his voice betraying a mix of frustration and rare vulnerability.

My word. He could stare down a mob boss without flinching, rob a bank in his sleep, and shoot his way out of no fewer than twelve speakeasies (and counting), but he couldn't accept help from a friend—when he needed it desperately.

I gave a small sigh. "It goes like this—Hey, Verity. You are my friend and you've seen me through some crazy dark times. I am your friend. I've saved your life more than once—"

"Three times," he corrected with trademark bravado.

Look who's counting. "So instead of killing myself by giving you all my energy and supporting Molly," I continued for him, "I'm going to let you handle this one."

Frankie's face went as still as a pond with no breeze.

He ground his jaw, his expression iced over. But behind the frost, there was a plea, a silent desperation to save his girlfriend, no matter the cost.

I softened my stance, the fight draining out of me as I took a step toward him. "You're killing yourself, aren't you?"

His figure solidified with his resolve, his voice low and steady. "It's my business."

"Frankie—" I began. He had to see reason.

His voice rose, the words sharp and clipped. "You don't get it. You don't get it and you never will! I. Can't. Trust. Anybody. Ever."

I felt a pang of hurt at his words, a sting of betrayal that he'd lump me in with "anybody." I realized he'd had a tough time of it. I did. And I never took that for granted. But I didn't understand why he couldn't stand with me right here, right now. "Why—"

"Because I can't!" he cried, raw and ragged. "It never works out for me. I'm not the kind of guy people look out for."

"That's not true. Molly—"

The name softened his expression for a fleeting second before he steeled himself again. "I support Molly. I love her. I'd die for her."

"You *are* dying for her."

And there it was, the tragic truth laid bare.

He swallowed hard and didn't bother to deny it. "Fine. But I won't depend on her."

Did he realize how that sounded? "Maybe you should." He wouldn't be able to love her all the way until he let her in all the way.

"Maybe you should mind your own damn business." He sank back onto the bench, his face gaunt. "Don't say a word," he ordered.

He'd gotten paler and thinner just arguing with me.

I joined him on the swing. "I want you to depend on me," I said, noticing Lucy curl up next to where his feet would be.

"Verity—" he began weakly, and for a second, I thought I had reached him. But then he looked at me, his gaze laden with incredulity as if I was missing some obvious, critical point. "Verity." He uttered my name again as though it explained everything, as though it was the punchline of a joke I didn't get.

"When have I ever let you down?" I challenged.

He let out a short, humorless laugh. "How about when you dumped my urn onto a rosebush and put me on the train to crazy town."

I barked out a short laugh, but my voice remained firm. "That's ancient history, and we both know it's not the same. Answer the question. When have I ever let you down when it really mattered?" My eyes locked onto his, waiting for an answer I knew he didn't have.

"I—" Frankie hesitated.

"You're really trying hard to think of something, aren't you?" I prodded.

"I would love to prove you wrong right now," he admitted with a touch of his usual defiance.

"This isn't a competition," I said gently.

"I think I'd prefer that," he said wryly. Then he sighed. "Look, I get what you're asking, but I can't rely on anyone to have my back. Not you. Not anybody." He paused, his gaze dropping to the painted white boards of the porch. "I never could. Not when my parents skipped out. Not when I raised my brother and tried to keep him out of the mob. Not when he betrayed me and put a bullet in my head."

Over the years, we'd uncovered a lot of harsh truths from Frankie's past, the betrayals he couldn't easily overlook.

Still.

"You forgave your brother," I reminded him.

He let out a bitter laugh, glancing away. "Yeah, and ask me how often I see him. It proves my point. I'm alone. Always will be." His shoulders slumped ever so slightly—a rare crack in his armor. "Don't give me that look," he said with a rough edge to his whisper.

"What look?" I was only trying to have a conversation here.

He blinked in rapid succession like he'd gotten something in his eyes. "Those sad, puppy-dog eyes. Makes me feel like a charity case." He shook his head, trying to reset his bravado. "I've got Molly as long as I keep proving I'm worth her love. But that's it. I don't have anything else."

"You have me," I reminded him.

"I don't need you," he scoffed, but his heart wasn't in it.

"Right now, you do," I pointed out. "And for the sake of argument, let's say we do it your way. And you're totally fine with running your power down and draining yourself until you no longer exist in order to keep Molly alive for a few days, hours, or minutes more."

He winced, the thought clearly paining him. "I'm kind of hoping to free Molly before that happens."

"Me too." We could do it. I knew we could. "I'm fine with you focusing your energy on her. Do what you need to do to keep her with us. Just let me handle the rest." I edged closer. "Let me try to do this without your power. Trust me to know when to call for you, despite the toll it takes." I drew so close I felt the chill of the ghost. "Trust me to be your partner. Believe that I'm here for you. Always. Not just when it's safe or convenient." His bottom lip quivered a bit, but I wasn't finished. "Oh, and let me blow your sockets. I'm here because we're friends—that's it. You don't have to earn it or deserve it. You don't need to be anyone other than Frankie, the annoying gangster." The nutty guy who built a moonshine still in my yard. "I love you just the way you are."

The swing rocked gently, almost undetectable as he stared at me for a second. "Because you're a crazy person," he concluded.

Yet the shadow of a smile crossed his lips, and I could tell he understood.

"Maybe I'm crazy too," I admitted. "But I'm your brand of crazy, and you're the one who decided to be friends with me."

His brows furrowed. "I don't remember any deciding. I think it just kind of happened."

"Well, now you're stuck," I concluded. "So that's it. It's you and me. Okay?"

"Okay," Frankie said with new resolve. He also looked more solid now. His eyes were less hollowed. And he'd gotten his arms back all the way to his fingertips! Wow. Look at that. I didn't know how we'd done it, but I was so stinking thankful. Now we just had to keep him on *save* mode.

The gangster frowned at me. "I also think I know a way you can learn once and for all if the Irish were behind Kitty's death." He screwed up his face as if he were about to say something distasteful. "It's on the mortal plane, so you wouldn't need my power."

I clapped my hands together. "Now we're talking."

The gangster was less amused. "You have to promise to take me along when you go out. That way, I can ask questions if anyone's around."

"Right into the Irish headquarters?" I asked. "You blew your cover, remember?" He'd have to go in as Frankie. That was like taking a stick of dynamite into a house fire. The Irish knew he was around. They were mad at him already. "You can't afford to get shot."

He notched up his chin. "Anything for Molly." He pressed his lips together, inviting no more debate. "Now listen close. Seamus O'Reilly was a cocky son of a gun. In his gang, if a hit was on, Seamus posted a picture in his office with a red *X* over the unlucky slub's face. If you wanted the job, you went in and wrote your name underneath for everybody to see."

"And it would still be there," I said, hope flaring. We'd know once and for all if Seamus never called off the hit. And if not, who had been gunning for Kitty.

"If the office is intact," Frankie cautioned. "If I had to guess, I'd say there's a good chance it's still there. The boss's office is downstairs in a private area just for him."

"That's even riskier for you because the Irish will shoot you on sight."

"I'm good at sneaking around," he said as if that would solve everything.

I had a bad feeling about it, but there was no time to play it safe. "Fine, but no shooting anybody."

"No unnecessary shooting," he corrected, not helping my nerves one bit.

The gangster was saved from another debate when my cell phone let out a sharp *ping*.

I stood as I drew it out of my back pocket. Ellis had answered my text:

Yes, I would be glad to go to the old Irish bar with you. I would be more interested to know why.

The building is locked, but I can get us a key. You shouldn't go alone anyway. I'm just getting home from last night's investigation and need to sleep. Let's go tomorrow during the day. Good night and I love you.

I loved him, too, but I wasn't waiting until tomorrow.

"Forget it. I can't wait for you," Frankie said, backtracking with amazing speed as he read over my shoulder. "Molly doesn't have that kind of time."

"We'll both go now," I vowed, heading for the house to fetch his urn.

"You can't get in," he said on my heels.

"I think I know a way," I promised. I hoped.

I'd just have to call in a favor and pray that Ellis understood.

Chapter Eighteen

My well-loved Cadillac grumbled to a halt on the street in front of a tidy white bungalow. The engine gave one last clank of protest before settling into silence. I twisted the key and pulled it out, taking a moment to appreciate the mature trees lining the street, as well as the look of pure horror on Frankie's face.

He sat stiffly in the passenger seat next to me. "This is Ellis's house." He said it like an accusation. "Don't tell me you want to bring the fuzz to Seamus's headquarters after the cops already raided and torched the place."

"Don't worry," I said, slipping the keys into my purse. "He'll be asleep by now." It had been at least ten or fifteen minutes since I'd gotten off the phone with my boyfriend, and he could nod off as quick as a cat on a sunny porch.

Frankie's confusion melted into a conspiratorial grin. "I get it. He has a key to his dad's property, and you're going to steal it." Thievery was one of Frankie's favorite pastimes.

"Absolutely not," I said, my voice firm, trying to mask the mortification that he'd dared suggest it. "Why do you always consider stealing a first resort?"

"Why do you consider it last?" Frankie asked, with no trace of irony.

Morals. Common decency. A consideration for other people.

I grabbed my brown hemp bag from the bench seat between us, the texture rough under my fingers as I chanced a glance at the gangster to my right. His fingers deftly checked the bullets in his gun as if they were rosary beads. I sighed. Forget it. He'd never understand.

I slung the bag over my shoulder and pushed open the car door, the afternoon sun warm on my face. "The last time I talked to Ellis, he told me his dad forced his mom out of the family mansion." She'd been shocked, blindsided. "At least while Leland is in town, I have a feeling she's holed up here."

Frankie snapped the cylinder closed. "And you *want* to see the Iron Matron," he clarified as if I'd volunteered to go skinny-dipping with the shark from *Jaws*.

I slammed the car door shut, feeling the uneven weight of Frankie's urn bump against my side. "Today, I do."

Frankie glided out the passenger-side door. "You remember how she tried to bankrupt you. How she tried to make you lose your house after you rejected her perfect boy, Beau. How she thought you weren't good enough for Ellis, never mind the fact she doesn't like Ellis half the time. In fact, I can't believe Ellis would let her stay with him."

"She's his mother," I said, skirting around the front of the Cadillac to join Frankie on the sidewalk. "Plus, he's a good person."

"Nobody's that good," Frankie said as we headed for the house.

Ellis was. Even if Frankie couldn't comprehend it.

I looked at Ellis's simple, sturdy home with its tidy black shutters under a crisp blue sky. "Knowing her, he's forbidden to say a word. And Ellis would be noble and honor that." Saying it out loud made me all the more sure of it. "Virginia is a proud woman. I doubt she'd want it known around town she's been driven out of Tara."

Years ago, Virginia had torn down the historical Wydell homestead and replaced it with a sprawling McMansion. She wouldn't be able to stay at the Sugarland Hotel or anywhere else public. She was on shaky terms with her extended family. Her son Leland IV had taken his father's side in the divorce, and even though she considered her youngest son, Beau, the perfect child, he wasn't the type to look out for her in return.

That left Ellis.

"You might be right," Frankie said as we made our way up the asphalt driveway, his gaze sweeping our surroundings as if anticipating an ambush. He paused, an eyebrow arching as he took in the trio of terra cotta planters, each holding a perfectly trimmed lemon tree. The once sparse porch now boasted a sleek, black wicker seating set with plush white cushions, and a brass knocker had been added to the front door, shining ostentatiously in the sunlight. "Looks like she's made herself at home."

"How very Virginia," I said. Although I had to admit all of it looked great. Virginia Wydell had many faults, but her taste wasn't one of them.

Frankie glided in front of me, blocking my path. "I still don't get why we want to see her. Remember, we're out to learn who killed Kitty. And I don't think Virginia has the answer."

I sidestepped around Frankie, not missing a beat. "She owes me a favor."

"You're as endearing to her as a splinter," he pointed out.

"As if that ever stopped us from working together." I stepped up onto the front porch, the wood creaking slightly underfoot. "Besides, I think I'm growing on her," I added, tapping on the door.

"You might want to think again," Frankie said a moment after it swung open.

Virginia stood in the entryway, her frown as tight as the blonde hair artfully twisted at the nape of her neck. She wore a crisp white jacket with matching pants, set off by a pale blue silk shirt and pearl earrings. The crease between her perfectly plucked eyebrows deepened at the sight of me.

I did my best to seem unfazed. "Virginia," I greeted her warmly, my voice carrying a cheer I didn't quite feel. Despite everything, I was glad to see her. I wouldn't be here if I didn't need her help. "I was hoping you were in."

Her frown didn't waver. Suspicion painted every feature of her still-striking face. "How did you know I was here?" she demanded, her tone icy.

"I heard what happened," I admitted. "I didn't tell anyone," I rushed to assure her when she appeared alarmed. It wasn't like Virginia to show her emotions so freely. Leland had seriously knocked her off her game. "Can I come inside?" I added, squeezing past her into the front room.

What I saw made me pause. Ellis's comfortable bachelor living room had undergone a subtle but unmistakable transformation. The black leather sofa, always so stark against the white-painted wall, now had the company of soft, dove-gray throw pillows. I looked at Ellis's black leather coffee table. It doubled as storage and most days appeared as if it were giving birth to a bunch of video game controllers hanging from their wires. But now they were neatly corralled by a sleek, black leather organizer, their wires tamed and out of sight.

An immense TV hung on the opposite wall, but it was no longer a lone monolith in a desert of minimalism. A slim glass vase with a single, sculptural white lily stood on a floating shelf beneath it, its simplicity a statement in itself. The touches were few, but they were Virginia. Expensive, tasteful, and efficient.

I wondered how she'd managed it. I'd asked Ellis a dozen times if he'd like me to help organize. Then I realized Virginia probably hadn't asked.

From the corner of my eye, I caught her hard gaze. Her voice dropped to a whisper. "Ellis is asleep, and I refuse to let you wake him." She crossed her arms over her chest. "The poor boy has been working too hard. Way harder than if he would have listened to my advice and joined the family law firm."

"To be more like your husband, Leland?" I asked innocently.

Ellis had always been the black sheep of the family. And in his family, that meant he'd dodged a bullet.

Virginia's posture softened slightly. "Ellis is a better man than his father, a better man than I could ever have hoped to raise. I'd just like things to go easier for him sometimes."

At least we had that in common. "I'm here because I need your help."

She raised a brow. "Then you might not want to insult me first."

Since when was the truth an insult? "I need to borrow the keys to a property you own—I'm investigating the abandoned Irish bar near the old drive-in. Ellis said he could get me in, which means he was most likely going to ask you." Leland would never let us snoop around his property without a fuss. "Ellis offered to accompany me tomorrow, but I need to go now. It's sort of an emergency."

Virginia tilted her head slightly. I could tell she was intrigued. "Does this have something to do with the wrecked police cruiser you found last night?" Clearly, Ellis had filled her in.

"Yes." And more. "I'm trying to figure out what really happened to Kitty Cunningham."

Virginia's expression lit up. "I remember that." Then, with a conspiratorial grin, she added, "Will you be ghost hunting?"

"Hopefully not," I said. Frankie was too weak as it was.

"But sometimes it's unavoidable, isn't it?" Virginia concluded.

"You said it, sister." The voice came from behind me, and I flinched. Frankie was supposed to be resting, saving his strength.

Virginia pursed her lips and nodded. "We've had a lot of security problems at the old Irish bar. It's not safe, even during the day." She plucked a tiny piece of lint from her jacket. "I won't be responsible for you getting yourself into trouble."

"I'm perfectly capable—"

She waved me off. "You could do with another set of eyes. Backup in case things go south."

"True." But that was impossible. "But I can't wait for Ellis—"

"I'm coming with you," she declared.

That was worse. Much worse.

Virginia strutted through an arched doorway into the small adjoining dining room. A fresh vase of peonies sat atop Ellis's simple wood table. She plucked a Louis Vuitton purse from one of the chairs, slipped it over her forearm, and turned to face me, her expression resolute. "Sorry, sweetheart. You're either taking me, or you're not going."

I was shocked she'd want to join me. It wasn't as if Virginia enjoyed exploring abandoned properties, especially ones she owned. And she wasn't exactly dressed for it. But I couldn't help but be glad I'd wagered correctly. She had the key. "You're as pushy as Frankie," I said, the words slipping out before I could weigh them.

"I'll take that as a compliment," the gangster said.

"I get things done," Virginia stated matter-of-factly. She draped a paisley scarf around her hair with a practiced hand and slid on a pair of oversized sunglasses that would've made Jackie O envious.

"Do you have the key on you?" I asked, just to be clear. It was almost too convenient that she'd have it ready in her purse.

Her ruby-red lips formed a thin line. "I suspect Leland has been meeting his latest mistress at the old motel. At least he's found plenty of excuses to go out there. I was hoping to catch him in the act."

That seemed extreme, even for her. "You're already divorcing him." What else could she do?

She squared her shoulders. "I know. It shouldn't matter so much. And it's unsafe out there. That's why I haven't done it," she replied, her voice carrying a hint of vulnerability.

Had she loved Leland? I mean truly? Her marriage had always seemed to me like more of a business proposition, a union for money and prestige.

I noticed then how fragile she looked—like a porcelain doll

that had been handled too roughly. The divorce was taking its toll on her, and despite our differences, I almost felt sorry for her. "You look nice," I said, offering a small olive branch.

"Of course I do," she responded. As if it were expected, required. "Now, let's go solve your case."

Chapter Nineteen

Of course, Virginia had insisted on driving.

Too bad for her, I'd insisted right back. I wanted to have the land yacht handy in case we ran into trouble.

And so, Virginia sat, back stiff, in the passenger seat of my 1978 avocado green Cadillac, her seatbelt secured tightly. She kept one immaculately manicured hand braced on the purple velvet bench seat. The other against the dash.

As if that could stop it from rattling.

Frankie stewed in the back seat. "I feel naked without the knife in my sock."

"There's no helping it," I said, with a toss of my hair and a sympathetic glance. He didn't have legs.

Then I snuck a glance at Virginia, who appeared as though she'd accidentally sat down on a bench streaked with bird poop.

There was no helping any of it.

The whole thing felt a bit surreal, to be honest. Ellis would have been a much better partner. He would have been on the case, with me one hundred percent.

Instead, I was sneaking in with his mother.

Still, Ellis had asked me not to go alone. And in an emergency, his mother would have to do.

We eased through the same entrance as before. Only this time, we rolled past the abandoned drive-in with its faded marquee and the skeletal remains of its speaker stands poking up like the ribs of some long-forgotten beast. I followed the chain-link fence and noticed the exact spot where I'd slipped through.

That had worked out better than I'd expected. At least we'd found Kitty.

Beyond the drive-in, on the right, I saw the overgrown walkway we'd used to sneak over to the no-tell motel.

And a bit farther up on the left, the hulking remains of O'Reilly's Pub, its brick exterior intact, yet exuding the tiredness of a once-cheerful place that had long ago given up the fight. Several of the Tudor-style stained-glass windows had been boarded over, and graffiti curled around the edges.

"You might not even need my key," Virginia huffed. "You could just knock it over and sift through the rubble."

"I have a feeling it's sturdier than it looks," I told her, eyeing the thickset bricks and the solid-looking door. Especially if vagrants had been hiding out in there.

I sincerely hoped we'd find it abandoned today.

The lot was a sea of cracks and overgrown weeds. I parked as close as the pavement allowed, the engine sputtering to a halt like an old man settling into a favorite chair. Virginia made a face. I ignored her and glanced behind us.

The rusted fence that marked the rear of the old drive-in loomed in the distance, the back gate sagging on its hinges. Whoever stole the chief's cruiser would have had a direct line to Kitty waiting by the fence.

I could almost hear the screech of tires, the shouted commands, and the adrenaline-fueled chaos of Kitty's last moments.

"Well, let's get to it." Virginia unclasped her seatbelt, her movements precise, like everything she did. She reached for the door handle, pausing momentarily to smooth the fabric of her pantsuit.

This was a criminal investigation, not a board meeting. But I had a feeling she wouldn't appreciate the reminder as we stepped out of the car and onto the uneven lot.

The ground was littered with rocks and glass, even the odd beer can.

The O'Reilly's Pub sign, though faded, still swung with a certain dignity above the doorway, the letters barely legible after years of neglect. A shamrock, once a vibrant green, was now just a ghostly outline against the peeling paint.

Virginia and I stopped in front of a solid, four-paneled red door, padlocked shut. Above it, a wrought-iron lamp, now rusted and lifeless, had once welcomed patrons with its warm glow.

"Have you ever been here?" I asked.

"Not inside," she said, ghosting a hand over the flaking paint. "I've come out here a few times with Leland after he bought the property." She gazed at the building with a mixture of fondness and sorrow. "We used to explore while tipsy after a bottle of Château Latour. We liked to pull into the drive-in and relive the old days."

"That's sweet. You two at the drive-in." It made them seem almost...normal. Two people, sharing a moment, and not the king and queen of Sugarland, determined to rule with an iron fist.

The stained-glass windows were Tudor style with small leaded panes that created a patchwork of colors. Most of the glass was intact, but here and there, jagged holes punctured the artwork. Bullet holes.

Makeshift seals fashioned from soggy cardboard, yellowed newspaper, and what looked like bits of old rags were stuffed into the gaps. They fluttered slightly in the breeze, a feeble last stand.

Virginia's eyes softened, the corners crinkling with a hint of a smile that hadn't quite decided to stay. "Leland used to pack a picnic basket full of my favorite things—crusty baguettes, gourmet cheeses, and these little chocolate truffles that I adore. We'd lay out a blanket in the bed of his old pickup truck, right there at the drive-in." She traced the outline of a shamrock on the door with her finger, her touch gentle as if it could summon the memories held in the wood. "I used to surprise him with mixtapes of songs from when we first started dating. We'd listen and just forget the world for a while."

She paused, a sigh escaping her lips, the weight of the years pressing down on it. "Some people think I married him for the money, but I didn't. Not entirely. He was such a sweet man when I first met him." Her eyes clouded over, the smile gone as if it had been nothing but a trick of the light. The corners of her mouth drooped, and she wrapped her arms around herself, a self-embrace that suggested the warmth she once felt was now a cold absence. "It took me a long time to realize he's not that man anymore."

"How long has it been since you felt connected like that?" I asked, kicking at a pile of debris near the door.

"Too long," she murmured, her gaze fixed on some unseen point in the distance.

"Look at this." Near the front door, wedged against the wall, was a triangular piece of rough-cut wood. It looked out of place against the antique architecture, its edges too clean, its surface not yet worn by time or weather. I bent to pick it up, the wood still carrying the scent of being freshly cut.

Virginia recoiled. "Don't touch it."

"It won't bite," I said, showing her. "In fact, it looks like a prop to hold the door open. See?" I demonstrated by wedging it under the door, noting how it fit the gap at the bottom with an unexpected precision. "And it's newer."

Strange that it would be here.

Unless...

The cold realization hit. "Someone must be going inside."

Virginia stiffened. "I don't know how." She reached into her purse, her movements deliberate. "Leland keeps it padlocked." The key she produced glinted in the sunlight. "This is the only way in."

"You'd better hold that thought," I cautioned.

With a resolute turn, the padlock clicked open.

Virginia slipped inside first. "What a mess."

I used the triangle of scrap wood to prop open the door, noting how it fit perfectly into the gap as if it had been made for that purpose.

This was bad.

I pulled it free and followed Virginia inside.

The door swung closed behind me with a hushed thud. The interior of the bar dimmed. Dust motes danced in the few shafts of light that managed to pierce through the stained-glass windows, casting a kaleidoscope of muted colors across the room. The air was thick with the scent of soot and rotting wood.

A pool table, its felt long since eaten away by time, stood sentinel in the center of the room, and a turn-of-the-century carved wood bar stretched along the right wall. Glasses hung from a rack above, coated in decades' worth of grime.

But it was the walls that caught my attention. Bullet holes scattered across the plaster like malignant constellations. Splintered chairs and the shattered remains of liquor bottles lay testament to the shoot-out that had brought down the bar and the Irish mob.

As my eyes adjusted, the evidence of fire damage became clear. Charred beams overhead bore the scars of flames, and the walls were streaked with soot. Remarkably, the building's integrity seemed untouched by the blaze that had tried to consume it.

Frankie hovered next to me. His body tensed, and his eyes narrowed a fraction.

"What?" I asked. "Is there trouble on the other side?" There was no way for me to tell without being tuned in, and I wanted him to stay safe. "Maybe you should wait in the car."

Frankie looked at me like I'd told him to strip naked. "I'd rather die."

"I'd rather you not," I told him. It was one thing to risk everything for Molly and quite another to be reckless. "What's going on?"

He surveyed the room with suspicion. "Nothing's going on.

That's the problem. A lot of guys bit it in here, and nobody stuck around?" He tipped the brim of his white Panama hat down over the bullet hole in the center of his forehead. "It's too quiet."

"Let's consider that a good thing." We could use the break.

"That's usually when the hammer drops," he gritted out.

He wasn't wrong.

Frankie couldn't afford to be shot. For one thing, it would put him out of commission at a critical point in our investigation. Worse, he didn't have the strength to endure an energy hit like that. One bullet could be the end of him. For real this time.

I swallowed hard. "If you run into anything bad, just say the word and I'll get you out of here." On the double. I'd hightail him and his urn back to my house faster than he could say *Bob's your uncle.*

He drifted away from me. "I told you I'm here for Molly, no matter what."

That was what I was afraid of.

Virginia's voice cut through the silence. "Look at this." She stood behind the bar and held up a bundle wrapped in a newer-looking leather case.

"What is it?" I asked, skirting past a table turned on its side and riddled with bullet holes.

"I'm not sure," she said, depositing it on the counter. "The back bar is a mess. All the bottles are empty. I found this tucked behind one of them."

She unfolded the case to reveal a set of tools delicate enough for surgery. They were various shapes and sizes, some slender and pointed, others curved like the back of a spoon.

"I've never seen anything like it," I said, picking up a flat one with a corkscrew tip and turning it over in my hand.

"Seriously?" Frankie's voice sounded behind me. "Have you learned nothing during our time together?"

I shot him a look. "I've learned that you can be helpful if you want to be. So if you know what these are, please tell us."

"They're advanced lock-picking tools. Professional grade," he said, as if that explained everything.

"Truly?" I said, turning back to the kit. "Your lock-picking set doesn't look anything like this." Frankie's prized tools were basically three hooks and a spoon-looking thing.

"Don't go picking on my kit," Frankie shot back. "Suds gave me that set as a gift."

Suds had also decorated his ugly urn.

Virginia's skepticism was palpable. "Why would someone leave a lock-picking set inside the building they'd need to pick the lock to get into?"

Frankie scoffed. "You don't need a set like these to get into a building. That'd be like Michelangelo painting a barn." He hovered his fingers over the lot of them. "These are the brushes he'd use in the Sistine Chapel."

I relayed Frankie's analogy to Virginia while Frankie petted the tools with reverence.

Virginia furrowed a brow. "Is he always this obtuse?"

I shrugged a shoulder. "Only when he thinks he's educating me."

"Stop with the insults. You're not getting rid of me," Frankie snapped. "I swear these are tools you'd use for more advanced crime."

"Behind the bar?" I said, gesturing to the space around us.

Frankie rolled his eyes so far back into his head I thought they might get stuck there. "You don't stash it where you use it. It's got to be meant for someplace else around here," Frankie said, his gaze sweeping the room.

"Where?" I asked. The place was a wreck.

"That's the question," Frankie murmured, thinking.

As I filled Virginia in, she grew more wary. "I don't like the idea of live people in here," she said, her voice hushed.

I agreed. "Let's find the boss's office, see who he might have hired to kill Kitty, and get out of here."

Frankie gave a stiff nod. "From what I've heard, Seamus O'Reilly kept his office down in the basement."

"There's a basement?" I asked, not at all delighted at the thought. Basements tended to be dark, full of spiders, and hard to escape—three of my least favorite things. I turned my attention to a door next to the bar. It was pocked with bullet holes. "Let's hope this is his office," I said, pulling the door open.

A narrow wooden staircase led down into the dark. It stank of dank wet brick and a century of dust.

Darn it.

"You want to stay here while I go down?" I asked him.

"Never," Frankie vowed.

"Of course not," Virginia shot back.

"I wasn't talking to you," I told her as she folded up the kit she'd found behind the bar. I'd been trying to keep my lug-headed gangster safe. "And you'd best leave that where you found it," I added as she slipped the lock-picking kit under her arm.

"I want to see if they fit anything," she said as if it were the obvious thing to do.

She was as bad as Frankie.

Her ruby lips twisted into a wry grin. "Aren't you curious?" she pressed.

Yes, but survival trumped curiosity. "We want to get in and out," I warned before any dead gangsters or live interlopers discovered us.

"I've got my flashlight," Virginia said, drawing a keychain light out of her purse. "It's stronger than it looks," she added when I stared a moment too long.

"It's not that," I said, my own flashlight—a hefty Maglite— now in hand. Her little light reminded me of my early days, of a younger, less prepared me.

But when had Virginia ever been innocent?

My beam revealed the first five steps and then...the dark unknown.

Frankie shrank down into an orb.

If anything, I figured he'd be leading the way.

"Since when are you afraid of basements?" I asked, stepping down as the wood stairs creaked under my weight.

"The Irish are onto me," he said, his voice hovering over my right shoulder as we ventured down into the dark. "I keep thinking of all the things I did to them, before and after I was dead."

"We don't know that they're down here," I reassured him, my flashlight cutting through the oppressive darkness, revealing more steep stairs.

"If they're not up top, they're down there," he warned, his words like ice.

My stomach sank. He was most likely right.

"Stick close," I ordered, my voice echoing slightly against the brick walls. Frankie was a part of this, no matter the risk, and there was no use telling him otherwise.

The staircase creaked in protest with every step we took.

At the bottom, the Maglite's beam revealed a narrow hallway, the walls bricked like the inside of a tomb. It was cooler here, the air still and heavy with a silence that seemed to press against my ears.

I swiveled my beam to the right and lit upon an old door, the wood swollen with years of moisture. "Look!" I hurried over the uneven dirt floor to get a closer look.

It would be a convenient place for the head of the mob to hole up.

With any luck, we could be in and out of Seamus's office in no time, with the answers we needed and with no harm to my friend.

I reached to open the door, my hand inches from the rusted metal handle, when an icy blast of wind slammed into me. I shrieked, the chill cutting through my clothes and sinking into my bones.

"Don't," Frankie hissed in my ear, so close I could feel the urgency of his breath. "The entire gang is in there."

"Oh wow." I let out an involuntary shiver. I withdrew my

hand slowly as if the air itself had turned to glass, fragile and sharp.

A *click* echoed in my ear as Frankie cocked his gun. "If they heard us, I'm done."

"What?" Virginia pressed.

I held up a hand. Frankie hovered off to my right. I stood stock-still and held my breath as if the sound of it might betray us.

"They're back there drinking and playing cards," he murmured after a second, his words whisper-thin.

I hadn't heard. I didn't want to hear. I sincerely wished now that I had been tuned in. That I could have avoided going anywhere near that door. Closing my eyes, I sent a silent plea into the darkness, hoping that the raucous laughter and clinking of glasses inside would be enough to cover the sound of one ghost's whispers and the racing of my heart.

We'd know soon enough.

Chapter Twenty

I stared at Frankie. Frankie stared at me. Both of us on the alert, wide-eyed, and waiting. If the dead Irish gangsters discovered us, we were done for.

Frankie clutched his revolver. I... Well, I had nothing except my flashlight. I didn't even have his power. I wouldn't know if the ghosts were on us until my buddy started shooting or until he dropped down dead.

This time for good if his energy didn't hold out.

The seconds ticked by. The attack never came.

I unclenched my muscles as much as I dared and realized I'd been holding my breath. We backed away slowly, hardly daring to make a sound.

Virginia stood a few feet down the corridor with her back to the wall. Her eyes flicked from the stairwell we'd come down to us. She raised her brows as if asking if we were okay.

I nodded, glad she had the presence of mind to realize we'd been in trouble with the dead, and to keep an eye on our one and only escape route just in case the living showed up.

A grin tickled my lips despite the gravity of the situation. I never thought I'd see the day that Virginia had our backs.

I touched her lightly on the shoulder. "We'll go this way," I whispered, my voice hardly registering even to me.

"They can hear us?" she mouthed.

In theory. I nodded to her. Ghosts didn't usually pay much attention to the living, but there was no telling how aggressive the Irish would be. And if they decided to try to scare me, or even see what I was up to, they'd for sure find Frankie.

We couldn't afford that. We needed to keep moving, find what we came for, and get out.

If Seamus O'Reilly's office was down here, we'd find it. We'd search it. And we'd learn once and for all if the hit had been out on Kitty and if it was one of his men who had run her down that night.

The pitch black of the basement was absolute, a void where the end of the hallway should have been. We moved through the dark, my hand trailing along the cold brick for guidance, the other clutching the flashlight like a lifeline.

The narrow hallway seemed to stretch into oblivion, each brick soaked in the dank, earthy smell of abandonment and decay. The air was thick, clinging to my lungs like a second skin.

Then my light landed on a second door.

It was less imposing than the first, almost nondescript, but for the old tarnished brass nameplate affixed to it. The etching was obscured by years of tarnish and grime. The wood of the door rotted at the edges and splintered near the bottom.

The knob turned slowly, the metal resisting. With a concerted effort, I pushed it open. It protested with stiff hinges and a prolonged creak that echoed down the hall.

"Quiet," Frankie hissed.

"I'm trying," I shot back under my breath, stepping forward into what appeared to be an old storage room. Dust rained down, glittering briefly in the beam of my flashlight before settling on my skin and clothes.

I felt the delicate tickle of cobwebs breaking across my face.

Ew, ew, ew. I brushed them away with quick, jerky fingers and tried my best not to imagine them tangled in my hair.

The room beyond was a time capsule, untouched by the decades. Gun racks lined the walls, each shelf hauntingly empty in the beam of my Maglite. Frankie stepped in behind me and let out a low, appreciative whistle.

"Ain't that beautiful," he murmured, his voice carrying a note of awe.

"What is it?" I whipped the beam of my light across the water-stained brick walls, over the barren racks under rusted-out wall hooks.

"Looks like tetanus waiting to happen," Virginia murmured, her voice a soft echo in the dark space.

Frankie's eyes scanned the room with the eagerness of a kid on Christmas morning. "Tommy guns. Too many to count, with those gorgeous round drums that hold a hundred shots easy. And ah..." He ran a hand along a shelf. "M1911 pistols." He selected one, and it materialized in his hand, a large, ugly gun with a heavy black barrel. "This baby's like having a few aces up your sleeve at a poker game. Always reliable."

"Put it down," I gasped. "The Irish might know you're touching their things."

Frankie slipped it into his coat pocket.

"Frankie!" I protested.

"Look at this"—he bebopped to the next rack and reached out to touch something I couldn't see—"a Winchester Model 1897. That's a trench gun, used in the Great War."

"You'd better not steal that too," I warned.

"I like pistols," he said as if that were the only reason to let it be. His attention shifted, and he lit up. "But I will take this." He snatched something off a low shelf.

In his hand appeared a crude but no doubt deadly Molotov cocktail. The glass bottle's vintage label was peeling at the edges, the cloth wick frayed but functional. It smelled like gasoline and moonshine had a baby and would no doubt go up like a Roman candle if Frankie so much as lit a cigarette near it.

He had to stop getting distracted. "That's dangerous," I warned.

"I know," he said with glee, stuffing it into his coat pocket, leaving a large lump.

"Are we investigating this room, or are you just stealing things?" I demanded.

He reminded me of a hamster storing carrots in its cheeks.

"A little of both?" he ventured.

"Frankie!" I scolded as loud as I dared. We had things to do, and him loading up on weapons was only going to encourage him to want to use them.

"Hey." He pointed at me. "We're in the Irish headquarters. I'm outnumbered and outgunned. I need a little extra firepower. At least I'm not taking a Chicago Typewriter."

"Chicago Typewriter?" I echoed, unfamiliar with the term.

I had a feeling I didn't want to know.

"Yeah." Frankie notched his chin up. "You know, the Thompson submachine guns. They make that distinctive *rat-a-tat-tat* sound."

"How can you resist?" I asked dryly.

But the gangster had gone grim as he looked over the stash only he could see. "It's like they were preparing for a war."

"Let's go," I urged. We'd seen enough.

"Yeah," Frankie said, grabbing one last Molotov cocktail for the road.

"Seamus's gang was preparing for something big," I said as the door closed behind us with a decisive thud. "There's a huge arsenal down here."

"We'll figure it out," Virginia assured me from the hall.

She'd had our backs. Again.

She'd also stolen my line.

"We will figure this out," I agreed. We had no choice.

I shone my light farther down the darkened hallway.

We moved on, deeper into the bowels of the bar's basement, the earthen floor uneven under our feet, the beam of my flashlight bouncing off the walls until we came upon a staircase. It was wider than the one we'd used to come down from the bar, and the steps were concrete instead of wood.

I exchanged a glance with Virginia.

"I don't think that's the way to the boss's office," she said. "Let's keep going."

"I want to see what we're dealing with down here." There was staying on task, and there was staying *too much* on task. "Let's check it out."

"Absolutely not," Virginia insisted. "Focus. I don't want to be down here if that live person comes back looking for this," she hissed, waving the lock-picking kit at me.

I took to the stairs. "You're the one who stole it."

She gasped as she hurried up the stairs after me.

Well, it was true. My hand skimmed the cold, damp railing, the metal flaking away beneath my touch. "I'd like to point out I'm the only one who hasn't swiped anything here at the Irish bar." It wasn't much of a win, but I'd take it.

"I—" she began, but she had nothing. Which had to be a first for Virginia.

At the top, the stairway ended at a formidable steel door. I tried to open it, but it wouldn't budge. Locked.

"Dead end," Virginia said behind me.

"Not quite." My light caught hold of a sliding peephole.

It resisted as I tried to slide it open. Like it had been wedged shut by time and rust. I braced a foot on the wall and yanked with all my strength. The gangster peephole protested with a screech of metal against metal. But with one last forceful tug, I managed to get it mostly open.

I looked out at a double-lane covered drive at the rear of the bar. A tall brick wall shielded it from outside view, and the roof of the bar stretched out to cover it. In the few feet left exposed, I could see the highway beyond.

"This door is perfectly placed," I realized. "The Irish could move their smuggled goods out of storage, load the trucks without being seen, and have a straight shot out to the highway."

"For the first time, I'm jealous of the Irish," Frankie murmured.

"This isn't what we came to see," Virginia pointed out.

True. It seemed Virginia had a gift for lasering in on a goal.

"You're right." I forced the peephole shut. "Let's find the office."

We made it back to the hallway and hadn't gone far when we stumbled upon a door that seemed to be hanging onto its frame by sheer willpower. The wood was old, the varnish long since worn away to a dull, lifeless finish. A rusted iron handle lay drunkenly, threatening to snap off in my hand if I so much as turned it.

Virginia glanced at me. "This could be it."

"It would make sense for the boss to be right here, overseeing shipments." I gave the door a gentle push, and it creaked open.

But that was where our luck ended. Instead of the heart of the operation, we were greeted by the ghosts of a whiskey cellar past. The room was barren save for the remnants of its former life, a few broken bottles with labels faded beyond reading and empty crates left to rot.

The back wall was a patchwork of old shiplap wood, damp and moldering. I was about to swing the door shut when Virginia caught it.

"Wait. What's that?"

"You see something?" I followed her gaze, but all I saw was more of the same—wood, shadows, and emptiness. "I don't see anything." At least this room was easy to pass up.

I glanced at Frankie.

"No, boss. No booze. We're moving on," the gangster concluded.

"Sounds about right to me," I said.

But Virginia was undeterred, her eyes narrowing. "The woodwork doesn't line up at all."

"If she's looking to the Irish for decorating tips, she's going to be sorely disappointed," Frankie snarked.

"It's an old cellar," I said to her, taking the diplomatic route. "Nothing's going to line up perfectly."

The office was our prize, not some carpenter's mistake.

"I care," Virginia insisted, stepping into the room. "It's wrong. Nobody would lay boards like that unless..." She put her hands on the wall. "Give me some light."

"Give me a break," Frankie said.

I gave her the light, watching her trace the lines of mismatched wood. She pressed here, tapped there, and then, with a suddenness that made me jump, she stepped back as a section of the wall swung outward.

"Oh, my word," I managed.

"I knew it," she gushed.

I shone my light inside to reveal a bank vault, the metal door gleaming dully. "Wow," I breathed out, impressed despite myself.

Ellis's mom broke into a genuine smile like I'd never seen on her before. "This is fun." She smoothed a single errant lock of hair back into place. "I could get used to ghost hunting."

"More like ghost avoiding," I reminded her. At least today. "Does the vault open?"

She tugged at the door. I did as well, but it was locked tight.

"Look," I said, locating two separate keyholes. "This door needs two keys."

"Or one lock-picking kit," Virginia said, holding up the one she'd pilfered.

She was worse than Frankie. "You can't pick this safe."

Frankie leaned in, giving the lock a once-over with a connoisseur's eye. "I'm not even sure I could pick this safe. Oh, who am I kidding? I'm great at this."

I turned to Frankie. "There's an easier way to see what's in the vault." My gangster could walk through the door.

He sighed, the theatrics of a man resigned to his fate. "Fine. Only because we're desperate."

With that, he stepped straight through the vault's door.

While he was in there, I explained to Virginia where he was. Good thing I was quick about it because Frankie emerged seconds later, his eyes as wide as saucers. "It's bourbon! So much bourbon." He tossed up his arms. "The best stuff. Cases and cases of Pappy Van Winkle!"

His weakness. My stomach knotted. We'd had trouble with Frankie getting distracted by alcohol before. It hadn't been too long ago that he'd been caught like a trout by a bottle of Old Rip Van Winkle on a string, so his affinity for the modern brand was understandable.

If by *modern*, you meant starting in 1935.

"Focus," I instructed.

"It's made with wheat instead of rye, so it's smoother," Frankie went on.

"Is the whiskey in your world or mine?" I asked.

"Both," he said, still excited. "And it tastes even better when you steal it."

I stepped closer to him, my voice firm. "Don't touch them. It could be another trap."

"Or it could be delicious," the gangster countered.

"Come on." This time, I made sure Frankie was ahead of me as we stepped back out into the hall. We couldn't afford to get sidetracked, not when we were so close.

The beam of my Maglite cut through the darkness, sending shadows scuttling into the corners like wary rats.

"So the Irish were dealing in premium bourbon when they were brought down," Virginia mused, her voice echoing faintly down the hall.

"My bet is the police never found the vault," I said as we moved down the hallway side by side, with Frankie in the lead. Virginia's shadow, elongated and distorted on the walls, danced with each flicker of my light. While Frankie had no shadow at all.

"McAvoy was interested in taking down the mob, destroying

their operation," she murmured. "At least that's how I remember hearing it. He wouldn't have cared what was in storage."

"Maybe," I said, my eyes catching a spider scurrying up the wall. "Or maybe the police found the cheaper stuff in the front room and took that as evidence." I'd have to ask Steve and see if he knew.

There was one thing that puzzled me. "When Patrick escaped, he told Kitty he had the money for them to start a new life. He couldn't have stolen any Pappy Van Winkle to do that."

"His father would have noticed," Virginia agreed, sneezing slightly. The air in this part of the tunnel had grown mustier.

"It would also be hard to move it in the quantity it would take to buy a new start," I said.

"Then where'd he get the money?" Virginia's question hung in the air.

"It wasn't down here," Frankie said as we came upon a door at the dead end of the hallway. "Unless we're about to find it."

I nudged the door open with a cautious push and was rewarded with a plume of dust coming off the doorframe.

Coughing, I drew back. "This place hasn't been touched in a long time."

Virginia edged past. "Let me see—" She let out a high-pitched squeal. "Ew! Cobweb."

I shone my light past her, and the thrill of discovery ran through me. "This is it!" Seamus O'Reilly's office.

Or at least it sure looked like it.

The desk faced the door, a sentinel of dark wood standing guard. Behind it, the wall was adorned with black-and-white photos, each marred with a stark red X. Names scribbled at the bottom of each photo told the tale of all those who'd been killed in Seamus's name.

Frankie was already at the wall, scanning the photos. I joined him as his eyes locked onto one at the bottom. The photo was curled at the edges and caked in decades' worth of dust. I brushed it off, and what I saw sent a jolt through my heart.

A pretty blonde smiled coyly, her innocence clashing with the violence of the red slash across her face. It was Kitty Cunningham.

Beneath her photo, scrawled with a chilling finality, was the name *Patrick*.

"He didn't." My breath hitched, and a cold shiver ran down my spine.

"Patrick loved Kitty," Frankie protested with a rare lack of guile. "He wouldn't kill her. He was supposed to marry her."

He slammed his mouth shut as if he couldn't believe he'd said that. Fair enough, because I couldn't believe what I'd seen.

Could it really be true?

This would break her heart.

Then Frankie's eyes widened, and he cursed under his breath.

"What?" I demanded. Was there a piece of the puzzle we'd missed?

Frankie hesitated, and his demeanor shifted like he was bracing for a blow.

"Have out with it," I urged. "We need to figure this out."

My gangster winced, and I felt his energy flow over me. *Oh, no, no, no.* "That's not what I meant, and you know it."

The photos began to glow with a ghostly gray. But they appeared the same on the other side as they had in the realm of the living, and I honestly had no idea why Frankie needed me to see it. "What's going on?" He'd better have thought this through.

He gave a tip of the hat and a shrug of apology, then shot up through the ceiling and out of sight.

What was he doing? Abandoning ship?

"Frankie!" I hollered after him.

The next instant, a cold blast of air struck my back.

I whirled around, flashlight in hand. But I didn't need it.

I didn't need any light at all.

There in the doorway, glowing ghostly gray, stood a stone-faced gangster. His eyes were sharp, the color of steel left out in the rain, and they fixed on me with an intensity that terrified me to the bone.

"Seamus." The name escaped my lips before I could catch it. And I prayed I was wrong.

His hair was slicked back, the gray at his temples giving him a distinguished and intimidating air. The cut of his suit was vintage, broad at the shoulders and pinched at the waist—a silhouette that commanded respect in an era when respect was harder to earn than money.

"Seamus O'Reilly," I managed to greet him, the words catching in my throat.

His left eye twitched, wrinkling the scar underneath. "You can see me." His voice was the rasp of a blade being drawn from its sheath.

Whoops.

Chapter Twenty-One

Seamus O'Reilly's stare bored into me, and I felt the temperature drop a few degrees.

"I've heard about you," he said, his voice low and laced with a threat that made the hairs on the back of my neck stand up.

I forced a smile, clutching my flashlight like a lifeline. "All good, I hope."

His form seemed to solidify with his suspicion, the air growing colder still. "Your associate blew up my car."

I swallowed hard and ignored the goosebumps racing up my arms. "Ah, yes." That. The memory of the explosion played in my mind, hot and violent. "You and I both know there's no controlling Frankie the German." And to my dismay, there was a tremble in my voice that I couldn't quite mask.

His left eye twitched, the scar beneath it pulling taut. "I hate that guy."

"He gets that a lot," I said, trying to steady my voice as I met his gaze.

The mob boss eyed me hard. "You think because you're alive you can waltz into my office? I've buried guys for less."

I fought the urge to shrink away. "I'm trying to piece together what happened on the night the police raided this place," I said, my voice gaining a little strength as I clung to my purpose. "I'm here looking for information that only you have."

Seamus O'Reilly stared at me, and for a moment, the only sounds in the room were the ragged breaths I was trying to steady.

The gangster harrumphed, unimpressed. He turned on his heel and sauntered over to a personal bar along the right wall—a heavy, dark wood affair that exuded an aura of power and wealth. Bottles of expensive liquor lined the polished shelves, their labels reflecting the golden age of the Rat Pack and the birth of Las Vegas, a time when the art of a good drink was akin to a religion. With deliberate movements, he poured a deep amber liquid into a cut-crystal glass.

"Who's the hot dame?" he asked, shooting a glance over his shoulder, his gaze slipping past me to the hallway where Virginia stood vigil.

"She's a friend of mine," I ventured, not quite sure what he was getting at or if what I'd said was even true. "She has my back."

"Classy," Seamus remarked, his eyes lingering on Virginia in a way that made me glad she couldn't see him. She stood outside in the hall, reflected in the ghostly glow of the room. Her jaw was set firm and her stance wide, her flashlight trained on me as if it could tether me in place and keep me safe.

The gangster smirked, and in one swift second, his office door slammed shut on a startled Virginia. The force of it rattled the room, and my stomach tightened as the lock clicked shut.

"She can't save you," Seamus said. "Nobody can." He lifted his drink in a mock toast. "If you were smart, you'd know that."

I did. I watched him take a sip of his drink, noting the way he savored it. It had been a risk coming down here, even without Frankie's powers. But now that my housemate had opened me up to the other side and promptly fled, I was at the mercy of the mob boss. And my own wits.

"I think if you wanted to hurt me, you'd have done it by now," I ventured.

His stare was unyielding, searching for a crack in my facade. I let him look, lifting my chin ever so slightly.

Inside, I was taut as a wire. But showing weakness to a man like Seamus O'Reilly was akin to signing my own death warrant.

He strolled toward me like a predator stalking prey. "You're with the South Town Boys."

"Hardly." I made a show of glancing to my left and right. "Do you see any of them?" I planted a fist on my hip. "Frankie the German ditched me. Ice Pick Charlie gives me the creeps. And Crazy Louie... Well, he's had it out for me since I accidentally knocked the head off his real-life body down in a fairly gruesome speakeasy." After a massacre that had been long forgotten by the living, but not the dead.

Seamus's lips curled into a semblance of a smile, a predator amused by the antics of its prey. "I heard you punted it like a football. Good job."

More like knocked it with my elbow. "I barely escaped with my life."

He shrugged as if saying *tomayto, tomahto*. "And now you come to me, needing *information*," he mused, parroting the way I'd said the word as he casually sat on the edge of his desk. "It's funny because I don't need anything from you."

"This is important," I insisted. He wouldn't want to hear about Kitty or Molly or any noble pursuit to save them, but he might care about something closer to home. "People need to know the truth."

"What people? I don't care about people," he mused, swirling the liquor in his glass.

Oh, come on. The man had to have an ego. He was the head of the Irish mob, for goodness' sake.

Plus, he hadn't tried to kill me yet. I must have something he wanted.

"Posterity," I said, taking a casual step toward him. "You're still a legend around town."

He took a sip of his drink. "You flatter me," he remarked

dryly, the glass making a soft clink as he set it back down on the desk.

"Maybe. But it's also the truth." I glanced at the photos on display behind his desk—the hits he'd ordered. "Did your son, Patrick, really kill Kitty Cunningham?" I ventured another step. "Did he run her down in cold blood?" I pressed, watching for the telltale hardening of his stare, the clench of his jaw, any sign that I'd struck home.

Seamus's eyes glinted with a sinister amusement. "Yes, Patrick handled her," he said, his voice casual as he drew a cigar out of his coat pocket with the ease of a man who ritualized every motion.

"You're sure of it?" I pressed. This was important.

He looked at me as if I'd just asked him if the sky was blue. With the unlit cigar in hand, he gestured dismissively. "He's my son. My number two." When that didn't ring a bell with me, he leaned forward slightly. "Patrick is the one I trust the most," he declared with pride. But it didn't last. His expression darkened. "Too late, though." He bit the end of the cigar and spit it onto the floor. "She'd already ratted us out to McAvoy. Told him we were moving a big score."

"Which was..." I trailed off, giving him room to chat.

Seamus struck a match against the desk, the flare briefly illuminating his hardened features. "Nice try," he said through the glow, the corner of his mouth tilting up as he lit the cigar.

Oh, come on. "What does it matter now?"

He took a deliberate puff of the cigar, the smoke curling into the air between us. "Okay, I'll tell you." He pulled the cigar from his mouth, holding it aloft like a professor ready to deliver a lecture. "You ready?"

"Always," I vowed.

The corner of his mouth ticked up. "It was puppy dogs."

Har-de-har. "So you're not going to tell me." I crossed my arms.

Seamus couldn't help but grin, the smoke playing around his teeth. He was clearly amused with himself, enjoying this game of cat and mouse. But then, as he caught the sheer determination on my face, he removed the cigar from his mouth, his humor fading. "I will tell you that somebody wanted our puppy dogs and not us." His voice carried a sharp edge. "All that talk of the Sugarland PD taking down the Irish was bullshit." He slammed the cigar hand down on the edge of the desk, his anger flaring. "Somebody on the force wanted our score. And Kitty led them right to it." The cigar rolled slightly, leaving a smoldering trail on the polished wood.

"But nothing is missing in the vault," I countered, realizing my mistake the second I said it.

The way Seamus glared at me, I felt like a bug under glass. "How can you possibly know that?" he demanded.

I'd rather not say. "Why do you think somebody wanted the score and not you?" I countered.

Seamus shoved himself off the desk. "Because they didn't arrest anybody." He pointed the cigar at me. "They gunned us all down. They left no witnesses. It wasn't all of 'em, or the word would have gotten out. But it was at least one of 'em. Probably more."

If that was true, there was a lot more going on than we realized. "Who was it? Who were the dirty cops?" It seemed McAvoy had missed a few.

Seamus shoved the cigar back into his mouth and began to pace. "We don't know."

Didn't know, or wouldn't tell? "Your guys had to see who shot them."

"They set the fire first," he gritted out. "The smoke camouflaged the killer cops until it was too late."

Wow. "Okay, well, how do you know for sure that it was Kitty who betrayed you?"

Seamus whipped around to face me, his eyes alight with a cold fury. "Because my men are loyal. Even in death. My son is loyal." He spread his hands wide as if to encompass the entirety of his unwavering empire. "That leaves his dippy girlfriend."

"Fiancée," I corrected, a slight edge to my voice. I wasn't going to let him diminish her, even in name.

"Hardly," he spat the word out like it left a sour taste.

I had no doubt many of his men had remained true to him. They'd stuck with him to this day. We'd narrowly avoided them earlier. But he had Kitty all wrong. And what about his son? "I haven't seen Patrick here today," I bluffed as if I'd seen the rest of them.

Seamus stiffened as if the name itself was a barb. "We have our differences. He'll come around."

Maybe so, maybe not. "I saw him kissing Kitty after the drag race."

Seamus's face twisted into a mask of rage so quickly it was frightening. "I ordered him to end it, and he did!" His fists clenched at his sides, the veins in his neck standing out like cords.

"Didn't look like it," I said, knowing I was poking the tiger. But I couldn't stop now. "I saw serious lip-locking."

His jaw worked, muscles bulging as he dug in. "That was the last time he defied me. He only did it to get her alone so he could kill her." He twisted his hands as if imagining them wrapped around her neck.

"Or did *you* kill her?" I shot back.

The ghost of a smile crossed his lips. "I wish." The admission settled him down, the storm passing as quickly as it had come. He cleared his throat. "Look. I'm being honest with you, kid. There was no score that day. It was all a setup."

"Right." It seemed as far-fetched as his puppy story.

"Fine. Don't believe me." He reached back to the desk for his glass. "But we both know the police never found anything," Seamus said, turning back to me. "There was nothing here."

It was true that the police had reported no big score. Still, somebody was lying. "If there's nothing to guard, why are you still here?"

The gangster shrugged. "It's my place."

A real-life knock at the door made me jump. "Verity."

Virginia's fear-laced voice seeped through the wood. "There's someone upstairs."

My stomach hollowed. Was it real, or was it ghostly?

"It'd better not be the Germans." Seamus chewed on his cigar and added under his breath, "bunch of schnitzelheads who couldn't fix a game of solitaire."

Virginia might not be able to hear Frankie up there, but a dozen gangsters throttling him might cause a bump or two in the mortal realm. "You might need to call off your men."

Seamus shook his head, a sneer twisting his lips. "I don't need to do anything for you, and that's not any of my guys up there."

I heard it too then—the hollow footsteps of a live person walking upstairs. The floorboards creaked above our heads. There was no good reason for anybody else to be here. Or prop the door outside. Or stash a lock-picking kit. If they realized we were down here, if they trapped us, we'd be in real trouble.

"I need to go," I said, backing toward the door.

Seamus tilted his head, unbothered by the fact that a live person could attack me in the basement and no living person would hear me scream. Save for Virginia, who was out in the hall alone.

"Do me a favor and stay gone." He ashed his cigar, the tip falling and fading to nothing. "I might not be so nice next time."

"Sure thing," I said, although I couldn't make any promises. I fumbled with the lock, half expecting it not to yield. But the door opened, and I slipped out into the hall, closing the door on Seamus and his threats.

Virginia had killed her light, plunging the hall into darkness save for the gray glow of the ghostly brick on either side. I could make out her silhouette crouched in the shadows, yet she couldn't see me. She jumped when I touched her on the shoulder.

"Don't worry. It's me," I whispered, my voice as soft as a shadow passing.

She closed her hand over mine. "There's at least one live person up there. It could be the owner of the lock-picking set or

one of the vagrants Ellis told me about. Or worse, someone trying
to kill you."

I gasped. "Why would you say that?"

She straightened, leading the way through the dark. "Because
someone's always trying to kill you."

I couldn't argue with her on that.

We hurried down the hallway, careful not to make a sound.
We passed the liquor cellar and the stairwell. We were almost upon
the ghostly armory when a door behind us slammed.

"Go faster," I urged Virginia before venturing a glance over
my shoulder.

Seamus stood outside his office, a Tommy gun in his grasp
with its ugly round drum and the butt of it balanced against
his hip.

He was on us in a second.

"I like to use trespassers for target practice," Seamus said, the
corners of his mouth tilting up in a cruel smirk.

Is he talking about me?

His chin ticked up toward the floor above, and he smiled.

Okay, them. I whooshed out a breath.

Of course, that was still bad because I needed to get outside,
and if Seamus and his gang started shooting up there, I could get
hit in the crossfire.

Or shot on sight since I was also here without the gangster's
say-so.

"Hold off," I hissed. "Please," I added, remembering my
manners. "Only until my friend and I get out of here." Then he
could shoot whomever he wanted.

His laugh was predatory, a sound that made my skin crawl.
"My place. My shooting gallery. And I don't take orders from
you."

With that, he zipped straight up through the ceiling.

Oh no. I could only pray he didn't encounter Frankie—who
should have warned us about the intruder. I sincerely hoped my
gangster was okay.

Virginia and I exchanged a glance, the unspoken agreement that she'd follow my lead in this. That I knew more. And I did.

We could hide and hope the intruders didn't come downstairs. Or we could realize that anyone with a lock-picking set was most likely coming down those stairs sooner rather than later. If we stayed and hid, we'd not only risk discovery, but we could still get caught in the crossfire when the Irish decided to defend their vault.

We needed to get out fast. To sneak upstairs. To make it out that door.

I grabbed her hand and led her down the hallway as quickly as I dared. "Stairs," I whispered when we made the turn and ventured up-up-up.

Virginia squeezed my hand. I could feel the drum of my heart, and every stair creak sounded like gunfire to my ears.

We could make it.

We *would* make it.

We'd almost reached the door to the main bar when Frankie's head materialized through the brick, startling me so hard that I missed a step and stumbled. His hair was mussed and his cheeks ruddy. "There's a live guy, armed, at three o'clock," he warned.

"What o'clock?" I whispered. "Where?" I had no frame of reference with his head protruding from the wall.

I could hear the muffled shouts of Seamus. He was in the hall below, rallying the mob, which wouldn't end well. The cadence of his orders sharpened the air. A fight was brewing, and the last thing we needed was to be anywhere near it.

But Virginia kept us on track. She eased open the door to the main bar and crept around it, dragging me behind her.

The shadows stretched long and thin in the late afternoon light, casting diamond patterns on the floor. Virginia's grip on my arm was like a vise as she pointed toward the bar. Someone was cursing behind it, bottles clinking and rattling in their wake. The door to the outside stood propped open, exactly as I'd warned it might be.

The sliver of freedom beckoned us.

We were so close.

We exchanged a glance.

"Now," Virginia mouthed.

She dashed ahead, the stolen lock-picking kit clutched under her arm like a football. I was on her tail, my breath sharp in my throat.

She made it out first, and I wanted to cheer. I was almost there when a hand clamped down on my arm, and a live person's grip, firm and unyielding, yanked me backward.

Chapter Twenty-Two

I turned and saw—"Maisie!" Her knuckles were white as she locked her grip around the barrel of her shotgun.

"Verity!" Her voice hitched. "You're lucky I didn't shoot you."

Wouldn't that be awful? To escape the mob only to get plugged by my old friend.

"Come with us." I hurried her away from the bar. Our secret exit was no longer secret, and we had to get out of there.

"Why?" she demanded, but her feet were already moving, her work boots crunching the gravel of the weedy parking lot. The land yacht lay dead ahead.

"I'll explain later," I promised.

Virginia flung the back-seat door open, and we ushered Maisie in, slamming the door.

"What are you two doing together?" Maisie balked.

My eyes darted back to the bar as I clambered into the driver's seat, Virginia sliding into the passenger side next to me.

"Escaping," Virginia said.

I turned the key and made a hard reverse that tossed Maisie against the back seat before Virginia had her door all the way closed.

"There's an armed man inside," I said, meeting Maisie's startled expression in the rearview mirror.

"Well then, drop me back off," she ordered, struggling to shove herself off the back seat and reach the door handle.

"Not a chance." I hit the gas, and the land yacht leaped forward, pinning Maisie to her seat as we made our escape. "You said it yourself. It's dangerous."

My ancient Cadillac kicked up a cloud of loose gravel as we peeled out of the parking lot, bouncing like a bingo ball over the broken asphalt.

Maisie picked herself up and stared out the back window at the rapidly fading bar front. "They probably saw you. Don't you want to go back and see them?"

"Not today," I said, speeding past the drive-in. And not if they were armed like Maisie was.

"I feel like I'm in la-la land," Maisie protested. "And suddenly *Virginia* cares about this property? The Wydells are the ones letting it rot!"

"It's ours," she snapped. "We can do what we want."

"We're not discussing this now," I said. Even if Maisie had a point, we weren't going to solve the issue in the car.

"It should be mine," Maisie countered. "All of it. If you hadn't swindled me out of my inheritance."

On a previous adventure, I'd learned the truth behind Maisie's birth, and the fact that she should have inherited a portion of the estate that had gone to Leland Wydell. Her efforts to gain it back had so far come to naught.

"You can't prove that," Virginia stated as if that made it fact. As if that made it right.

"We'll figure it out," I promised.

Maisie huffed down into her seat.

"There." Virginia's finger stabbed toward a break in the road. "Take that to double back and get on the highway."

The faster, the better.

Virginia's face was a mask of calm, but her hands betrayed her as they clutched the dashboard. "Three people have been found dead in that bar in the last ten years," she said, her eyes never leaving the road ahead.

"I know," Maisie said. She planted her elbows on the bench seat between me and Virginia. "I found two of them."

"While trespassing," Virginia snapped.

"In the bar?" I asked Maisie.

"One of 'em behind the bar on the main floor," Maisie confirmed, "another down in the basement hallway."

My heart skipped a beat. "Please don't tell me they were murdered."

"I can't tell you anything," Maisie insisted. "They were just dead."

I gripped the wheel tighter. "Well, what did the police say?" I pressed, steering us onto the main road to the highway.

"They had no reason to suspect anything," Virginia said. "They've been battling the criminal element out there for years. The trouble spills out from the interstate, and the abandoned bar is an easy pit stop."

"Why have I never heard of this?" I asked, not even sure where we were headed.

Away seemed to be the best option.

Virginia twisted the ring on her finger, an emerald band where the diamond wedding set used to be. "Leland kept it out of the papers."

"And I didn't want any looky-loos coming out and getting hurt," Maisie chimed in.

I still didn't get it. "Why? What's going on in that bar?"

I almost wished I'd stuck around to find out, but my sense of self-preservation had been too strong.

"I've been trying to figure that out for years," Maisie said. "It'll sit empty for months, and just when I start to think there's nothing to it, I find my tape disturbed."

Virginia scrunched her brows together and ventured a glance at Maisie. "Tape?"

"I tape the doors," Maisie stated plainly, as though it were the most natural thing in the world. "Front and back. If the tape is broken, I know somebody's been in there."

"Have both doors been opened?" I asked. I didn't see any upstanding reason for anyone to be unloading from the back. Or to be going in the front for that matter.

"The front door is opened at least every month. The back, once, twice a year. Every year," she confirmed. "Sometimes more often than that."

"So it gets visitors," I said, exiting at the Stop 'n Go. "Three of them dead in the last decade." I wondered if they'd had anything to do with the person who'd hidden the lock-picking kit. Or the intruder we'd dodged on the way out. They could be one and the same. After all, the person had been rooting around behind the bar.

The car hummed beneath us as we took a side road past the Stop 'n Go, doubling back to Maisie's house.

Unfortunately, I'd forgotten the road was more pothole than pavement, but we made it soon enough. I turned at a weathered mailbox, its post leaning like a tired sentinel. I slowed down the narrow dirt drive, the woods crowding around it like curious onlookers.

Maisie lived in a simple cabin surrounded by stubby fall grass and mounds of colorful leaves. I brought the car to a gentle stop and leaned back to catch her eye as I said, "Promise me you won't go back to that bar tonight. Ellis is sleeping, and I don't want to wake him and come after you."

Maisie nodded and slid off the bench seat, her hand pausing on the door handle. "I promise," she said grudgingly. "The bunnies need to be fed, and the woodchuck I rescued last week is due for his medicine." She perked up. "Want to see him? His name is Ellis, too."

Of course it was. She looked at my boyfriend like a son.

"Later," I promised, watching her step out of the car and head for the cabin, the shotgun slung over her shoulder.

I waited until she'd reached the door and let herself in before firing up the engine. I had to get Virginia home, and then Frankie and I had to figure out our next move.

Frankie, I realized, retreating down the drive. I hadn't seen him since our escape.

"Hey, Frank," I prodded, steering with one hand and reaching for the hemp bag on the seat next to me with the other. I gave his urn a rattle. "Are you with us?"

A groan echoed throughout the car. "For the five-hundredth time," he grated out, "I'm not *inside* the urn, and don't call me Frank!"

"Somebody's in a bad mood," I said to Virginia.

"Didn't he run off and leave you alone with the head of the Irish mob?" she tsked.

"He did," I confirmed, pulling back onto the road. "I hope you were doing something productive with your time."

"Count on it." Frankie materialized in the space between the seats that Maisie had vacated, a smug look on his face. Never mind that he was missing an ear. "I learned there's a big horse race in Jackson tonight. Seamus always goes to those." When I wasn't impressed, he added, "I also watered down all the booze at the bar. The Irish will have a conniption!"

That would show them.

I sincerely hoped my housemate had used his dwindling energy resources to do some investigating as well. "Did you get a good look at the real live person rattling around back there?" I asked, hoping for a clue as to who had owned Virginia's stolen lock-picking kit.

The police would be interested as well.

Frankie's blank expression said it all.

He waved off my question. "Hey, I warned you on your way up the stairs."

He'd also left me to fend for myself against their leader. Although, I supposed I couldn't fault him for that, or for lending me his power without asking. Given the weak state my housemate was in, he couldn't have afforded a showdown with Seamus or any of them. And he had enabled me to talk with O'Reilly.

I kept my peace as I steered us into town, toward the tidy bungalows of Magnolia Street. We passed Kitty's old house, its windows dark. Then Steve's. And as we approached Ellis's place, I saw his front door open.

Ellis, dressed in jeans and a button-down, descended the steps. He wore sunglasses and had a duffel bag slung over his shoulder. His stride was purposeful as he headed toward the black Jeep parked in the driveway.

"Where does he think he's going?" Virginia asked as I pulled up to the curb.

Ellis tossed the bag into the back of the Jeep and looked up. We locked eyes for a moment, brief and charged.

"Verity!" he said, surprised yet happy as I swung the car door open. "Mom," he added, more than a little shocked when Virginia emerged as well. "You're...together." He took off his sunglasses, holding them loosely in one hand as he looked from me to Virginia, trying to piece together the unexpected picture. "What's wrong?"

"Frankie is in a bad state," I said, slamming my door closed. "We needed to check out the Irish bar as soon as we could."

"And I kept an eye on her," Virginia added, striding across the lawn toward the house, her movements purposeful yet discreet as she clutched the lock-picking set just out of Ellis's line of sight.

Ellis's attention flicked from me to his mother, a frown creasing his brow. "She's up to something," he said, joining me at the curb. "I've never seen my mom cut straight across a lawn."

"You look like you're up to something, too," I said, tugging at the bag over his shoulder. "Are you skipping town on me?"

His shoulders tensed, and he glanced down at the bag. "Actually, yes," he admitted, his voice lowering a note. "I dropped in on Steve McAvoy this morning shortly after you did."

"About his dad's stolen police cruiser," I offered.

He leaned against the land yacht, arms folded. "I am the lead detective on the case," he said with a twinge of irony.

Sure, but I was always glad to lend a hand.

I planted my butt next to him as he continued, "Steve made a few calls after your visit, and he was able to point me to a witness in town who placed Seamus O'Reilly in the driver's seat on the night Kitty died."

I sucked in a breath. "Who's your source?"

Ellis pushed himself off my car. "I'm not at liberty to say. At least not yet. Come on." He began walking me to his Jeep. "Now get this. The Irish mob reestablished itself in Vegas around the same time, under a boss named O'Reilly."

Amazing. "So O'Reilly didn't go down with his guys." He went out and got new guys.

Or Patrick started up out there.

Ellis opened the back of the Jeep, the hatch rising with a soft hydraulic hiss. "It's a common name, and I'm not making any assumptions," he cautioned, tossing his bag in.

"But you're flying out to Vegas." That much was clear.

He closed the hatch and turned to me. "I'm not officially telling you."

"Of course not." This could be huge.

He drew his keys out of his pocket, the jingle of metal on metal punctuating his concern. "I'm on the red-eye tonight to question a witness out there. The reestablished mob might still be operating, and if they are, they might still be using the old bar. I don't know why or what could be there."

"I do." I shared our discovery of the hidden vault full of vintage Pappy Van Winkle bourbon.

His eyes flickered with interest as he considered the implications. "Rare, aged bourbon goes for a lot of money. But if it's still there, then nobody has taken it yet."

I leaned against the Jeep, feeling the cold metal through my white jeans. "Your mom also found a lock-picking set hidden behind the bar," I told him.

"So why is she hiding it from me?" he wondered.

"Maybe she feels like a rebel." For once. "And then there's Maisie. She's been taping the bar doors for years to see when people are going in and out."

Ellis raised a brow. "How many people went without me?" he asked, only half-joking.

"You snooze, you lose," I joked. I'd tell him later how we ran into Maisie. "There's evidence that people have been coming and going regularly. In fact, a man came in while we were down in the basement. We had to sneak out past him."

And not very successfully.

"That's why I didn't want you out there alone," Ellis said, his concern no longer veiled.

"I wasn't alone," I reminded him.

"Did you get a look at him?" Ellis asked, the detective in him taking over, his keys now forgotten in his hand.

"I didn't," I admitted, wishing Frankie had.

But no, he'd used his limited energy to mess with the Irish. I supposed in his mind, it was a noble cause.

My poor ghost hadn't even gotten out of the car at Ellis's house. He was running on fumes.

I looked to Ellis. "I just heard about the bodies found in there over the years."

His expression darkened. "They weren't my cases, but yes, three that we know of."

I wrapped my arms around myself, the late afternoon chill seeping into my bones. "Why did I not hear about this before? I mean, this is Sugarland." A place where rumors didn't just run rampant, they stampeded like bulls in Pamplona.

"Because it wasn't anyone from Sugarland," he replied somberly. "From what we can tell, two of the victims were vagrants who came off the highway and holed up in there. One was a confirmed criminal. We found one car. Stolen. The other two, we don't know how they got there." He exhaled a cloud of breath visible in the cooling air. "Two were ruled accidental, one drug-related. But in light of what we're learning now"—his expression grew grim—"maybe not."

A gust of wind sent a shiver through me, and I hugged my arms tighter to my chest. "I didn't run into any of them on the ghostly side." Although I hadn't been tuned in until the end. "The new Irish mob could have killed them to protect their score."

Ellis's gaze met mine with an intensity that held me in place. "If the new Irish mob knows about the haul, why are the bottles still there?"

"They might not have both keys." I laid it out for him, describing the vault door we'd discovered. "The lock has a double-key mechanism." It was clear both were essential to get inside. "Then again, if Seamus made it out, he probably had both keys."

"Not necessarily," Ellis hedged. "I mean, why build a double-key vault if you're not going to give a key to someone else?"

"I don't know, but I met Seamus, and he doesn't strike me as a guy who'd share his vault key."

Ellis gave a sharp nod. "In any case, now someone's trying to pick the lock." He rubbed the back of his neck. "Just be cautious, all right? Try to steer clear of this mess until I'm back tomorrow night. It's hard to say what's happening, but it seems like we're dealing with people who will kill to get what they want."

I leaned up and gave him a soft, sweet kiss. "You be careful, too."

He cracked a half-smile, the worry lines around his eyes softening. "Hands down, this is the best part of my day."

"I aim to please," I said, threading my fingers through his.

His grip tightened gently around my hand. "Thanks for spending time with my mom today. I know you two have your differences."

I brushed my thumb across the stubble on his chin, the rough texture a stark contrast to the softness in his eyes. "Don't get your hopes up. It just kind of happened." And I wasn't going to make a habit of it.

His laughter rumbled through him, that easy sound that never failed to warm my heart. "I know how she can be. But I'm grateful for your patience."

"I like who you are too," I said simply.

He drew me in, his hands resting comfortably on my waist as mine found the solid warmth of his chest. We kissed—a sweet, electrifying connection that warmed my heart and sent shivers down to my toes.

This was all I really wanted.

Him.

The moment was shattered by Frankie's scoff. "What is this?" he demanded as if he were the wronged party. "I thought you were exchanging information, not cooties."

"You're such a romantic," I said, pulling away.

Ellis leveled me with a saucy grin. "Just wait until I get back."

"I'm only a romantic for Molly," Frankie said as if anything else would be unthinkable.

"My gangster's here," I said, running a hand down Ellis's chest. "I have to go."

"And I've got a plane to catch," he said, planting a final kiss on my forehead.

"Call me when you land," I reminded him, reluctant to let go.

"Always," he assured me, opening the lock on his door.

I headed back to the land yacht and gave him one last look as he fired up his Jeep and pulled out into the road right after me.

One way or another, we'd get to the bottom of this.

Of course, that was before I realized what awaited Frankie and me when we arrived home.

Chapter Twenty-Three

Violet, Lottie, and Ruth clustered on my back porch, their bodies tense as they circled a ghostly figure slumped on the swing.

"Molly!" The urgency in Frankie's voice was like a physical force as he bolted through the passenger-side door before I'd had a chance to park.

Or even stop.

Oh my. It seemed the girls had found Molly, and she was in a sorry state.

I threw the car into a haphazard park near the rosebushes and hurried to join them.

"How is she?" I asked, taking the back steps two at a time, passing Lucy as she high-tailed it from Frankie. Now that I'd gotten closer, I could see the ghost's head and shoulders as she sat hunched on the swing. The rest of her form had dissolved into nothingness.

"She's weak," Violet said, her voice a tight knot of worry.

Kitty's youthful face, framed by tendrils of blonde hair, flickered into view as she gathered the strength to materialize fully. Her voice trembled. "My legs are gone. My hands are gone," she stammered, each word steeped in terror. "I'm fading away, and soon I'll be nothing!"

Frankie squared up to her. "You gotta let Molly go," he insisted. "End it now."

"I've tried... I can't." Kitty's voice cracked, her form shimmering as if her tears might cause her to vanish completely.

"She's too upset," Ruth said, wringing her hands.

Violet's eyes darted to me, then back to Kitty. "She doesn't know how."

Kitty's whole being trembled. "I want to release her. Honestly, I do," she insisted, her panic rising again. "It's like something's holding me back. I'm stuck."

She'd been stuck since the night she'd died waiting for Patrick. For almost seventy years, she had lingered, anchored by uncertainty and longing, waiting for him to come for her. Needing to know if he had betrayed her or if he still loved her. Craving him with the same intensity as when she was alive.

Wanting to let go was one thing. Convincing a soul to abandon its one true love was another. Kitty could try to talk herself into giving up, into letting go. She could rationalize it all she wanted, but deep down, her soul was grasping for the truth.

She deserved that truth. She needed it like I craved air. But her tie to Molly was deadly, a poison, and it would kill both of them unless we could figure out a way for her to let go.

And the only way we could do that was to answer her question.

I just didn't know how.

I ushered Violet aside, catching the worry etched deep into her face. "How long does she have?"

Violet's eyes shimmered with unshed tears. "Hours," she whispered, her voice barely a thread.

I slammed my eyes closed.

"I blame myself," Ruth fretted, joining us. "We found her at the site of the old malt shop where Kitty used to work. We should have looked there first."

"You did the best you could," I assured her. They all had. It was all any of us could do.

Still, we needed answers *now*. We had to figure this out.

Lottie's fingers trembled as they traced the outline of her cameo necklace. "I caught a glimpse of Molly while we were helping her up onto the porch."

Frankie reached out, his fingers brushing the cheek of the ethereal figure on the swing. "I see Molly," he said, his voice firm and tender. The image of Kitty shifted, and for a moment, I could have sworn I saw her too. "That's right. I see you," he assured her. "And I'm going to save you. Tonight."

It was an impossible promise.

"Okay, let's think," I said to her friends, trying not to betray how helpless I felt. How afraid. The trouble was we weren't ready. "We don't know enough." We were still piecing together the events surrounding her death.

"We know plenty," Frankie insisted, easing himself onto the bench beside Molly with a tenderness that belied his usual rough-and-tumble ways. "We know who killed you."

Kitty gasped and jolted upright. Violet's hand flew to her mouth, and Lottie grasped Ruth's hand.

"Frankie, don't say it," I urged, the words tumbling out. Kitty was already weak, and telling her that her one true love was the one who'd pledged to kill her would devastate her. "We don't have proof, not *real* proof. We only have a scrawled signature on a picture."

Kitty's attention snapped to Frankie, and her image grew stronger, as if she was drawing upon every last bit of strength, as if she needed to know. "Did Patrick sign his name to the hit?"

She was right. She knew far more about the mob ways than a girlfriend should.

Frankie nodded grimly. "We saw it clear as day. Patrick's name under the red X on a photo in Seamus's office."

Kitty's laughter rang out, shocking us all. It was a fragile sound, like the tinkling of fine China on the verge of shattering. "I could believe he might betray me in the moment. But to be my hitman? No." She gulped. "It's absurd." Her gaze swept across our startled faces. "The only reason he'd do it is to keep me safe," she insisted, pleading with her eyes. "He'd take the hit so nobody else would kill me, and then we could run away."

Frankie stood and looked down at her as if he couldn't quite believe she hadn't collapsed into a pile. "Hold up, sweetheart. You said before you weren't sure whether or not he hurt you. That you couldn't leave unless you knew whether or not Patrick loved you."

Her bottom lip quivered. "I know he loved me," she insisted, but the tremor in her voice betrayed her uncertainty.

The gangster squinted at her. "But you're still here."

Tears welled in Kitty's eyes, her image gaining more strength and becoming clearer. "Maybe...maybe you're right." As she grew more visible, Frankie winced, and I saw his left shoulder begin to blur and fade.

"Enough," I said sharply. Like I'd said, Patrick's name on a piece of paper wasn't definitive proof of anything. The last thing we needed was for Frankie to lose any more parts. And he'd make her flee again if he kept agitating her.

Kitty had to understand that we were on her side.

I squatted in front of the desperate girl, my voice softening despite the urgency I felt. "From what I saw tonight, I'd be more willing to believe Seamus killed you," I said plainly. "We know he was after you. And if Patrick remained loyal to you over his father, I have no doubt Seamus would take revenge personally."

Frankie's shoulders stiffened. "He'd also kill his son if he wasn't loyal."

I braced a hand on the porch post and stood. "That's the thing," I said, attempting to recall every nuance of my conversation with the mob leader. "He went out of his way to tell me how loyal Patrick was. It's like he was protesting really hard."

Kitty perched on the edge of the swing, the chains jangling softly. "If he doubted Patrick, he was right. Patrick did betray him that night."

"But did Seamus know that?" Frankie gritted out.

"If he did, he'd have killed both Patrick and Kitty," I said. I'd bet my life on it.

Kitty nodded. "He would have. He was ruthless."

"We found his big score," I said, pacing toward where Molly's friends gathered on the other side of the stairs, taking in every word. "Seamus was running rare bourbon."

"Long after prohibition," Frankie added. "Some habits die hard."

I stopped, glancing back at Kitty. "It's still in the old bar in a hidden vault. My boyfriend Ellis is with the police. He says it's even more valuable today, and he thinks the live Irish mob might know it's there." I rested a hand on my hip. "Although I have to think that if that was the case, they'd have taken it already."

Kitty chewed her lip. "Maybe they can't get in. The vault has a double-key lock."

Frankie disappeared and materialized nose-to-nose with Kitty. "How did you know about the vault door?"

She gasped and shot backward, straight through the swing. "Seamus had one, and Patrick had the other," she insisted. "Patrick said so!"

Kitty knew more than we'd imagined. "What happened to Patrick's key?" I asked, approaching her carefully. "This is important," I added when she hesitated.

Kitty glided away, toward my back door. "I don't know. I wasn't involved in that. He should have given it back to his dad. We were leaving."

"Or he didn't give it back to his dad, and Seamus killed him for it," Frankie said.

I nodded slowly. "I could see that. But I still don't understand how Seamus could have stolen the chief's cruiser and fled while being surrounded by police." Something didn't add up. I paused, trying to think. "We know they were moving the bourbon out of the vault the night Patrick gave them up. Seamus seemed to honestly believe at least some of the police officers were dirty and after his big score." I rubbed a hand over my chin. "Although,

McAvoy's son, Steve, said his dad had people watching both Mac and Buzz."

Kitty paused under the porch light. "There could have been more."

"Or maybe the chief was dirty," Frankie said.

"Trouble is, I don't trust a thing Seamus said," I told him.

The gangster didn't even try to reassure me. "Yeah, Seamus was a liar. It was one of the things that made him good at his job." He shrugged a shoulder. "But even liars tell the truth sometimes."

When it offered an advantage to them. And in this case, he'd no doubt been hoping to tamp down my suspicion and get me out of his bar.

Kitty nibbled her bottom lip, the flickering porch light shining straight through her nearly transparent features. "Patrick was feeding information to Chief McAvoy. That might have included the names of men the chief suspected of being bad officers. Chief McAvoy was cleaning up the force. That much I know. I wish I'd asked..."

"He wouldn't have told you," I said, the porch boards creaking under my feet as I ventured over to comfort her. "He might not have even told his son the whole truth even decades later." The former officer hadn't shared that with us in any case. Or maybe Steve had held back a little. He could have been protecting some of their families who were still in Sugarland. "Either way, we don't have enough information."

Or any real proof to support our theories of what went down the night of the raid.

I ran a hand through my hair. Heck, Ellis was still looking for proof that the Irish mob from Vegas might be after what we'd found in the vault. I mean, three modern people had gotten killed in that bar. Maisie had been right—it was a dangerous place.

"So, what do we do?" Kitty asked, gliding to me, her voice a mix of fear and determination.

I looked back to Frankie, the weight of our next move settling on my shoulders. I couldn't believe I was about to say this, but it was our only option. "We have to kick the hornet's nest and see who starts buzzing."

Frankie cocked his head. "What are you talking about?"

It was simple. Almost too simple. "It seems everything revolves around this big score that triggered the raid and the murder."

"So?" Kitty pressed, gathering close.

Violet broke away from the group near the porch rail. "Yes, I mean, what does money have to do with love?"

"Absolutely nothing," I assured her. "But it's at the heart of this mystery, and the only way to solve this fast is to stir up trouble." I paused, my plan taking shape. It was daring. It was crazy. And it might just work. "We need to steal the big score."

Frankie spun a circle and whooped. "Yes! Yes! Yes!"

"But in a big, big way," I said, the idea growing bolder in my mind.

"Finally!" Frankie crowed. "I finally got through to you. And we're going to save Molly at the same time!" For a second, I thought the gangster was going to kiss me. "Don't worry about guns. I've got an arsenal."

"Frankie—" I started.

But there was no stopping him now.

"Don't worry about men," he insisted. "I'll call in the South Town Boys."

That I could get on board with. "As many as you can find. Tell them we need to make a big splash. We want them to raid the main bar. Shoot up the place."

"This just keeps getting better and better," Frankie said, rubbing his hands together.

Anything to make him happy. "While they keep the Irish busy, you and I will rob the vault on both the ghostly and mortal realms—just to be sure we're ticking all the boxes—and see who cares enough to show up and stop us."

Kitty gaped at me with a mix of excitement and awe, and

perhaps a bit of train wreck tossed in. "Seamus is going to kill you."

"Maybe so, maybe not," I countered, the thrill of the chase sparking life in my voice. "A lot of this hinges on Patrick," I said to her surprise. "Think of it this way," I said, pacing, trying to get it crystal clear in my mind. "We haven't seen Patrick at all since you played back your memory of the night you died."

"Why did he tease me like that?" Kitty lamented.

"It's not bad that he hasn't shown up," I assured her. Although it wasn't necessarily good, either. When her face fell, I added, "I mean, yes, you need to see him and ask him what went wrong that night. And it would be wonderful for both of you to be reunited. But I also think it could mean you're right about him."

I spun on my heel and paced along the edge of the porch. "If what we hope is true, then Patrick betrayed his father and stole— something—so he could run away and start a new life with you. Then he's going to be super cautious about coming back or placing you in danger. He loves you. He wants to protect you by staying away from you so that Seamus doesn't find you and go after you. If that's the case, Patrick also has no reason to be at the mob bar because he's given up that part of his life. So if we raid and Patrick is a no-show, he's yours. He's in love."

"But where is he?" Kitty pleaded, trailing me.

"I don't know." Maybe we'd learn more on the raid. I turned to Frankie. "If Patrick is guilty and he killed Kitty to get back in with his dad and take over the operation—" Kitty's stricken face gave me pause. "If that's true, then Patrick will show up at our raid in order to defend the bar as his dad's second in command."

"I still say Seamus did it," Kitty insisted.

"You might be right," I told her. "Seamus didn't trust you, and I'm not so sure he trusted his son." The gangster's insistence on his son's undying loyalty struck me as too much. "Today, down in his office, I think he *wanted* to believe in Patrick very much."

Frankie leaned up against a porch post. "I hear that's a tell with him—an overinflated bravado. But you gotta realize, he's also an egomaniac."

"Have you seen Patrick at all since 1956?" I pressed.

Frankie looked like he'd smelled something foul. "No. But he's also with the Irish. We tend to avoid those *arschlochs*. Sorry for the language," he added to the ladies.

"Seamus could have killed both you and Patrick," I said to Kitty. "If so, he'll have no reason to show up to the raid tonight. He died with his big score in the vault, so us stealing it tonight won't make a difference."

Frankie barked out a laugh. "You just have to take the fun out of stealing, don't you?"

I pointed a finger at him. "You said there's a big horse race tonight and that Seamus always goes."

"It's a great night to mess up his place," Frankie agreed heartily. "Seamus never liked to be in the thick of things. He'd trust his guys to protect the bar."

Right. "So logically, he'll be out. Unless..."

"What?" Frankie pressed.

"Well, if Seamus is guilty of the murder, there's no need for him to find out what he already knows," I said. "He knows he killed Kitty. He knows Patrick betrayed him, and he knows he killed Patrick, too. It's over. He'd have no reason to miss the race for a bunch of schnitzelheads who couldn't fix a game of solitaire."

"Hey," Frankie shot back.

"His words, not mine." If Seamus did it, Patrick was literally dead to him despite how he tried to save face with me. "Unless, of course, he didn't kill anybody," I said to Kitty.

She stiffened at the idea that the mob boss could be innocent, at least of that.

"Seamus had one key, and he supposedly trusted Patrick so much that he gave him the other key. But," I said, tapping my chin, "the bar was raided on the night of his big score, and you're telling us Patrick gave them up. Seamus would have had to suspect if and when his son never showed up to defend him. So if he's innocent of the murders, he's going to be desperate to know if Patrick betrayed him. And if we bring Kitty there and Patrick shows up but not to stand by his dad, then Seamus gets his answer."

"I think Patrick will come for me," Kitty insisted.

I sincerely hoped he would.

"I think I need a chalkboard," Ruth fretted.

I had it all in my head.

"Wait," Violet said. "So if Patrick stays away, he's innocent, but if he shows up at his father's side, he's guilty."

"Exactly," I said. "And if Seamus stays at the horse race, we know he was lying and probably killed Kitty and Patrick both. But if he was unsure about his son's loyalty, he will show up at the bar to find out. Which means he's innocent."

"Okay," Violet said, tucking an errant strand of hair behind her ear, "so that's everything."

"No, wait," I said to the group. "There's a third possibility. It could have been the crooked police."

"Finally!" Frankie threw his hands up.

"What are they after?" Ruth asked, clasping her hands together.

"They were after the score for themselves," I said.

"That's right," Frankie agreed. "They never found it."

Virginia had.

I braced my rear against the porch rail. "If McAvoy and his men were raiding in order to clean up Sugarland all those years ago, they were done when they brought down the Irish. They'd have looked into the main storage room, confiscated what they saw, and called it a day. And they certainly wouldn't show up seventy years later. I mean, you gangsters get in immortal scuffs all the time. Do the police ever show up?"

"No," Frankie insisted. "Only when they're bored. They

know we can't really do anything to one another. Loot goes back to whoever died with it, and we all wake up in an hour."

Kitty glided toward the swing. "So if the police stay home, everyone is on the up and up."

I pushed off the porch rail. "But if the police show up, it'll be to keep you quiet again, Kitty. The only thing anyone has that's worth anything in the afterlife is their reputation."

Frankie had been trying to protect his for years since I grounded him.

My housemate nodded thoughtfully, then smiled. "So we basically go in there and wait for all hell to break loose."

"In a manner of speaking," I agreed.

"Oh, Frankie," Molly's voice gushed.

I spun at the sound and saw her standing by the swing.

Her face was sweet, her eyes alight. "I never thought I'd get to go on a heist with you."

"It's me and you, babe," he said, rushing to her. His image surged, strengthened by her presence. Her excitement. Her love. "I'll get you out of this," he promised, kissing her on the cheek.

She smiled and faded, gone as soon as she'd appeared.

"I'll get you back," he vowed as if she could still hear him.

"When do we go?" Kitty pressed.

"Tonight," I said. We didn't have any time to lose.

Frankie nodded. "Tonight it is. We'll stop by the South Town Boys' hideout on the way."

"We'd like to go too," Violet offered. Although Ruth didn't look so sure.

"Meet us outside the drive-in," Frankie ordered. "We'll position you as lookouts."

Then it was settled. Frankie and I would lead his mob in a raid against the Irish. We had the South Town Boys. We had the girls. I could try to catch Ellis before he boarded his plane, but barring that, I needed one more person to help me break into the vault, and it wasn't Frankie.

I looked at my gangster. "Let's go."

Chapter Twenty-Four

On the way, we stopped by a few of Frankie's old haunts. The first was a dilapidated speakeasy tucked away out back behind the Southern Spirits distillery. I waited in the car for that one, considering I still hadn't put Crazy Louie's head back on his shoulders where it belonged.

How could I when the dead Louie would use me for target practice the second I stepped inside?

The second hideout we visited was located inside a run-down railway car, half of it swallowed by overgrowth. It was off an abandoned set of tracks and looked like it hadn't seen life since the days of prohibition.

But the third place was a surprise. I did a double take when Frankie directed me to stop in front of the *New For You* resale shop, right on Main Street. I used my waiting time productively—googling photos of Seamus O'Reilly—and raised a brow when Frankie hurried back outside.

"Really?" I gestured toward the busy shop. "I mean, wouldn't you all rather stay inconspicuous?"

Frankie exhaled a stream of smoke and chuckled, flicking the ash from his cigarette as he passed through the passenger-side door and flopped down in the seat. "You should hear their new piano player. And his buddy on the sax." He took a long, fond drag on his smoke. "It's the place to be. For gangsters who can go places," he added with a frown.

We'd deal with that later. As long as he'd found the gangsters we needed now.

The streetlights flared to life as I pulled back out onto Main Street. "Did you assemble the crew?"

Frankie rested an elbow on the doorframe. "Sweetheart, I got a crew bigger than the one we used to hijack the circus train."

I nearly choked. "You hijacked the what now?"

He waved a dismissive hand. "There was no money in it, but Suds had a beef with the bearded lady."

So naturally they'd been forced to hijack a circus train.

"Okay, then," I said, taking a left onto Magnolia Street. I had to admit it sounded like Frankie had everything under control. But then, he usually did—right up until the moment he didn't.

Of course, now it was my turn to surprise him.

Frankie shot me a curious look as I pulled up to Ellis's driveway and killed the engine.

My housemate used his cigarette to light a new cigarette and tossed the spent butt out the window, where it disintegrated. "I think your boyfriend is on an airplane right now."

He was. I'd called and left him a message, but it appeared we'd missed him.

"We need to borrow Virginia's lock-picking kit," I said, grabbing my bag.

"That she stole," he pointed out, with a tinge of pride.

He didn't have to sound so happy about it. Then again, in retrospect, I was really glad for Virginia's sticky fingers. "The plan hinges on us opening the vault in both realms," I said, sliding out of the car. It was the only way to guarantee a full freak-out.

Frankie puffed as he smirked, blowing smoke out of his nose as he joined me outside. "No worries. Listen to me and you'll be in like Flynn." He grinned. "You know," he said, waiting for me to walk around the front of the car, "I've been waiting years for you to realize stealing's fun. I'm proud of you, kid."

"Gee, thanks," I said. He might as well enjoy it while it lasted.

We walked up to the house, and the motion lights flared to life, illuminating a stone fountain amid the holly bushes at the front of the house. When did Virginia find the time? Although the lights, I had to admit, were a good idea.

I knocked on the door, and it swung open almost immediately. Virginia stood dressed in figure-skimming black cargo pants that somehow managed to appear both practical and stylish. She wore a tank top under a tailored zip-up black jacket, her hair done up in an elaborate braid. It was Lara Croft meets Martha Stewart.

"I thought you'd be here by now," she said with absolutely no trace of guile.

"Where do you think you're going?" The words slipped out sharper than I intended, but I couldn't mask my surprise. Virginia wasn't dressed for a quiet evening in.

She pressed her lips together primly. "You can't leave a message on Ellis's machine and not expect me to listen," she said as if it were obvious. Yet the slight flush on her cheeks betrayed her. "I mean, think about what went down this afternoon," she said, trying another tack. "It's obvious you can use a hand."

She had been a help, but that didn't mean I wanted her around tonight. "I only stopped by for the lock-picking kit."

"I've got it ready to go." She swooped up a crossbody bag from behind the door, the contents jingling softly as she slung it over her shoulder and across her chest. "I also have water, snacks, extra flashlights, scotch tape, and an emergency horn." She patted her bag. "I'm going with you. You can't deny I'm a good lookout. I know the bar." She paused, her tone softening. "Besides, Ellis would have my hide if something happened to you because I didn't help."

"Fine," I said grudgingly. We didn't have time to argue. Plus, I could use a live lookout who could call for help if things got dicey.

And they always did.

This time, Virginia voluntarily took the back seat, which was interesting to say the least. Meanwhile, Frankie made himself at home in the shotgun seat. He pulled a cigarette from behind his ear and planted it on his bottom lip.

"Do you have to smoke in my car?" I asked as he flicked a match to life against the brim of his hat.

"Yes," he said, taking a deep drag as I pulled out of the driveway. Smoke curled out of his nose as he rested an elbow on the window ledge, the cigarette perched between his fingers. "I have to smoke as much as I can while I still have my arms. You and I both know it's going to get rough tonight."

I did. "Just...be careful." His willingness to gamble everything for Molly was both noble and terrifying. I'd do the same for Ellis or my sister. For Lucy, even. But he could still watch out for himself at the same time.

He leaned back, the smoke from his cigarette dancing upward before sinking and pooling between us. He was lucky I couldn't smell it.

I still didn't like it.

"This is going to be a blowout," he said with a half-smile, savoring the anticipation as much as the nicotine. The glow at the end of his cigarette flared with each inhale, and he stuck a hand through the closed window to catch the breeze. "The boys are talking up the raid all over town."

"Good," I said, trying to muster a bit of the same enthusiasm. It was what we wanted, wasn't it? To draw them out, to see who would come to challenge us. To learn what really happened the night Kitty died.

"Anything I'm missing?" Virginia asked from the back seat.

"No," Frankie and I said in unison. Although she only heard me.

The land yacht's headlights cut through the darkness as I steered us out of town and along the original route we'd taken to get to the drive-in. As we turned down the road leading to the abandoned property, it felt like the calm before the storm.

We would either arrive to an eerie quiet, the German mob our only company, or we'd be greeted by chaos incarnate.

Either way, we'd have our answer.

I caught sight of the crumbling Tennessee Oil gas station on the edge of the forgotten part of town. We passed the rusted pumps under an old tin awning. And then the diner with its chipped white-tile exterior. I remembered the way.

We turned left at the lump of a building completely overtaken by bushes and trees.

"Kitty is with Molly's friends," Frankie said. "She's going to be hiding out of sight until the timing is right."

"Okay, good." I nodded.

We drove until the asphalt road opened up into a field caged by a rusted chain-link fence. Then I about choked when I saw the sign for the Starlite Drive-In.

Ghosts. Dozens upon dozens of ghosts had staked out underneath the flickering glow of the Starlite sign.

"What's going on?" I craned my neck for a better look.

It had better not be the Irish.

"Relax," Frankie said, his voice steady as he flicked the ash from his cigarette. "I told the South Town Boys to meet up there." He took a quick, hard drag, the ember briefly flaring like a warning. "You know, so they're less conspicuous before the raid."

"So we're all supposed to believe they're going to the movies," I said dryly, pulling up near the chaos.

The Starlite sign stood sentinel above it all, a teetering watchtower ready to topple.

The place was swarming with more dead gangsters than I'd ever seen gathered, each looking exactly as they had when they died. I saw a lot of suits with gunshot holes, a guy with a tire mark down his back, and even a guy wearing cement shoes.

He wasn't moving too fast.

They were a timeline of the underworld, decked out in the mob finery of their respective eras—pinstripes from the 1920s and '30s, wide lapels from the '40s, slick suits from the '50s and

'60s, two leisure suits, and a conspicuously modern soul from the '90s.

"He's wearing Air Jordans," I said like an accusation. But really, I was more shocked than anything.

"Better than Handsome Henry, who died in his underwear," Frankie remarked.

He had a point. "Oh, look. I see Henry!" I said, pointing to the hitman with a dad bod. He wore white silk boxers and braced a Tommy gun on his hip while he chatted.

All of the mobsters were packing heat like it was going out of style—which, I guess for them, it never did. Tommy guns, pistols, rifles, snub-nosed automatics. Those were illegal.

Not that they cared.

They goofed around like schoolboys teasing each other. A rockabilly-era ghost sent bullets dancing into the sky, while his compatriot, snug in a leisure suit, swiped a fedora off another thug and flung it high like a makeshift clay pigeon.

Then I spotted Miss Felicia in the crowd, blazing her way through the mob like a salmon swimming upstream. She pointed at things nobody looked at. She shouted orders that nobody listened to. The Sunday school teacher with her sensible sneakers and long skirt was a commander without an army, her attempts to corral the ghostly wiseguys as futile as trying to catch smoke with a net.

"You remember Miss Felicia?" I asked Virginia. When she nodded, I added, "She's in her own kind of hell right now."

Virginia's face blanched. "Do we need to save her?"

"No." I couldn't help but smile. "She'll be right as rain as soon as we get the Germans out of her drive-in."

As I watched the ghosts, a small satisfaction settled in. This gathering had its uses. If any of the Irish were here for a show, they'd surely notice the South Town Boys' reunion.

They wouldn't confront Frankie's crew outright—not when they were so badly outnumbered. But they'd know trouble was on the way.

"Time to gather the troops," I said to Frankie, who gave a curt nod and tossed his cigarette out the window. "See you in five," he said, slipping through the passenger-side door.

"Frankie!" several of the South Town Boys called out. Ice Pick Charlie stepped from the crowd, sporting his distinctive crew cut. The scar along his cheek crinkled as he gave me a wink. Suds ducked past him and clapped Frankie hard on the back. "Just like old times, right?"

I didn't stick around to find out. I hit the gas and steered past the reunion, toward the bar just beyond. After the chaos of the gangsters, I almost welcomed the dark.

The place was desolate, the parking lot a tangle of weeds and cracked asphalt. I saw no sign of the intruders from earlier, which didn't mean they wouldn't be back. No sign of ghosts, either. Except for the three waiting for me in the parking lot.

I parked near them with the passenger side of my car facing the bar.

Ruth rushed up to me in a rustle of silk.

"You're here," she exclaimed.

"We were getting worried," Violet said, her elegant hands clasped together.

"Yes, well, we had to gather the mob," I explained.

"I don't see anyone," Lottie remarked, scanning the empty lot.

"You will," I assured her. "Is Kitty all right?"

She nodded.

"Good. Gather close, if you please," I said, positioning the girls on the side of the car that shielded us from the bar's view. "Here's the plan; in a couple of minutes, Frankie is going to lead the Germans up here for a full-on raid. I need you to be our lookouts. Stay out of the fray and find somewhere safe. Keep an eye out for this man." I held up my phone, showing them the images I had saved of Seamus O'Reilly. "If you see this man, warn Frankie and me immediately. We'll be down in the basement raiding the vault."

"And I'll be with you down there," Virginia said as if it were a foregone conclusion.

"Actually, I need you up top as well," I told her.

Virginia's lips pursed, then she crossed her arms with a haughty tilt of her chin. "That's hardly the best use of my talents," she snipped. "I know the basement. I found the vault." She rested a hand on her packed crossbody bag. "You need me."

I squared up with her. "You said it yourself. People are ending up dead inside that bar. It's not safe, especially after dark, and we both know it."

"Do as I say, not as I do," she muttered under her breath.

Come to think of it... "Yes, that's it exactly." And what was this sudden passion for ghost hunting? This sudden concern for me and what I was doing in the basement of her property? "Just trust me, okay?" This wasn't my first rodeo.

She crossed her arms over her chest. "I spoke to Ellis after he left. He told me his plans. For all we know, Ellis's trip to Vegas could be riling up the real mob. They might decide to swoop in and claim that bourbon before the police get a chance."

"That's comforting." I mean, it was true. I just didn't need to hear it at the moment.

"A single bottle of that vintage Pappy Van Winkle could fetch thousands," Virginia said, her eyes alight with the thrill of the hunt. "All together, the booze in those crates could be worth millions."

"And it all belongs to you," I said, feeling a cold twist in my gut. It was her property. Technically, at least. Hers and Leland's. Maybe I didn't want Virginia guarding me after all.

For the first time, I wondered if she'd discovered the vault when she was down there with me or if she known it was there all along.

Maybe she just needed me to open it.

Tonight.

With no other live witnesses around to tell the story.

Virginia had never liked me. She'd never considered me good

enough for her son. And now I was threatening to tell the world about the fortune hidden on her property.

A property Maisie would contest if she could wrangle the means.

"Stay outside," I ordered. "Or I'll tell Ellis you didn't back me up."

"You're making a mistake," she warned.

"I'll have Frankie." As long as he stuck around. But it was better than worrying about Virginia. "Keep a lookout from here," I told the frowning socialite. "If you see any live people sneaking in, call the police and then send one of Molly's friends in to warn me."

Virginia looked at me like I was nuts. "How do I talk to a ghost I can't see?"

I gave Lottie a reassuring nod, and she touched one of her perfectly curled ringlets as if to steady herself. "Lottie will be right by your side, no matter what."

Lottie's eyes sparkled with a mixture of pride and determination. "You can count on me."

"Lottie can see and hear you even if you can't see or hear her," I assured Virginia. She opened her mouth to protest, but I fixed her with a firm gaze, the kind that brooked no argument. "Lottie will also warn me if you so much as think about coming inside," I added, making sure my tone left no room for doubt.

Virginia's lips thinned, and she gave a small, exasperated sigh. "Is that truly necessary?" she asked, her voice laced with annoyance.

"Yes." Yes, it was. "Now give me the lock-picking kit."

And we'd pray Frankie could tell me how to use it.

Virginia gave me a long look before she unzipped a pocket in her bag and drew out the kit. "Here," she said, grudgingly handing it over.

"Thanks." I tucked it under my arm and turned to the others. "Ruth and Violet, make sure you stay clear of the shooting and keep a lookout for trouble outside. Ghostly or otherwise. If something goes wrong, one of you can come down and get us out fast."

Ruth's eyes lit up. "This is so exciting," she said, clasping her hands together.

"I'd kind of like to date a gangster," Lottie admitted to her friends.

Then I was glad she was stuck shadowing Virginia.

"Ready?" Frankie's voice sounded in my ear.

I almost dropped the lock-picking kit.

"No." I hated when he popped up on me like that. "I need to be inside the bar before the shoot-out."

"Ahhh...too late," he said.

A wave of ghostly energy rippled through the air, leaving my skin tingling and my stomach dancing. It felt like static on the wind. Like an invasion.

And then...

"Go!" Suds shouted.

The night erupted in the blink of an eye as a mob of gangsters materialized in the parking lot. "Ding-dong!" one shouted. "It's the South Town Boys!" hollered another. They began hurling Molotov cocktails through the bar's windows, the sound of breaking glass shattering the calm of the night.

Frankie shimmered into existence at my side in mid-throw as he lobbed a Molotov cocktail over my car and through one of the stained-glass Tudor windows. "This is one of the ones I stole from the Irish!" he shouted, bubbling with a mix of pride and adrenaline. He pulled another from his coat. "This one too!"

My heart raced. "We need to get in there now before the Irish start shooting back," I urged. "Come on." I hoped the South Town Boys would hold their fire until I at least made it to the door.

No such luck.

I ran full tilt, dodging the fiery bottles that sailed past, some falling short and igniting the ground on either side of me in bursts of fire.

Frankie pranced like a gazelle next to me—despite his lack of legs—*whooping* the entire time.

It was a wonder he'd survived mob life long enough to get shot in the forehead.

We reached the red door, and I yanked the handle hard. It didn't budge. It was locked!

A jolt of shock surged through me. The intruder had locked the door this afternoon?

"Still don't need me?" The voice came from behind, laced with a hint of smugness.

Virginia.

Without a moment's hesitation, she reached around and shoved her key into the padlock. One twist and we were in.

"Thanks. Now man your post," I said, slipping through the entrance and slamming the door behind me.

When I made it inside, I saw that Frankie had already passed through the wall. He picked up an unexploded Molotov cocktail and, with a flick of his wrist, sent it spinning onto the pool table. It erupted into a fiery inferno, consuming the green felt and sending billiard balls scattering like comets.

"Gorgeous!" he shouted at the flames.

"Insane," I corrected as ghosts of the Irish mobsters began to appear, their outlines hazy in the smoke and firelight. "You see what you did?"

He grinned at me.

"Watch out!" I shouted. The nearest Irishman, brandishing a Tommy gun, unleashed a line of bullets toward Frankie, who danced to the side like a showgirl.

"Look!" Frankie called to the shooter as a ghostly stick of dynamite crashed through the front window and landed on the floor way too close to us.

The man dropped the gun and dove for the explosive.

"Come on," Frankie called to me, zipping to the basement door and flinging it open.

"You people are crazy!" I hollered, watching the Irishman toss the dynamite back at the South Town Boys.

"Thanks," Frankie barked over his shoulder as he careened down the stairs. He wasn't even watching where he was going. I barreled after him. Despite the fact that it was a horrible idea to go *into* the basement of a burning building. A basement that might or might not still be full of the Irish mob.

"We told them to create a distraction, not burn the place down with us in it," I panted, my voice echoing slightly in the stairwell as we descended.

"Sometimes the difference is small," Frankie said, racing down ahead of me.

I just hoped a bunch of Irish weren't getting ready to charge up the stairs we were going down, or this was going to be a really short heist.

"I didn't see Seamus," I said, my breath coming in short gasps. I blamed the smoke. And the stress.

"Not yet." Frankie stopped on the bottom step and crouched, gun poised, his gaze flicking left and right with a predator's attentiveness.

"I didn't see the police, either," I said in a hoarse whisper, joining him. The hallway stretched out empty, the silence almost as jarring as the chaos above.

"I still say the cops are dirty," Frankie muttered, his eyes narrowing as he made a left toward the vault.

"What makes you think that?" I asked, hurrying over the uneven dirt floor, the toe of my sneaker sending a rusted Coke can skittering across the floor.

"Because they're cops," he said.

Well, I for one, was glad the cops weren't dirty after all. Chief McAvoy had managed to turn Sugarland into a better place, even if it had cost him his cruiser.

"Let's just pick the lock on the vault," I suggested, eager to shift our focus. We passed the door to the armory. It glowed a ghostly gray.

"You don't know how long I've waited for you to say that." Frankie beamed over his shoulder. "This is better than the Pappy."

"What is?" I glanced up the darkened smuggler's stairs.

"You," he said like a proud papa. "Picking a lock. Adopting a life of crime," he gushed, stepping aside with a flourish to let me enter before him. "You know how long I've waited to teach you to steal?"

He was going to have to wait longer because the door to the vault stood wide open—in my world and in his.

Chapter Twenty-Five

We stood for a moment in shock, the vault door yawning open before us.

"Somebody robbed the place?" Frankie barked, somehow managing to sound both shocked and offended.

"To be fair, we're here to rob the place," I pointed out.

They must have broken in this afternoon after we left. Worse, if the door was still open, they might be in the building or at least on their way back soon.

I hadn't seen anyone upstairs. But then again, we'd been busy with the mob war. And down in the basement, there were plenty of places to hide.

They could even be inside the vault right now.

The heavy door hung open enough for a person to slip through, but not enough to see inside.

"I'm checking it out," I whispered. I had to.

My gut twisted as I edged past Frankie, my sneakers whispering against the threshold, adrenaline sharpening my senses.

What greeted me inside stopped me cold.

I could usually count on Frankie to exaggerate, but his earlier description had not done the place justice.

Stacks and stacks of wooden bourbon crates crowded the

space, the rich, dark wood a stark contrast to the stark metal walls of the vault. They were piled five and six deep in meticulous rows thigh-high on the left and right, and as tall as me against the back wall.

It was clear they'd been there a while, the edges of the crates fraying and beginning to succumb to rot. Each crate was labeled in an elegant, faded script, *Pappy Van Winkle Handmade Bourbon 107 Proof Aged 30 Years*. It was a cache that would make any connoisseur's heart skip a beat—as well as any thief's.

If these crates were full, we had millions of dollars in booze on our hands.

It made me a little dizzy. I hadn't realized there'd be so much. "So, are we still robbing the place?" A bead of sweat trailed down my back. I didn't see how we could pull it off.

I should have known better than to ask Frankie.

"New plan," my housemate announced, drawing up beside me. He had three rifles slung over both of his shoulders, a pair of Tommy Guns tucked under his arms, and his suit coat bulged with what I could only assume was a brand-new stash of Molotov cocktails.

Because it had better not be dynamite.

"We're staking the place out," he announced, unloading the guns onto the crates. "We're going to ambush the competition. And *then* we're going to rob the place."

It was a terrible, terrible plan.

My mouth must have been hanging open because he added, "Don't worry. There's plenty more guns in the ammunition room, and the crooks have got to be back soon."

What a comfort.

"Who's worried?" I asked, my voice cracking. I was just trapped down in a vault in the middle of the haul men had killed for while a mob war went on upstairs. I was holed up with a gangster who didn't realize other dead guys could steal the same guns he had. At the same time, I was completely not prepared to confront dead killers or the real-life Irish crime syndicate from Vegas. Both of whom wanted the big score.

Meanwhile, Frankie grew weaker by the minute, and we still didn't have the answers we needed to solve Kitty's murder. And if we couldn't give Kitty the peace she needed—soon—Frankie, Molly, and Kitty would be dead. And it would be all over. Permanently.

The weight of our predicament settled like lead in my stomach.

Frankie, as usual, remained blissfully overconfident. "It always looks a little dicey before the gunfire starts."

"And perhaps while it's going on," I suggested.

What a mess.

I watched him struggle to lift a ghostly bourbon crate. This was bad.

"Forget it," he huffed, giving up. "I don't need to make a barricade. Not with grade-A hooch," he said, patting the top of the box.

"Maybe we should get out of here while we still can." I despised saying it, but we'd do no good to anyone dead in the vault.

Frankie looked at me like I'd told him I wanted to give up the Alamo. "You can't quit now." He spread his arms wide. "We're about to blow this thing sky-high."

"That's what I'm afraid of," I said, eyeing the Molotov cocktails hanging out of his inside coat pockets.

He dropped his hands. "You can do whatever you want," he said, jabbing a finger at me. "I'm staying here for Molly." When I hesitated, he added, "You said it yourself—the only way to get answers is to stir up trouble."

That was before I realized trouble would be coming right for us.

"You know what the weirdest thing is about tonight?" Frankie asked, planting his hands on his hips, revealing the pistols he'd stuffed into his pants pockets.

"I could give you a list."

He ignored me. "The dirty cops aren't here. They don't care."

"That's because the police weren't dirty," I informed him. Okay, maybe Mac and Buzz, but McAvoy had taken care of them. My housemate had to stop assuming it was the police. "We're playing a different game now."

Frankie ran a hand through his hair, knocking off his hat. He didn't notice.

"Okay, well, who are the dead guys robbing Seamus's vault?" he demanded, gliding back toward the crates along the wall. "It isn't Seamus."

"It could be Patrick," I said, trying it on.

Only it couldn't be because all he wanted to do was run off with Kitty. And he'd already secured the funding he needed to start their new life.

Unless we were wrong about him.

"We'll find out soon enough," Frankie said, hefting one of the Tommy guns.

That was what I was afraid of. "I'm not so eager to meet the real-life thief." Or gang. Or whoever it was. I glanced out at the dark hallway, half expecting to see shadowy figures emerge.

How bad was it when I was hoping it was a local criminal and not the Irish mob? "I mean, it has to be that guy you saw upstairs searching for his lock-picking set, right?" The Irish mob wouldn't be so sneaky. I cringed at how close I'd come to the man. "Though how he got in without this—" I wondered, holding up his tool set.

"Everybody's got a spare," Frankie said as if it were obvious.

"Either that or somebody in the real world has both keys." I eased out of the vault, my gaze sweeping over the locks on the outside. Not a key in sight. Wishful thinking, but a part of me had hoped for an easy clue.

"Nothing," I said, rejoining the mobster, who was deep in thought.

Crime was his specialty.

He ran a hand over his chin. "If Seamus got away, he could have passed his key down to his new branch of the Irish mob." The thought hung heavy between us.

"He could have passed down both keys if he killed Patrick for double-crossing him."

"I need a drink," Frankie muttered, reaching into his coat. Instead of a flask, his hand came out with a pistol. In one swift move, he used the barrel to flip open the nearest crate of expensive booze.

"You think this is helping?" I asked. A gunfight would be bad enough, but a boozy gunfight would be worse. Maybe I needed to start building my own barricade.

He froze, his hand hovering above a bottle. "Shoot me now."

I'd rather not.

"I can't drink this," he choked out.

Finally, a sensible choice. Maybe I was rubbing off on him. "What?" I asked when he remained rooted to the spot. "Frankie?" I prodded, going to see for myself.

When I peered into the crate, what I saw took a moment to register.

Gold bars, meticulously stacked in tidy rows and cushioned in straw, glowed gray in the ghostly realm. Oh my heavens. "Seamus wasn't moving bourbon."

"He was dealing in stolen gold," Frankie finished for me.

My heart skipped a beat.

I dashed out of the vault and grabbed a splintered plank from the storage room debris. With it, I pried the lid off the crate next to Frankie's. I had to see our find in the real world, and I knew better than to touch the gangster's haul.

Frankie had a gun, and old habits die hard.

The lid gave way, and I shone my light over the find, gasping all over again. Stacks and stacks of gold bars, very real and very precious, gleamed brightly. "I don't believe it," I said breathlessly.

Each ingot bore a United States eagle stamp and a mark of 200 ounces. Just in this crate alone, there were a dozen or more. I lifted one out. I had to use two hands! The thing weighed more than my skunk. No wonder Frankie had been unable to lift the ghostly crate full of them.

I stared at the gold in my hands. Real gold. Right here. The abundance was almost obscene. I placed it back on top of the others. The sheer value of the find, the weight of wealth in one wooden crate, was staggering.

It was the kind of wealth that changed lives—or ended them.

"It's my big score," Frankie said softly, his fingers grazing the bars on top of the crate he'd opened. "It's my score!" he whooped, lifting a bar with both hands and kissing it. "We're going to save Molly. We're going to be set for eternity!"

"You can't keep what you didn't die with," I reminded him.

"Then I'll steal it again," he said with relish, trying to find a spot for it in his overloaded coat pockets.

This was getting out of hand. "This isn't our gold."

"It is now," Frankie said as the temperature in the room plummeted.

We weren't alone anymore.

Chapter Twenty-Six

The vault door creaked all the way open on its own. Seamus O'Reilly stood outside in the hall, his imposing figure blocking our only way out.

The stone-faced gangster's steely eyes fixed on me with an intensity that could cut glass.

"Hello," I said, trying to sound both casual and friendly as I stepped in front of Frankie, who was still holding a bar of Seamus's gold.

But the mob leader didn't knock it out of his hand, or shoot us, or attack.

"Where's Patrick?" he demanded, craning his neck to peer behind us, his voice a growl. "Have you seen him tonight? Did he come back?" He made a low, throaty sound, almost like a snarl. "Tell him all can be forgiven. But he's got to talk to me."

Before I could speak, the sharp crack of a gunshot echoed from down the hall. Seamus's head snapped sideways, and he crumpled to the ground.

Dead once more.

Shock rooted me to the spot. My heart pounded in my chest, the echo of the gunshot still ringing in my ears.

I heard a hollow chuckle. Then the ghostly image of Sugarland's beloved Police Chief McAvoy emerged from the shadows. He appeared as he had in all the old pictures—fit and trim, with a shock of white hair and deep lines around his eyes and mouth.

"Funny." He stepped over Seamus's body as if it were no more than a forgotten coat on the floor. "That's how I killed him the first time." He grinned, holding the smoking gun. "He didn't see it coming then, either."

My breath caught. "You knew about the vault." McAvoy hadn't shown the slightest surprise upon discovering us among the crates with Frankie holding a bar of gold.

His lip curled into a self-satisfied smirk. "I'm a good detective," he said, resting a hand on his utility belt. "Don't forget I wiped out the Irish mob."

"So you could steal their gold," I said.

I didn't want to be right.

But I was.

He shot me a glare designed to pin me to the wall before he broke it with an ominous chuckle. "They're the ones who stole it," he coaxed. "I merely acquired it while making Sugarland a better place."

I felt my hands curl into fists. "Did you kill Kitty?"

His facade cracked, a brief flicker of sadness passing over his features. "That was the worst part of the job. My girls adored her, and I liked her too." His gaze shifted, stealing a glance toward the hall. "But a job's a job. Although I'm really going to hate to do it again," he ground out through clenched teeth.

In one swift motion, his hand shot back into the hall, and with a sickening tug, he yanked Kitty into the room by the neck. She trembled with terror as she struggled helplessly against his grip.

"Kitty!" I cried out, shocked.

She was supposed to be waiting outside.

"Molly!" Frankie dropped the gold with a thud and fired his pistol, the shot echoing in the vault and splintering the doorframe right next to McAvoy's head.

McAvoy fired back, and he didn't miss.

Frankie hit the floor, blood blossoming on his temple.

Ohmygosh. "Frankie!" I turned to go help, but he was already dead.

"Frankie." Molly's face appeared over Kitty's for a brief moment, sobbing.

Then Kitty's countenance slammed over her once more. "Don't shoot us," Kitty pleaded.

"Not yet, love," McAvoy said, cold as ice. "Not until we talk."

I couldn't move. I couldn't breathe. I'd seen Frankie dead before, but not like this. The other times, it knocked him out for an hour, but he could regenerate, like any other ghost. This time, I watched with horror as his hands melted like wax in a flame. His wrists. His elbows. He was going fast.

His spirit was trying to heal, but it didn't have the power. Instead, he was bleeding the last of his energy to keep Molly alive for another second, another minute.

Soon he'd be gone forever.

"What do you want, McAvoy?" I demanded. We needed to know now and be done with it.

McAvoy held Kitty up to his face, her feet dangling, her terror clear. "I want to finish my business with this little strumpet." He locked eyes with her.

And I wanted to save her.

And Molly.

And Frankie.

McAvoy tightened his grip on Kitty's neck. "You bragged about Patrick having a special key, how his father trusted him so much." He gave her a shake. "Where is it?"

"I don't know—" she said, her words tumbling over themselves.

"You do," McAvoy insisted in her face.

I looked down at Frankie. He'd melted to the shoulders, and he'd lost most of his chest.

My gut churned as a plan formed in my mind. If I could use

McAvoy to learn what happened on the night of Kitty's death, if we could show Kitty that Patrick loved her or give her any kind of closure, then maybe, just maybe, she'd find her peace and find a way to free herself before she drained the life out of Frankie and Molly too.

To do that, I needed to get McAvoy talking. Fast. "Why couldn't you just let Kitty run away with Patrick?" I shot out.

He looked at me like I was crazy. "I needed a babysitter," he joked, giving her a hard shake. He looked at her like a child ready to tear the wings off a butterfly. "You were gone for so many years, I thought you went to the light." He tilted his head. "Bet now you're wishing you had."

"I-I was lost. In the cemetery behind the Heritage Society," Kitty stammered, her voice trembling like leaves in a storm.

"That's where I buried you the first time," he responded coldly, the words falling from his lips like stones. With a callous shove, he tossed her onto the ground.

"I was stuck there," she protested.

He studied her trembling form on the basement floor. "When I dug you up, you didn't have that pretty ring on your finger. I'd have kept it," he added just to taunt her.

She covered her ring with her right hand.

"I wouldn't have buried you there at all except I was in a hurry after I shot your lover."

"You?" Kitty gaped up at him. "You killed Patrick?"

McAvoy's posture was rigid, smug. "Don't you think you'd better cooperate?"

"She will if you tell us what happened the night of the raid," I said, promising for her. Frankie had melted to his shoulders, and his chin was missing.

McAvoy caught my horrified expression and smirked. "We raided the bar. I knew the score was big. I followed Seamus down and plugged him when he went to check on it. But he only had one vault key on him."

"And the vault was locked," I said with a furtive glance at

Frankie on the floor, my heart hammering in my chest. He'd lost both ears.

"Of course it was locked," McAvoy scoffed. "Seamus wasn't stupid." A sneer twisted his face as he looked down at Kitty. "Good thing Patrick had his special key," he said, chuckling when she gasped. "So I went out and grabbed my cruiser."

Wait. "During the raid?" I asked. Steve said the cruiser went missing before it started.

Then again, Steve wasn't there. He was only going on the word of a dirty cop—his father.

"It was complete chaos," McAvoy gloated. "Nobody missed me." He looked at the young girl he'd sworn to serve and protect. "Kitty had told me all about their special room at the motel. Lucky number seven. I found Patrick heading there and pulled him over. Lo and behold, the boy had a trunk full of gold. All the better to run off with you." He winked at her. "He offered me the key in exchange for your life."

"He did?" Kitty's voice cracked.

"He loved you!" I exclaimed. He did. He really did. And now she could go.

I watched in horror as Frankie's neck melted away.

"He loved me." Tears blossomed in her eyes.

"I shot him anyway," McAvoy said as if discussing the weather.

Kitty lay rooted to the spot in shock.

McAvoy waved her off. "He was no good for you. I tossed him in the trunk, but the lying SOB didn't even have the decency to have the key on him."

The truth hit me with sickening clarity. "That's why you went after Kitty."

"Messed up my car something awful, but she'd have started telling everybody everything once Patrick came up missing." He said it as if it was part of the job, just regular cleanup. "I had to stash my cruiser quickly in the no-tell motel. I didn't plan on keeping it there, but where else can you go in Sugarland? The owner knew better than to rent that room or we'd shut him down for indecency." His expression hardened. "Now where is that key?"

"I don't know!" Kitty protested. Her chin quivered, and her mouth set in a hard line. "It doesn't matter," she declared. Her luminous spirit surged, gaining strength and clarity.

"Watch it," I warned, sick and ready to scream as Frankie's face melted away. "You're killing him!"

But Kitty didn't notice. She scrambled to her feet. "Patrick died for me. Don't you see?" she asked, turning to me. "He loved me."

"He did," I said. "He always did. Now do the right thing!"

"I died trying to run away with him." She brought her hands to her chest. "I stood by him. I loved him back." She swallowed hard, and an air of peace came over her. "It's okay now. I can go."

"You can," I said as Frankie's forehead glowed on the floor near her feet.

Kitty closed her eyes and held out her hands, ready for her spirit to be lifted.

But nothing happened.

Terror crossed her features. "It's not letting me go." She turned to me in terror. "What's wrong? Maybe it's because I haven't seen Patrick yet."

McAvoy pointed the gun at her. "Try that again and I'll plug you. You're not going anywhere until you find that key for me."

Kitty held still as if she could conserve the last bit of Frankie's energy through sheer willpower. "I couldn't begin to know where it is. Patrick left the key for his father. To show him Patrick still loved him, even if he didn't want to live like him. That's all I know. That's why he left me at the hotel and told me to meet him later at the fence. He went to leave the key in the one place his dad would find it."

McAvoy leaned in, his voice a serpent's hiss. "I've got eternity."

"My friends don't," Kitty said. "Patrick loved me. I made this as right as I could, and now it's time to go. Thank you, Molly," she whispered. "Thank you, Frankie." She teared up at the smidge of a glow on the floor as her image began to fade and her spirit rose.

"Not so fast, Kitty." McAvoy pointed his gun at me. "Stay right here, or I'll kill the live girl." He gave me a grim wink. "My bullet will kill you just fine, won't it?"

Yes. But we didn't have time to discuss it. "What do you want?" I demanded.

The corner of his mouth ticked up. "You've met Seamus. And from what I hear, you're good with the living and the dead. I want you to help her find the key."

"Let Kitty go first," I demanded. "Let her save our friends. Then we'll talk."

Only a glimmer of Frankie's forehead remained. A white haze with an ugly round bullet hole in the center. I choked up. He hated that hole.

I glared down the barrel of McAvoy's gun.

"Sorry, kid." He hitched a shoulder. "Collateral damage."

The edges of Frankie's bullet hole began to melt away.

A shot rang out, and I braced for the impact.

But McAvoy fell forward, bleeding from the head, falling on top of what little remained of Frankie.

A wickedly handsome young man stepped into the room.

"Patrick!" Kitty rushed to him, flinging her arms around him.

He held her tight and buried his face in her hair. "I was trying to stay away. I was trying to protect you. McAvoy wanted me, not you."

"Help me," she said, drawing away, holding his hands in hers.

"I'd do anything for you," he promised.

With his love and his support, she stepped out of Molly's ghostly form.

Her image faded away, at least in my eyes. Patrick still held her where her hands had been, gazing down at her with pure love.

"I don't need a body." Her voice floated softly in the air. "I just need you."

I rushed to where Molly lay on the floor. It was her body now, her face. "Are you all right?" I asked as she sat up. "Can you direct some energy to Frankie?" I pleaded, motioning to where McAvoy lay dead on the floor.

"I already am," she said, holding her head as she scrambled on her hands and knees toward where we'd last seen the gangster. "Frankie, Frankie, Frankie," she implored as she shoved the body off him.

I didn't dare touch it. Contact with me could make ghostly things disappear, and the last thing I needed to do was make this worse.

She rolled McAvoy away to reveal a faint outline of Frankie as if he were done in police chalk. His face shimmered dully in the bleak basement room. But he was alive.

"He made it!" I clapped my hands together, whooshing out a sigh of relief.

Molly beamed at me. "He did."

They both had.

"He really loves me," Molly said, stroking his head. "I mean, I knew he did before, but I never knew how much."

"You're his other half," I told her. "It's a rare thing."

"It is." She smiled down at him. "And I can't wait to spend the rest of my afterlife loving him."

I stood and left her stroking his hair while whispering sweet nothings into his ear. Patrick sat on a crate of gold in the vault, head bent lovingly, with his arm around an invisible Kitty.

It was time to give them all a moment.

Plus, I'd rather not be caught in the vault by whoever had opened it on my side of the veil.

I stepped out into the pitch-black hallway, my ankle brushing a discarded plastic grocery bag. Voices echoed above—gangsters celebrating. I hoped it was our side. I dug out my Maglite, closed the door behind me, and made a right toward Seamus's office.

I was curious about something Kitty had said.

She'd talked about a place where Seamus would surely find Patrick's key.

I'd just about made it when a light flashed from behind me, and a hand grabbed my shoulder from behind. I spun around, but my attacker yanked me against him.

"Sorry, kid," he said low under his breath as he shoved a plastic grocery bag over my head.

Chapter Twenty-Seven

My heart slammed against my ribcage as the grocery bag slipped over my head, sealing the world out. Panic clawed up my throat as I tried to shove it away, but he held my back tight against his chest, my arms trapped at my sides.

I flailed and screamed, the slick plastic clinging to my mouth. But my cries came out weak, trapped by the bag, my answering gasp sucking plastic instead of air. I heaved, my breath hot against the suffocating grip, my lungs burning for air that wouldn't come.

The bag tightened with every inhale. I felt the hand on my throat, and the iron grip of an arm slung across my chest, tying me down.

I pitched forward, lunging for the ground, but my attacker was glued to my back. His hand, a vise on my neck, held fast as I writhed, my back arching against his chest.

With a surge of adrenaline, I jackknifed forward and kicked my heel backward, aiming for his balls.

The blind strike found its mark.

A guttural grunt erupted from behind me, and the iron clamp around my neck faltered. I wrenched one hand free, my fingers clawing at the bag until they broke through.

A rush of cold air flooded my lungs. Sweet, pure air. I sucked it down. I felt my face wet against the bag as he yanked the sack off.

"Bitch," he snarled, cramming the bag into my mouth before I could breathe enough to scream.

He clamped one hand around my mouth and the other across my chest as he hauled me away from Seamus's office, the only light the erratic dance of his headlamp on damp bricks.

His grip was tighter this time, like bands of steel as he forced me down the corridor.

We passed the door behind which my friends, my lifeline, celebrated unaware. Frankie, Molly, Kitty, Patrick...

The light flickered over the familiar door, a beacon of safety just out of reach as I was dragged farther into the dark.

The corridor seemed to stretch into eternity, my feet dragging against my will, my heart pounding in my ears. The gag muffled every desperate noise that clawed up my throat.

We came upon the smugglers' stairs. The wide concrete steps appeared skeletal in the harsh glare of camping lanterns strategically placed on every third or fourth step. Their cold beams cut through the darkness, casting long, ominous shadows that reached out like fingers toward the steel door at the top.

My captor's grip steered me toward the stairs with a terrifying efficiency—up the first step, the second. I twisted in his grasp, turning just enough to catch a glimpse of him.

It was Steve McAvoy!

The deep-blue eyes that once seemed lively and expressive were now cold and calculating. His salt-and-pepper hair seemed to bristle with menace.

Steve's voice was mechanical, clinical. "I'm sorry about this, Verity. I truly am."

It was Steve breaking into the vault. Steve taking the gold.

I yanked my legs up and kicked the brick stairwell. Hard. For a fleeting moment, he wobbled, his balance shifting.

He caught himself and steadied us both, but in doing so, he had to take his hand off my mouth.

"It's a family business, you see," he grunted, his breath hot against my ear. "Well, at least for me and my dad."

The truth hit me with a sickening twist in the gut.

I used my tongue and what little space I had to push against the plastic bag and force it out of my mouth. "Your dad double-crossed the gangsters," I gasped, the words laced with venom and revelation. I'd seen him, Steve's father. I'd watched him kill Seamus before the mobster knew what hit him. According to him, it hadn't been the first time. "Your dad killed everyone who knew about the gold." The massacre had been a cover. "Then he kept the gold for himself."

Steve's steps didn't falter, but his voice did.

"Seamus made it easy. The vault was behind his whiskey room. My dad cleared out the obvious booze and claimed the mob was moving some cheap stuff they stole. He hid the vault door—and the real treasure—behind a bunch of empty crates."

"And you hid it better with some fancy woodworking."

I lunged for the wall again, but he was ready this time.

Steve chuckled and drew me tighter against him, his breath harsh against my ear. "That was also my dad. He taught me how to use a saw. But I kept it up over the years."

I should have seen it! Steve lived a posh life for a retired police officer. His house was high-end. His trips were exotic and expensive. I just hadn't put it together. None of us had.

He'd lived well, but not so extravagantly that he drew attention.

It was the perfect crime.

And now I was the only loose end.

I had to escape—somehow. Because there was no one coming for me.

I struggled with everything I had as he dragged me up, up, up the stairs.

Ellis was on a flight. I'd ordered Virginia to stay out—or else. And my sister didn't know the basement of this mob bar existed.

I had to keep him talking. Buy myself some time. And keep the gag out of my mouth.

If he took me to a third location, I was as good as dead.

"So you've been siphoning gold this entire time," I panted, voice ragged but loud enough to pierce the heavy air between us.

"A slow, steady drip. That's the key," Steve grunted, the strain evident in his voice as he pulled me upward. "My dad taught me that."

"Your dad never even left the force, did he? He put in his full thirty before he retired. My grandma liked to tell me that," I said, my body going limp, trying to morph into an anchor. He stumbled slightly, his breath catching. It was working, but not well enough.

"Dad stayed on," he puffed out, the effort sounding in his strained tone. "And Dad cleaned up Sugarland. He liked to travel. Said he was a good poker player and won big in Vegas a few times a year."

"But he didn't play poker," I countered, lashing out with a foot. My heel connected with a lantern, sending it clattering and crashing down the concrete stairs. It bounced with a cacophony of echoes. But Steve didn't flinch, didn't pause. He just kept dragging me up like a machine.

"Dad had a nice house out there," he continued, his voice a strained wheeze now as he fought against my dead weight. "Took great vacations. He taught me how to live."

"And your sisters, are they in on it too?" I strained my neck, eyeing the next lantern we approached, the light flickering against the bare brick walls.

"No, but they live a charmed life in Florida, thanks to our investments," he said, a bitter edge of pride cutting through his fatigue.

His "investments" were in the basement of a mob bar.

I lashed out again, aiming for the lantern, but my timing was off. My foot swung through empty air, my miss costing me precious momentum. Steve's pace slowed, but he didn't stop dragging me upward.

And if he wanted me there, I didn't want to go.

"Dad wasn't greedy, nor am I. I took small withdrawals like he taught me. Fifty or eighty thousand here and there," Steve boasted, his voice steady as if he were discussing nothing more than withdrawals from a savings account.

"Do you have both keys, or was that your lock-picking kit upstairs?" I asked, my mind racing for any advantage, any oversight of his I could exploit.

He let out a hollow laugh, the sound echoing off the tight walls of the stairwell. "One key, courtesy of Seamus O'Reilly. Dad taught me how to pick the other lock."

"We stole your kit," I blurted out, hoping to agitate him into a mistake.

"I have a spare," Steve said as if discussing an everyday inconvenience. "I mean, no gold stash is perfect."

His was pretty close.

"You killed anyone who came near the vault." My voice was strained. He held me so tightly it was hard to breathe. "You killed those people Maisie found, didn't you?"

"Only three of them in the last decade." He grunted as I caught my heels on any step I could reach. "Damn highway." He pulled me up the last step, his grip cold and firm. "My dad killed more. Although he was better at getting rid of the bodies. I never had the stomach for that sort of thing." He paused, a momentary wince crossing his features before his expression hardened again. "But I'm good at making it look like an accident."

Oh no.

His words hung in the air as we reached the top of the stairwell. He spun me to face the formidable steel door at the top, the sliding peephole open to the starry night beyond. I caught a glimpse of freedom, but it was a cruel tease—such beauty on what could be my last night alive.

"I was going to have to move it out eventually if Leland sold the land," he said like we were chatting over coffee. "But after you dropped by my house, I knew I had to get the gold out fast."

I'd told him I was ghost hunting. I'd told him we'd found his dad's cruiser. I'd told him everything!

"You need to be more careful ghost hunting. One trip in the dark and you'll break your neck on these stairs," Steve said, his voice dripping with false concern.

I was terrified, every instinct screaming to fight, to flee, but where? I worked a hand free and grasped for the cold, damp railing.

Suddenly, Steve grabbed both my hands, pulling them behind me with a swift, practiced motion, pinning them like handcuffs. He edged me forward, holding me out over the long concrete stairwell. The lanterns, spaced every few steps, cast menacing shadows, and the basement yawned dark and gaping below us.

"I'm sorry, Verity. I really am. You seem like a nice girl."

Chapter Twenty-Eight

The metal door shrieked open. I barely had time to register the light pouring in or the loosening of Steve's grip as I felt a sickening thud behind me.

Then Steve let go.

I was falling. My heart leaped into my throat, my arms wild, flailing for something, anything.

Steve knocked me sideways, sending me careening toward the wall, reaching for me as he fell.

The basement loomed below, a gaping maw ready to swallow me whole. I could almost feel the cold, hard concrete, the crushing pain.

Then, out of the chaos, a force yanked me back from the edge, the grip ironclad around my wrist. My body swung around, my back slamming against the wall. I stared into Virginia's eyes, wide with fear, yet she held on.

I grabbed hold of her forearm, my grip just as desperate. Our arms made a bridge, a lifeline.

"Don't worry. I've got you," Virginia said, her clipped voice sure.

I let out a shuddering breath, nodding wordlessly, my fingers tightening on her arm as I heard the sickening crunch of Steve hitting the bottom.

~

An hour later, the adrenaline still hadn't worn off. I huddled next to Virginia on an old tire, its rubber cracked and worn, our backs to the brick wall that had hidden the mob operations from the highway beyond.

The gray door stood across from us, propped open with a bulky orange traffic cone that was out of place amid the dust and grime. The scene was bathed in the strobe of blue and red police lights. I could hear the Sugarland PD radios crackling, a constant back-and-forth as officers trudged up and down the back staircase, piecing together the scene of the crime.

They'd taken Steve away in an ambulance with multiple broken bones and a head injury. Despite what he'd tried to do to me, I hoped he'd make it. Or maybe it was because of his callousness that I'd like to see him behind bars.

I glanced at Virginia, whom I'd practically blackmailed to stay out front and not leave her post. I couldn't help but let out a shaky laugh. "You never do listen to me, and this time I'm glad."

I quite possibly owed my life to it.

Her lips twitched upward ever so slightly. "I was glad to have your back."

She fiddled with the emerald ring that had taken the place of her wedding band. "I kept watch out front for a while, as promised," she stated, her back straight as she watched the officers work. "But Ellis is always going on about the importance of checking the perimeter, so I did the same."

I couldn't help but smile at that. Virginia's relationship with her middle son—not to mention his career choice—had always been strained. But here she was, listening to him, putting his police training to use.

"Anyway," she continued, hands clasped firmly together,

"that's when I saw it—the black BMW parked under the covered driveway." Now that same car sat exposed under the flash of police cameras, its trunk gaping open like a confession, revealing a haul of gold.

"I sent Lottie down to warn you, but she refused to leave my side. She sent Kitty, instead."

And Kitty had been attacked by McAvoy before she could tell me anything.

Virginia's gaze shifted back to the gray door. "I debated going down myself. Instead, I made another lap. When I got back, the slider was open, so I took a look. That's when I saw Steve holding you over the stairs, one hand gripping your belt, the other poised to give you a push."

The image sent a shiver down my spine.

She gave my knee a light, reassuring pat. "I didn't have much time. There was a brick by my foot, so I picked it up, and... Well, you know the rest."

I did. And I thanked heaven for it.

We sat for a moment, watching the officers work—Virginia lost in thought, me just happy to be outside on solid ground, breathing the fresh evening air. Glad to be alive.

"We found a stash of gold bars in the vault in the basement," I told Virginia, watching her eyes widen. "There has to be millions down there. I doubt they can trace the original owners." The gold wasn't marked. "I wonder who it belongs to now."

Virginia considered it for a moment. "It belongs to whoever legally owns the bar and the vault."

It didn't surprise me. "That's Leland." Although it didn't seem fair for him to profit.

Virginia appeared unsettled as well. But there was nothing to do about it. "The important thing is you're safe," she said, ever the pragmatist.

"You're right." Even if things hadn't worked out exactly as I'd hoped. I was glad to be whole and alive. And more than that, I was thankful to say the same for Molly and for Frankie. Kitty and

Patrick were whole again as well. Even if Kitty didn't have a body, she had him.

Then I caught sight of a familiar figure approaching through the bustle of police lights and officers.

It was Maisie, rifle in hand.

"Verity!" she called when she caught sight of me. "I saw the police lights." She closed the distance between us and extended a hand to help me up. Her eyes darted around nervously as she did. "Don't let them see my gun."

"Maisie," Virginia greeted her, casually rising to her feet on the other side of me as if she were standing up from a table in a four-star restaurant.

Maisie stared at her for a second too long. "You're here again?" She glanced from Virginia to me, no doubt deciding it had been more likely for lightning to strike than for her to catch us together a second time. "What am I missing?"

"Absolutely nothing," I assured her, briefing her on what had really taken place at the mob bar.

Maisie's mouth dropped open. "Are there gangsters around now?"

"No," I said. At least I hadn't noticed any. I hadn't stopped to think about the gangsters since my near fall down the stairs. I took a quick look around. "It's strangely quiet on the ghostly side. At least back here."

The three of us walked around to the front of the bar. There I saw the aftermath of the mob battle in stark, ghostly gray.

Most of the South Town Boys I'd seen earlier lay dead. Again. Sprawled all over. It appeared they'd also tried to crash a Studebaker through the front of the bar, only to run over the guy who'd already had tire tracks up his back from the first time he'd died.

The door of the bar lay open with a pile of South Town Boys and Irish mobsters stacked like cordwood in the entryway and more inside. There wasn't a single survivor except for—"Suds!" I spotted him on the ground a few yards away, his head cradled in Ruth's lap.

Violet and Lottie stood a polite distance away.

His bowler hat lay askew, and his snub-nosed face shone as she wiped the sweat from his forehead with a lacy handkerchief.

"How were you the lone survivor?" I asked when I'd made it over to them.

He grinned, earning a kiss on the forehead from Ruth. "Someone had to help guard the ladies," he said with a modesty that didn't quite match the proud tilt of his chin.

"He got shot in the shoulder. For me," Ruth said dreamily. "He's my hero."

"Aww..." The gray of his cheeks darkened. "I'd get shot for a pretty girl like you anytime."

"I think Ruth likes the bad boys," Lottie said when I went to go stand with her.

"She doesn't know what she's in for," I said fondly, glad to see her so happy. She deserved it. We all did.

I caught the movement of real-life police inside the bar. Now wasn't the time, but I couldn't wait to check out what I suspected I'd find in Seamus's office.

Chapter Twenty-Nine

The next week, I bent to admire one of the last roses of the season, then stood to take in the day.

The air was heavy with the kind of warmth that seemed to borrow from summer, the kind that makes you question the calendar. The sky overhead was a clear, piercing blue.

Frankie and Molly were busy lounging on my back porch swing, passing a mason jar of Frankie's famous pine needle and chili pepper moonshine between them. The clear liquid caught the afternoon sun as it sloshed, potent enough to make your eyes water. But they sipped it like it was sweet tea, their laughter mingling with the clinking of ice.

Suds relaxed with Ruth out by the pond, enjoying a picnic in the shade of Frankie's moonshine still. I didn't think of it as a very romantic place, but they didn't seem to mind the hulking barrels and mess of coils. Or the smell.

They only had eyes for each other.

Suds had spread a checkered blanket over the grass and was lying on his side, propping his head up with one hand as he traced nonsensical patterns on Ruth's palm with the other. Every so often, he'd lean over and pluck a wildflower from the grass, tucking it behind her ear while she pretended not to notice, her lips twitching in a suppressed smile.

As for Lucy, she was sprawled out by the apple tree, her black-and-white fur soaking up the sun. She'd found a patch of grass that seemed to be just the right combination of sun-warmed and soft. She lay there, belly up, paws dangling in a posture of utter contentment that I liked to call "dead bug." Occasionally, her nose would twitch in her sleep, and a lazy paw would swat at a passing butterfly.

As for me? I still had one more thing to do.

I swung my bag over my shoulder and double-checked that my flashlight lay inside. Then I slipped into the land yacht and steered toward the old Irish bar.

The urn stayed behind, tucked under the rosebush in my parlor. I didn't need Frankie for this. I only needed to borrow a bit of his power, which he had in spades now that Molly was safe and well.

Before I knew it, I'd taken the familiar left past the crumbling building and skirted the drive-in.

I hadn't seen hide nor hair of Patrick or Kitty since that chaotic evening we'd spent in the vault. According to Molly, they'd made a break for it, eloping to Niagara Falls.

Just in case the Irish had taken over Las Vegas.

As I came to a crooked stop on the cracked asphalt, I detected the flicker of shadows behind the Tudor-paned windows of the mob bar.

The Irish might not be very happy to see me.

I screwed up my courage and pushed the car door open.

Ellis had reported no sign of the new Irish mob in Las Vegas. The source he'd flown out to interview turned out to be the mother of Steve's Vegas girlfriend. He'd gotten her to call in the hoax to get Ellis out of town while he moved the gold. Steve couldn't imagine me going in to investigate while Ellis wasn't around to escort me.

Steve had assumed wrong.

I heard the faint strains of Frank Sinatra's "I've Got the World on a String." I inserted the key I'd borrowed from Virginia and pushed open the red painted door.

As I walked inside, I saw a dozen or so round tables packed with mobsters. More at the pool table. More at the bar.

The music screeched to a halt.

A glass fell to the floor. A pool cue missed its mark. Johnny O'Toole stepped away from a table and cracked his knuckles. I'd forgotten how large he was.

Heads turned, and eyes narrowed. The atmosphere turned sharp in an instant.

Mobsters began rising from their tables, the sound of chairs scraping against the floor like the cocking of a gun. In unison, their hands reached inside jackets and behind backs.

Then I caught sight of Seamus. He stood up from a back table near the bar, his presence commanding the room. "What do you want?" His voice was a low rumble, a thinly disguised threat.

I could feel the weight of every gaze. But I'd come too far to let their cold stares deter me. I squared my shoulders and said my piece. "I think there's something you need to see," I told him. "It has to do with your son."

Seamus narrowed his eyes. "Patrick hasn't been back to see me. He's gone again."

"If I had to guess, I'd say he's afraid." He and Kitty both were. "Please come with me."

I made my way to the basement door, and without waiting for him to follow, I started down.

I made it all the way to the bottom before he shimmered into view next to me. The gray glow of the ghostly brick cast deep shadows across his face. "You got a lot of guts coming down here."

Maybe so, but there was one thing I hadn't made right.

The air was cooler here, the bricks damp. The ghostly glow cast a gray pallor that seemed to make the corridor stretch for miles.

I turned left and began to walk. "You wondered if Patrick was loyal, if he loved you."

The lines on Seamus's face seemed to harden. "He wasn't loyal to me," he said flatly. "You saw." But the flicker in his eyes betrayed a storm of emotions even the hardened gangster might not have understood.

We passed the door that led to the vault. Yellow and black stripes of police tape crisscrossed the entrance.

I pressed on.

"What would you do if you were brave enough to trust that your son really did care about you?" I asked simply.

"I'm plenty brave," Seamus shot back.

When it came to killing—yes. To stealing and plotting—no doubt. But to loving another person? I had to wonder.

I halted outside the battered wood door at the dead end of the hall, placing my hand on the rough surface. "Seamus," I said, turning to face him, my eyes searching his, "what would you say if I told you Patrick gave you your key back? That he wanted your forgiveness. That he loved you."

Seamus stiffened, pain crossing his features. "I told you. He wasn't loyal to me."

"If I may?" I asked, running a hand down the door.

Seamus nodded.

I pushed the door open and stepped into his office. The room was dominated by the heavy wood desk at the back, its surface gleaming dully in the half light. "Love isn't about following someone else's path."

"What?" Seamus growled. "You'd better not have brought me down here for a lecture."

Not exactly.

I leaned my rear against the front of the desk, feeling the cool press of the wood through my jeans. "Would you want Patrick to take over the mob even if he didn't want that lifestyle?"

Seamus frowned. "He'd learn to love it," he barked.

"Frankie says the same thing about me," I admitted. I

pushed away from the desk and walked to the wall behind it, where faded photographs hung like macabre trophies. "Patrick loved Kitty. And you," I said, grazing a finger against the curled edge of the nearest one. "He just wanted to follow a different path."

Seamus stood on the opposite side of the photo wall from me, his gaze fixed on the eight-by-ten photo of Kitty with the red X marring her features and the name *Patrick* scrawled underneath. "I think I know where the key is," he said flatly.

I was pretty sure I knew, too.

A muscle in his jaw clenched as he spoke. "I'd only take one of these down if I've forgiven the transgression," he said thickly. "If I called off the hit." His eyes met mine. "I never call off a hit."

He reached for the photograph with a hand that trembled slightly. "I'm calling this one off. The fight is over." He yanked it off the wall and flipped the photo over, revealing a gleaming gold key taped to the back.

The corner of his mouth ticked up, and his eyes misted as he crumpled the photo in his fist and tossed it into the wastebasket under the desk. "It's done."

He rolled the key between his fingers, lost in thought, when a voice sounded from the doorway.

"Dad?" Patrick's voice was tentative, his wide-shouldered silhouette framed by the dim ghostly glow in the hall.

Seamus turned, and the hard lines of his face softened. "Hey, kid," he said, his voice no more than a whisper.

The two men stood no more than ten feet apart, yet decades away. The years of pain and separation hung between them like a chasm, and it seemed like neither one of them knew what to do.

Then Seamus opened his arms. "Son."

Patrick stepped into the embrace, and they clung to each other at long, long last.

"I love you, Dad," Patrick murmured into the mob boss's shoulder.

"And I you, kid," Seamus said, his voice thick with emotion.

"Not for what you've done or haven't done, but because you're my boy."

Out in the hall, just outside the doorway, a tiny flickering flame caught my eye. "Kitty?" I ventured, taking the chance.

"I've always wanted this for him," she murmured when I reached her.

"I'm glad Seamus made it happen." He'd torn down the picture. He'd made his choice—that love was better than blind loyalty. That he wanted his son back, not to rob or steal, but to be part of his life. Or, I supposed, his afterlife.

"He's been wanting to come back." Kitty's light danced with her words. "He was just afraid. We both were."

That was over. "You don't have to be afraid anymore."

We watched as father and son began to talk, to laugh, to catch up on all the years they'd missed.

"I'm so glad," Kitty said. "And grateful," she added after a slight pause. "I just wish I had a body like most everyone else. I wish everyone could see *me*."

"I see you," I assured her.

But I knew what she meant. And I had an idea.

I turned to her, thinking back on what Chief McAvoy had said in the vault. "I think you might be stuck because you left something in the cemetery behind the Sugarland Heritage Society."

"But my body is down by the river. I heard the police talking. Steve confessed. That's where Chief McAvoy reburied me."

"I know." I'd heard the same. Ellis was working to have the body exhumed as part of the case against the McAvoys. "But in the vault, Chief McAvoy was surprised to see you wearing a ring. You had it in the ghostly realm because you died with it." But if he didn't remember seeing it when he was alive, she must have lost it in the physical realm sometime after her death. "My guess is that it's still buried in the ground behind the Heritage Society." It would explain why her spirit had been unable to move on from that place.

She'd been stuck in the loop of fear and anxiety over her death on the night of her elopement, and her worry about Patrick's love for her. We'd found Patrick for her. Now we just needed to find the ring.

Her flame surged with hope. "Can we look for it? Can we try?"

"Of course," I promised without hesitation. "We'll get started right away."

She'd been so brave, so giving once she'd realized what she'd done in taking over Molly's form. She'd even tried to leave Molly at the expense of her own eternal life and happiness. Kitty deserved for me to do everything I could to help set things right. And I had a feeling that with the help of a few friends, we might just pull it off.

Chapter Thirty

We found Kitty's ring buried under the old maple tree where it had spent the last seven decades.

I had it cleaned and polished and reburied with her at Holy Oak Cemetery. The town of Sugarland had taken up a collection to buy her a plot next to a small rose garden. Patrick, too. The police had found him in a shallow grave near the river.

The return of the ring worked. I wasn't sure if it was physics we didn't understand yet or if it was an emotional breakthrough, but at long last, Kitty had a ghostly body.

Smiling, I watched her with Patrick, playing lawn darts out behind Frankie's shed. She launched a dart and watched it soar through the air, landing with a satisfying *thunk* right at the heart of the grassy ring—a perfect bullseye. Her cheer was met with a kiss from Patrick.

Frankie used her distraction as an opportunity to move her dart off center, but he returned it to its rightful place after a long look from Molly that made both of them laugh.

Yes, Molly had her hands full. But she didn't seem to mind one bit.

I turned to my little skunk, who danced in the grass at my feet.

"Are you ready, girl?" Lucy's response was an excited spin, her black-and-white fur a blur. "Ramp," I instructed, heart swelling with pride as she dashed up the old washboard in a dead run. She spun a circle at the top and then toddled straight into a makeshift canvas tunnel. "Isn't she great?" I beamed, turning to Ellis and Maisie, who were comfortably ensconced in their lawn chairs, a bowl of pecans between them.

"She's a natural," Ellis said, tossing a pecan into his mouth with a proud smile.

"Where did she go?" asked Maisie when Lucy didn't immediately emerge from the tunnel.

I crouched down to peek inside and found Lucy playing with her tail as if she'd just discovered it. "She's researching aerodynamics," I reported with a laugh.

The rumble of an engine drew our attention to the side drive, where a fancy cream-colored Cadillac rolled to a stop near my grandmother's rosebushes. Virginia emerged, veiled behind a large pair of sunglasses and a silk driver's scarf.

"What's she doing here?" Maisie stiffened as if her chair had zapped her.

"Eventually, you'll stop being surprised," I told her. But the truth was I had no idea why Virginia would decide to visit.

She was dressed to the nines in a pink tweed business suit with a gray silk top and matching pumps. She wore pearls in her ears and around her neck, and her hair was done up in a classic French twist.

Virginia blazed straight past me as if we'd never met before, and planted a sharp kiss on Ellis's cheek as he stood to greet her.

"Hello, Verity," she said, turning to the rest of us. "Maisie," she added, her hands clasped in front of her, her greetings sterile. "I have something for you." And for the first time, I noticed she held a thin manilla envelope. "This," she said crisply, "is a letter from my lawyer."

"Mom—" Ellis protested.

Maisie's hands balled into fists, her knuckles whitening as she leaped to her feet. "On the day I left my shotgun at home!" she hollered.

Virginia rolled her eyes. "It's not a bad kind of letter." She gave the envelope a firm shake. "Take it." She held it out to Maisie. "Any competent lawyer will see it's good news." She squared her shoulders. "The reason Leland and I have been stalling on a court date for your inheritance case is because we knew we'd lose."

"What?" I asked flatly. Virginia never lost.

"The land you're living on is yours, Maisie," she continued. "The property you've been protecting is yours by birth. Retain a lawyer, show them this letter, and you'll win the case."

Maisie took the envelope gingerly, her eyes wide with a mixture of suspicion and hope. "I can't afford a lawyer."

"Trust me, dear," Virginia replied with an uncharacteristic twinkle in her eye, "they'll line up for a chance at this case."

Maisie looked like she might faint.

Ellis's face broke out into a genuine smile. "I'm proud of you, Mom."

"I'm proud of me, too," she admitted, rocking back on her heels.

Wow. "What's Leland going to say?" I wondered aloud. He was more of a shark than Virginia.

Virginia waved my question aside with a flick of her wrist, her pearls catching the light. "It's not his land, is it?" she said, her voice carrying a note of finality. "Leland will have to get used to disappointment."

"Is this really legal?" Ellis asked, drawing closer to Maisie as if the letter might jump out of her hand.

Virginia nodded, her posture softening. "The land and everything on it belongs to Maisie."

"The land is mine," Maisie said, letting the words sink in as she clutched the letter to her chest.

"It always was," Virginia admitted, with a tinge of regret. "I'm sorry for my part in this." She reached out, placing her hand gently over Maisie's. "Use it well. Make it come alive again."

Maisie's face split into a wide grin. "You bet I will."

∼

The following spring, when the weather warmed and spring buds bloomed, we visited the new farmers' market Maisie opened in the once barren area behind the old mob bar. The grass underfoot was a bright, hopeful green, and rows of saplings by the nearby picnic area promised generous shade in the summers to come.

Beyond, a neat array of fruit trees stood in the beginnings of a "you pick it yourself" orchard and pumpkin patch. The apple tree branches had just begun to swell with the first tender buds. In a few months, the peach trees would follow. Farther still, a tilled patch awaited the autumn pumpkins.

I imagined summer a few years from now, eager families waiting in line for fresh peach pie slices as a hometown band performed on the grandstand that was just beginning to go up. I imagined kids in Halloween masks chasing each other past hay bales, parents and grandparents with wheelbarrows loaded with fat pumpkins.

Toward the no-tell motel, Maisie's vision continued with a small flea market. It was a charming clutter of permanent stalls constructed with reclaimed wood, each one hosting treasures from different locals. The scents from the food stalls mingled together, too tempting to resist. At least I'd already snagged a treat —a flaky pastry that melted on my tongue, sweet and satisfying and baked by my good friend Lauralee, who had brought her food truck out.

"I'm excited to see what Maisie's doing with the Irish bar," I said, brushing the crumbs from my yellow shirt with the back of my hand.

Work trucks, splattered with mud and bearing the scars of

heavy labor, had taken up semipermanent residence in the newly renovated parking lot at the front of the bar.

Ellis took a hearty bite from the meat pie he'd bought from Sue Roan. "Maisie told me this morning she wants to restore the main floor into an Irish bar and restaurant." He grinned. "The menus will tell the story of Seamus O'Reilly and his big score. And I'm not supposed to tell you the next part," he teased.

"But you will," I concluded.

He wrapped an arm around my shoulders. "She's keeping the vault downstairs and turning the rooms into a local mob museum, honoring both the Irish and the Germans."

"Both sides will have a fit." I laughed.

"Then they don't have to go," Ellis teased back.

He took my hand, his fingers warm and steady, and steered me toward the old Starlite Drive-in. It stood like a sentinel to the past, its once-forgotten big screen now bustling with workers on ladders, the giant screen receiving a total makeover. The ticket booth gleamed with a new shine, yet retained its 1950s charm, the chrome accents polished to a mirror finish. Maisie had even had the old sign out front restored.

Miss Felicia bustled excitedly among the work crews, oohing and aahing at her favorite place, coming back to life in a whole new way.

"What about the no-tell motel?" I asked. Surely that place had some life in it still.

Ellis squeezed my hand. "She's turning it into a tourist attraction, a campy hotel for those who want to vacation retro-style. She's even adding a pool and some pickle ball courts. People can stay for a weekend getaway or just for the night."

They'd be stopping in Sugarland instead of racing past on the highway.

"That should help tourism along Main Street," I said. For years, it had been mostly locals shopping in our town. I had a feeling that was about to change.

Ellis grinned. "We've got a lot going on in our small slice of heaven. We might as well show it off."

I leaned my head against his shoulder. "Tell Maisie she did good." She never gave up. She made a difference.

"We all did," he said, kissing me on the head.

Ellis, Maisie, Frankie, Molly, Kitty, Patrick. Even Virginia.

And I was proud to be a part of it.

Note from Angie Fox

Thanks so much for hanging out with Verity and the gang. The thought of Maisie's new venture introducing more folks to the charm of Sugarland tickles me pink. I know I'd love to visit!

And speaking of visits, Verity's grandmother will stop by for the next book in the series, Secrets, Lies and Fireflies. She's a hoot. And the perfect partner-in-crime for Verity and Frankie as they solve a mystery that has them digging into the hidden history of Verity's home and family. Trust me, this is one family reunion you don't want to miss.

If you'd like an email when each new book releases, go to my website to sign up for new release updates. I don't email often, but when I do, it's always something good.

Happy reading!

Angie

**Check out the next
Southern Ghost Hunter mystery
Secrets, Lies and Fireflies**

Verity's grandmother returns to help Verity and Frankie solve a mystery that reveals a shocking family secret, as well as the heartwarming history of Verity's home.

This is one family reunion you don't want to miss!

About the Author

New York Times and *USA Today* best-selling author Angie Fox writes sweet, fun, action-packed mysteries. Her characters are clever and fearless, but in real life, Angie is afraid of basements, bees, and going up stairs when it's dark behind her. Let's face it: Angie wouldn't last five minutes in one of her books.

Angie earned a journalism degree from the University of Missouri. During that time, she also skipped class for an entire week so she could read Anne Rice's vampire series straight through. Angie has always loved books and is shocked, honored and tickled pink that she now gets to write books for a living. Although, she did skip writing for a week this past fall so she could read Victoria Laurie's Abby Cooper psychic eye mysteries straight through.

Angie makes her home in St. Louis, Missouri with a football-addicted husband, two kids, and Moxie the dog.

Connect with Angie Fox online:
www.angiefox.com
angie@angiefox.com